Strayed

Katherine Bitner

Copyright © 2024 by Katherine Bitner

All rights reserved.

No part of this publication may be reproduced, distributed, or transmitted in any form or by any means, including photocopying, recording, or other electronic or mechanical methods, without the prior written permission of the publisher, except as permitted by U.S. copyright law. For permission requests, contact [include publisher/author contact info].

The story, all names, characters, and incidents portrayed in this production are fictitious. No identification with actual persons (living or deceased), places, buildings, and products is intended or should be inferred.

Book Cover Design: Katherine Bitner [Image by Unsplash]

Editor: Kimberly Steinke [Parker Mayne Editorial]

Contents

Dear Reader ... VII

Dedication ... IX

... XI

1. Chapter 1 ... 1
2. Chapter 2 ... 7
3. Chapter 3 ... 17
4. Chapter 4 ... 21
5. Chapter 5 ... 29
6. Chapter 6 ... 33
7. Chapter 7 ... 41
8. Chapter 8 ... 49
9. Chapter 9 ... 55
10. Chapter 10 ... 63
11. Chapter 11 ... 69
12. Chapter 12 ... 77
13. Chapter 13 ... 81
14. Chapter 14 ... 89
15. Chapter 15 ... 97

16. Chapter 16 — 107
17. Chapter 17 — 117
18. Chapter 18 — 123
19. Chapter 19 — 133
20. Chapter 20 — 139
21. Chapter 21 — 143
22. Chapter 22 — 147
23. Chapter 23 — 155
24. Chapter 24 — 161
25. Chapter 25 — 175
26. Chapter 26 — 179
27. Chapter 27 — 185
28. Chapter 28 — 195
29. Chapter 29 — 205
30. Chapter 30 — 211
31. Chapter 31 — 221
32. Chapter 32 — 227
33. Chapter 33 — 237
34. Chapter 34 — 243
35. Chapter 35 — 247
36. Chapter 36 — 253
37. Chapter 37 — 257
38. Chapter 38 — 271
39. Chapter 39 — 277

40.	Chapter 40	281
41.	Chapter 41	285
42.	Chapter 42	293
43.	Chapter 43	301
Epilogue		303
Acknowledgments		309
Also by		311
About Author		313

DEAR READER

Before you read Strayed, I want to be transparent. There are subjects in this book that could be potentially sensitive, such as references to child abandonment, alcoholism, and death. As an author, I never want a reader to be triggered by my books and want you to know this before going into the story. Always put your mental health first.

To all who have ever felt like they were an outsider, this book is for you.

(and for the best boy, Wilbur)

"When you get into a tight place and everything goes against you, till it seems as though you could not hang on a minute longer, never give up then, for that is just the place and time that the tide will turn."
Harriet Beecher Stowe

Chapter One

April

The thickets are getting denser between the creek and the trailer, even though I trot this path daily. I know every rock, every leaf, every branch that falls on this path. And if I'm not walking it, Opie is. I make a mental note to go through the tools in the shed so I can clear this path. I have to push tree limbs out of the way, dodging the branches that poke out like little needles, threatening to tear my last good pair of jeans.

In a month, it will be the beginning of summer in North Carolina, but the heat hasn't met us in the mountains yet. April is my favorite month. The flowers begin to show their faces, and I can spend time outside without shivering while not worrying about Opie getting overheated.

Opie pads along next to me. He's quiet for a dog his size. I reach down to scratch his dirty, white fur, but he bolts ahead; a flash of brown fur zigzags right in front of him. He's always thought he was a hunting dog, like most dogs out here in the tree-lined hills. He isn't a fancy purebred with papers, though; he's a mutt with impossible-to-keep-clean short fur and paws that he never fully grew into. His vet papers say he's an American bulldog. People in town call him a pit bull. I wouldn't care less if Opie was actually a black bear.

He's got more love and loyalty in his blood than any person I've ever met.

I don't holler for him as he clumsily looks around, wondering where the rabbit went. He'll never catch it.

"Next time, buddy." I catch up to him, and his tongue flops to the side as he falls in line, trotting beside me as the clearing comes into view.

The black straps of my camera hang heavily around my neck, digging into my skin. I'm surprised there aren't permanent marks from the frayed, old nylon strap because it's always with me, just like Opie.

It itches, rubbing against my skin, but I can't bring myself to buy a new strap. It's not that I can't afford it; I refuse to. Every penny I've made since I bought this camera goes into an account. I call it the "great escape" fund for when I finally get the hell out of this town, out of this life.

The retired wedding photographer who sold me the camera apologized for its corded strap, which looked like it'd seen better days. But I have a deep love for worn things that had a life before me and now get to live on with me. I'm sure if I voiced this to anyone, they'd tell me that's strange. Lucky or not for me, I don't have friends. At least not anymore. I only have Opie.

I found him on a warm July morning—or he found me. I like to think he chose me. He's the only one who ever has. Any way you look at it, we were brought together, and nothing's ever been the same. They say you only get one great love in life, and sometimes I think mine is Opie.

It was a week after my graduation, and the town was already getting loud with summer tourists flocking from the surrounding cities, but the farm was quiet, as always. I didn't mind; I had learned to be my own best friend, to find peace in the trails I carved by foot on our land.

That same afternoon, I was in my own world, washing dishes, when the sounds of whimpering drifted through the open window above the sink, leading me outside to investigate. It wasn't uncommon for animals of all kinds to scurry around our land, but this crying was different. It was the cry of loneliness. That was when I saw him, a scraggly white puppy sitting in the shadow of the trailer. I clasped my hand to my mouth, looking around for more. Where there is one puppy, there is always more. When he continued to whine, I rushed to his side, kneeling in the dirt beside him.

His ribs stuck out where a round belly should've been, and his fur was caked in mud and burrs. He looked tired but lifted his head to peer at me with eyes as blue as the sky, eyes that would age into the color of honey.

"You poor thing. Come here," I cooed, scooping him up gently, and he let me. I brought him inside, out of the sun, and quickly filled a water bowl, then watched him lap it dry.

"Where are you from?" I had asked him as he gnawed on my finger for a few seconds before curling into a ball on my lap and quickly falling asleep.

I had dropped everything I had planned that afternoon, feeling like this puppy had found me for a reason. He needed me.

We went to the store together to get kibble, and after he ate properly and got a bath, I created a makeshift bed for him, glancing at him every few minutes while I tried to finish cleaning the camper.

"Your fur is so white. What're you doing out in these woods, buddy?"

White as an opal.

"I'm going to call you Opie, okay?"

He lifted his eyes to me, one ear perking up.

"You don't have to worry anymore. You're safe. I'm going to take care of you," I promised him.

I had meant it with all my heart.

Opie makes his way to the trailer door, pawing at it impatiently while I catch up. It cracks open with a simple nudge of his paw. The latch on the front door is thirty years old, and I've been meaning to fix it. I've been lazy about it, though. Mostly because I know that no one would mess with me out here in the woods. Mack is the only person who knows I even live out here, and he's too intoxicated half the time to remember he even has a daughter.

There was a life before Opie and I called this twenty-five-foot camping trailer home. But that life seems distant, like a memory fading in deep, murky water. What I do know is the day I decided I'd had enough of Mack's drunken ways and the string of women coming in and out of my life, I left the farmhouse for good. A winding path and a narrow dirt road about a quarter mile long separates the house I grew up in with the man who called himself my father and my own little sanctuary now.

It's a far cry from paradise, with a tarp over my roof and cinder blocks as steps into the trailer my grandparents used to take me camping in. But this patch of land is where I'd run to and play when I was little, and now it's mine. Up here, I'm hidden away, in all senses.

It's where I found Opie. Or he found me. And we made a home.

He didn't ask me why I was living in this trailer up the hill from a father who didn't acknowledge me, and I didn't ask Opie how he ended up in the dirt outside my door.

That's the thing I love most about dogs. They don't care if everyone else in the town thinks you're nothing but trash. *Or should be in prison.*

Opie thinks I'm gold.

Chapter Two

The metal bowl clangs on the floor, jolting me from the laptop screen I've been staring at for the last three hours.

"Opie, it's not time yet. It's only four." As I say it, his eyebrows scrunch together, and he lets out a little yelp like I'm lying to him, but I spring to my feet, snapping my computer shut and frantically looking around my living space for my phone.

Yet again, time has gotten away from me. It usually does when photography is involved—or Opie for that matter. The print shop closes at five, and I'd just finished developing my last two film photographs this morning. I love my secret darkroom. It's the old toolshed on the edge of the property. I don't think Mack even remembers it exists. I mean, the last time he even came near the trailer or shed was when he was searching for me to ask for change to buy a pack of cigarettes. That was nearly a month ago, merely a few days after he was released from prison. We haven't crossed paths since.

I knew I'd be cutting it close, waiting until the last day and the last hour to get the final pieces of my submission together, but I wanted it all to be perfect. Everything is riding on this—*everything*.

Grabbing my folder and tote bag, I fumble around, pushing papers and clothes out of the way until my hand meets my car key. Opie shoots me a disgruntled look.

"Sorry, buddy. I promise when I get back, you'll get dinner!"

I rush out the door, but Opie bounds out after me before I can close it. All eighty pounds of him slams into my legs as I jiggle the car handle open, nearly debilitating me.

"Fine. You can come, but sit in the back!" Opie gleefully waits patiently for me as I open the back door, and it squeaks on rusty hinges. He leaps onto the worn, green seats.

I kick the dirt off my hiking boots before getting in. Though it's pointless. The car is covered in fur and dirt already. The only thing older and messier than the trailer is this car my grandparents also graciously left me.

I pull the mirror down in the car and swab on mascara, hoping to look less feral. I glance down at my dirty-blonde hair, the shorts I cut myself from old jeans, and the two-day-old French braids hanging over my shoulders. It'll have to do.

The old car rumbles down the bumpy drive as the live oak trees cast shadows from the late afternoon sun. Mack's faded farmhouse comes into view, and I let out my breath when I notice his truck is gone from the driveway. It's not like he's at work. Mack hasn't had a job for six years; granted, he was locked away for three of them.

Six years ago, in the dead of winter, two things happened: Mack had his accident at the factory, ending his longest spell of employment. And Memaw died. Mack still walks with a slight limp, his once-handsome face now lined from years of painkillers and liquor. And Memaw's absence is the loudest silence I've ever known.

After ten minutes of winding hills down the mountain, I'm gliding into town through the main drag. Miscruz Hills is a town in the Blue Ridge Mountains, a place I like to think is stuck in time. That's probably why tourists are drawn to it. They find our quirky summer festivals and small stores charming, even though the town seems to prefer old technology and a slower pace. The charm shouldn't have been lost on me; I love old things. But Mack's reputation spread like a disease, infecting every bit I once found sacred here.

Opie's head hangs out the back window, his drool running down the side of the dirty car door, looking at everyone, hoping—I'm sure—they will acknowledge him back. My only gripe with Opie is he seeks attention wherever he goes, which means I'm forced to interact with more people than I ever feel comfortable with.

"Come on. You better behave. Stay by my side," I instruct, opening the back door to let Opie out. He listens, staying two inches from my side as I trek to the print shop. A chime rings overhead as I pull the door open, but I'm met with an empty shop.

"Be there in a second!" a familiar voice sounds from around the corner.

Opie sniffs the wood-paneled walls lining the small shop. All I smell is the mix of ink and vanilla air freshener. It's quiet, besides the gentle buzzing of printers. Sun shines on my back through the storefront windows, and I clear my throat. Levi Whitaker rounds the corner, and I'm suddenly face-to-face with him. I didn't think this through, but I also didn't have an option with this being the *only* print shop in town.

His faded jeans and white T-shirt match his laid-back vibes as he shoves his hands in his front pockets and smiles at me. "Hey . . ." he starts, stopping in his tracks when we make eye contact, slightly tilting his head as he speaks.

Levi's hazel eyes are kind as always, and it's instantly clear his charm has not diminished. Though I doubt he ever thought he'd see me here.

"Hi." I jump right into why I'm here and specifically don't address the elephant in the room—the fact that we used to be best friends and haven't exchanged more than a handful of words since middle school. Reaching into my canvas tote bag, I pull out the two photos from this morning and slide the folder across the counter. "I need these scanned. Highest quality, please." I tap my finger on the folder and avert my eyes to Opie, who is still sniffing around the small seating area.

"Okay. Yeah . . . not a problem." Levi stumbles over his words as he takes a few strides toward me and grabs the folder gingerly from the counter. "Hey, Opie!" He smiles, reaching over the counter with ease, getting too close to me to smile down at my dog.

I've been able to avoid most people outside my job, but over the last year, I've run into Levi twice with Opie. Once on a hike and once on Main Street as we were leaving the vet. Opie doesn't let me pass a stranger without saying hi, so Levi knows his name. And apparently, he hasn't forgotten it.

I haven't been forced to be around Levi since high school, and it's been a year since graduation. However, if I'm being honest, it doesn't seem that long ago. I could've told you everything about Levi—his likes, dislikes, what he eats for lunch, his favorite book, his annoying positive sayings, and his stubborn habits. But now, all I know is there are years of silence separating us, and nothing about him is *boyish* anymore.

His baby face has slimmed, giving way to an angular jaw. It still doesn't appear like he can grow facial hair, but he's grown his hair out a bit. I like it longer; it suits him. It's messy but styled, like he took time intentionally placing each piece of chestnut hair in the right place.

His hazel eyes falter, scanning from Opie to my face. A twinge of pink brushes across his cheeks, and I feel unnecessarily annoyed.

"You remember Opie, I'm assuming," is all I say, even though he obviously does.

Opie's soaking in all the ear scratches he can get, and I hate to deny him extra love, but I *am* in a time crunch.

"Will it take long, the scanning?" I attempt to maintain a relaxed tone, even if my heart rate is betraying me. I have less than six hours before the deadline.

"Yeah, for sure. You've got . . ." He thumbs open the folder.

"Careful, careful! Please . . . they are original film copies," I interject. My words come out rushed, and as Levi's eyes pique with curiosity, I regret not driving thirty minutes to the next town to get these scanned.

"Gotcha. I'll be careful. How's it going, the photography?" He nods at the folder.

My shoulders tense. Photography was something I picked up *after* everything—after Levi was out of my life—and making small talk with him wasn't something I had the capacity for today, if ever. I'm already faking pleasantries with customers at Peg's Diner for thirty hours a week. That's about thirty hours over my limit.

"It's good." I offer a weak smile, my hand instinctively finding Opie's velvet-soft ears to rub between my fingers.

Levi nods, looking a bit snubbed, and I feel bad. Because Levi has *always* been a nice guy. Though he stands over six feet now and isn't someone who anyone would mess with, he's a total golden retriever. The opposite of me.

"It's for a portfolio I have to submit by midnight. That's why I'm in a rush," I offer, more frustrated with myself for waiting until the last minute. In my defense, these last-minute additions are some of my best work and worth the added anxiety.

"You applying to photography school?" Levi asks, looking up at me briefly from the massive scanner before him.

I pinch my lips together and bob my head. It's not really school. But it will get me out of this town. Hopefully forever.

"Kind of," I reply.

Levi doesn't break eye contact, waiting for me to continue.

I shift my feet uncomfortably. "It's a program, a five-month intensive photography program in Charleston. It's taught by one of the top professors on the East Coast, and it's extremely competitive to get into. They only accept twenty people a year. Anyway, I figure it's worth a shot. It will get me out of here and could launch my career." I'm surprised by the enthusiasm and speed of my words, and by the look of Levi's lifted brows and curved lips, he is too. Photography is the only thing I've ever been good at.

"That's . . . that's really cool. I hope you get in." He picks his words slowly and cautiously. Levi slides the folder back to me across the counter, and the only sound between us now is the numbing whir of the machines.

"Yeah, thanks," I reply.

"You'll be missed," he adds.

I snap my eyes to his in pure reaction, holding back a scoff. The people in this town missing me? Highly doubtful. I'd bet my life on it. Actually, they'd throw a parade just to get one more Hayes family member out of this town.

All they see when they look at me is Mack Hayes's daughter, the town drunk's offspring. *The girl in the car that night.* The girl with the junkyard dog. Trash. That's what they think of me. They won't miss me. And I won't miss them.

"This town is . . ." I blew out a breath from deep within my lungs. "Aren't you curious what life is like . . . anywhere else?" I want to be annoyed with Levi and the uncanny way he can get me to talk, even at my most resistant.

After Memaw died when I was thirteen, and Mack's will to be a decent human being along with her, so did my childhood friendship with Levi. He gave me space to grieve, but when I pulled away, I never came back. Levi attempted to rekindle our friendship. He never stopped asking me if I was okay or if I wanted to come over after school. But then, a year passed of this back-and-forth, and Mack was deep into liquor and rage, casting his cloud of darkness over every aspect of my life.

So Levi continued to make new friends, do well in school, and simply moved on without me. As much as it hurt, I didn't blame him. Even after the accident, Levi was the only person at school who didn't look at me like I was evil. His passing smiles in the hallways reminded me of everything taken from me, everything I left behind.

But that was years ago, in the past, where it shall all remain.

I watch his shoulder shrug ever so slightly as he leans on the counter, revealing corded muscles that don't look like they belong to the little boy who used to chase me on the playground.

"You know tourism is one of our biggest economies, right?" He smirks sarcastically.

I glance down at Opie, who grew tired of the chatter and lies at my feet.

"I do . . . but there's a difference between visiting a place and living in it. Tourists get to leave," I add solemnly.

Levi looks tense, but then he perks up, his eyes shining as he looks at me. "Have you been to the new food truck park yet?" He runs one hand through his hair, messing it up in a way that still looks good.

I shake my head as an uneasiness takes over my stomach. The thing about being quiet is that your intuition skills are sharp as an ax. I know exactly what's coming, even if it does surprise me a bit.

"If you're ever up for giving this town another shot . . . I'd love to catch up and grab a bite with—"

I cut him off, smiling softly but digging my toes into the front of my boots in an attempt to steady my heartbeat. "I'm swamped between work and getting ready for—" I start, but Levi beats me to it, hiding his disappointment by waving his hand in the air.

"Photography school. I know."

I merely nod.

Levi *should* know by now that I don't go out. I'd never attended a party, a bonfire, or frequented any hangout spot like others my age. It's not like I know *his* life, but I can only imagine his social calendar isn't as depressingly empty as mine. For me, it's the diner and home. Every once in a blue moon, I'll stay after work to play a game of cards with Peg, only if she begs. But that's because Peg was my memaw's best friend, and she's the only person who still talks about her with me.

But dates with guys my age? Hell no. That would mean they'd risk being seen with Mack's daughter—an instant reputation ruiner. I prefer being ignored. It's better than being treated like I'm tainted.

"How much do I owe you?" I ask, sifting through my wallet.

The front door chimes, and a snappy voice fills the awkward silence. "What is that *dog* doing in *here*?"

I turn to see Levi's mom, her dark hair twisted in a knot at her neck and a silk blouse tucked in too tight. Her flowery perfume fills the air louder than her alarming presence. Even as a child, she rubbed me the wrong way.

With disgust, she stares at Opie and scurries toward the counter door, her heels clicking on the speckled linoleum floor. Opie misinterprets her body language, his body wiggling in anticipation of being pet. Instead, Mrs. Whitaker slams the half door in his face, and I stare, my jaw grinding in its socket.

"Mom, you remember Callie? I was just scanning her documents . . . and Opie's her dog." Levi's voice is tight and defensive as he stands rigid in his spot, staring at his mother.

Mrs. Whitaker, who pretends I didn't spend many afternoons at her house growing up, flashes me a fake smile with fake white teeth that are all straight as bowling pins.

"Sure, I do. But we have a strict no dogs allowed policy," she retorts, tapping red nails on the counter. She's tall, like her son, and suddenly, I feel so small in here.

"It's fine. I'm leaving." I slam down a five-dollar bill on the counter, not waiting for either of them to respond and turn sharply on my heel, nudging Opie to follow suit. I push the cold metal door open, the chime loud in my ear, and as the door closes behind me, a disgruntled argument between Levi and his mother starts up.

I want to whip my body around and offer Mrs. Whitaker some choice words, but I don't. I don't need to give anyone in this town more ammunition. Instead, I slide into my stuffy car, my voice cracking as I instruct Opie not to listen to that woman's nasty words. But my voice catches in my throat when I put the car in reverse and look up to see Levi standing alone at the counter, gazing at me through the glass windows. His face is long and full of hurt, and for a second, I only see the little boy on the playground who didn't care who I was or where I came from.

We break eye contact, and I pinch my lips together, reversing into the street and heading straight back up into the hills. Back to the trailer I call home, where I will finally submit all twenty photos to the school, along with an essay I've rewritten a dozen times. Back to where I can drown out the world and think about what lies ahead.

Because all I know is Charleston Photography Co. must accept me. I have to leave this town.

Chapter Three

June

On Tuesdays, I don't work at Peg's Diner, which has been my reluctant stomping ground for the past three years. When I got my license and could drive the old car Papa and Memaw left, I applied for a job there. Of course, the last thing I wanted was to serve burgers and milkshakes to my peers every weekend night. But it's still a small town, jobs are limited, and the tips are decent at Peg's, so I show up every shift to tie a faded white apron around my waist and count the pennies as they add up to dreams in my head.

Speaking of my dream, it's been two whole months since I clicked send on the email holding my fate. Other than Levi, no one knows about the photography program in Charleston. I plan on keeping it my secret—and leaving this town like a thief in the night.

Since I've been off all day, Opie and I have a designated lazy day—after a morning full of walks, of course. The weather is beautiful, sunshine and blue skies, so I take the chance to prop open all the windows of the trailer. The window over the dining table faces the meadow, so I sit there after our morning walk with a sweating glass of water, enjoying the warm breeze with my laptop open in front of me. Opie's sprawled on the vinyl floor, panting with his eyes closed.

I play videos and read articles, everything I can find, learning about Charleston and the photography program.

As my stomach starts to rumble, I close the screen of my laptop, stretching out my legs as Opie stirs on the floor. He's also hoping it's dinnertime. Dropping to sit on the floor next to him, with my back leaning up against the worn, wooden cabinets, Opie nuzzles me. From down here, I can see all the white fur coating the trailer floor. Actually, I can see most of the camper from this spot; it's not very big. Just big enough for us.

Looking down at my boy, I let myself get swept away in the dream of living in Charleston. I try to imagine the ocean breeze or what the city might smell like. It's hard to picture, even though I want it *so bad*. *If* I get accepted, I'll have to leave the first week of August. The program lasts only five months, but it's an intensive few months, with classes five days a week and the weekend full of assignments. It's like a semester-long masterclass; that's how the website describes it anyway. It costs a lot, too—almost equivalent to my entire savings. However, graduating from there would mean a world of opportunities, a professional portfolio, connections, and a new start.

My gaze is pulled down to Opie's fluttering eyes as he drifts in and out of sleep again, his heavy head resting on my legs. He's always too afraid to miss something I'm doing, yet he could sleep for days if I let him. Mindlessly drawing circles in the fur on his neck, I think about how the move will affect him too.

Every morning and night, I'll walk you through the beautiful, historic streets.

"It's for our future," I whisper to him as if he can hear my internal voice worrying about his adjustment to life in the city. We will make it work. Opie and I can make it through anything, I know.

One more week, and then we'll know whether we're getting out.

Chapter Four

Running my fingers quickly through my hair, I weave a braid that cascades down my back. Memaw taught me how to do it, and I had let her style my hair until the day she died, knowing it made her happy.

I always wondered how anyone so sweet could produce someone so rotten, though Mack didn't fully rot until Memaw was gone.

It's no excuse, Callie.

"Ready, Ope?"

He springs up as I slip on my hiking boots and drop my phone into the pockets of my thrifted sundress with yellow sunflowers. I only get in one moment of peaceful bird chirping and the sun shining before a cloud of dust kicks up behind the trailer. The old familiar sound of an uncapped diesel truck rumbles to a stop, blocking the trail to the creek.

With my mood soured, I plant myself stubbornly still as Mack jumps out of the truck, leaving it running, and marches right up to me. Squinting against the sun, I can barely bring myself to look him in the eyes—the same blue eyes I have.

"Carolina, I need a few bucks," he starts as he pulls his blue, beat-up baseball hat low over his eyes. It doesn't hide how bloodshot they are. Mack towers over me by at least a foot, and by the way his shirt wrinkles over his thin frame, it's safe to assume he's worn this outfit for days.

Scoffing in response, I turn to close the trailer door, whistling for Opie, who comes barreling out of the tall grass to sit at my side. He doesn't bother with acknowledging Mack; Opie's instincts are good. He knows when someone has ill intent.

"Carolina..." Mack pronounces every syllable of my name like he used to do when I was in trouble as a little girl.

"For the love of God, it's eight in the morning. And I don't have any cash anyway," I reply dryly, adjusting the water canteen in my arms. I have hundreds of dollars in bills in my trailer from tips, but the last thing I want to do is let Mack know that. For the most part, he leaves me to do what I please, but I wouldn't put it past him to steal from his own kin—or put one of his girlfriends up to it.

"Don't be lying to your daddy now. I know you got cash. I need it for gas."

"What about your disability check? I know you're not paying to keep up Papa's house, so where's it all going?" I ask, more out of spite than curiosity. I know where it's going.

"Don't get nasty. My money is *my money*. Been home for two months. That ain't enough time to get my shit together. I have a meeting with Officer Williams. So you either drive me or loan me some cash for gas."

Taking one look at his outstretched palm, my instinct is to slap it away, but it's too early in the morning to let Mack get under my skin. This is why I keep my distance. I wish I could put a fence on this part of the property. He has no business coming up here after he's the one who ruined everything.

And *loan* is a funny word. He's never once paid me back for all the times I had a moment of weakness and handed him a few dollars.

"Looks like you gotta call Officer Williams, then, and have your probation meeting at the house," I snap, but I know he can't do that. The farmhouse is riddled with bottles of alcohol and other things that would send Mack straight back to prison. He got out on good behavior, and his license was reinstated only a week ago. His girlfriend's been driving him everywhere, but I don't know where she is. Nor do I care.

"Or I miss it, they come up and search the house, I go back to prison, and guess what? You have to move off this land because they will take it too. Unless you'll pay for it, and if you don't even have five bucks for your old man, you can't afford this land—the land I'm letting you stay on for *free.*" His tone is hostile, and his icy blue eyes grow a shade darker. I hate this side of Mack more than most sides of him.

Without saying a word, I reach into my backpack and pull out a few crumpled dollars. It will get him there and back.

"That wasn't so hard, was it?" He shakes his head and jumps into his truck, revving it down the driveway, causing Opie to bark and chase the truck until I call for him to come back.

I don't know if what Mack's saying is true. If he misses a meeting, he's in trouble, considering his track record. But the land belonged to Mack's parents, passed down to him when they died. As far as I've been told, it's been paid off, and the only thing Mack's been owing is property tax. I don't know if I have any legal right to be on it other than the fact that my own blood tilled this land, carved these walking trails, and built this farmhouse.

It only feels like I belong here when I'm trekking through the pines and tall grasses with Opie by my side. I whistle, walking toward my favorite thing about this piece of mountainside land: the creek.

The creek has always been my reprieve. It's where I ran to when Memaw took her last breath, it's where I cried when Darren Peters broke my heart, and it's where I take Opie every morning. Mack never comes up this way; it's like my own paradise. As close to paradise as Miscruz Hills can offer me.

The creek is also where I learned to love photography. When the high school art teacher loaned me a crappy digital camera for my junior year project and told me to photograph something I love most, I took it home and made my way straight to the creek bed, where the trees reach across the narrowest part. I captured what I saw, unsure if the images were any good.

Maybe that's why I love photography. It's not always perfect. Sometimes, it's grainy, or I catch the light wrong. But those messed-up ones are my favorite, like the blurry photo of Opie hanging over my bed in the trailer. I took it a few months after he came into my life. I was still new at film photography, and Opie was still new at being someone's pet. The photo captured his wildness and my novice. It felt like we were blooming together.

Once I make it to the creek, I pick up a fallen branch, tossing it downstream, and watch with a grin as Opie clumsily runs through the rocky creek bed to chase it.

Sometimes, I wonder, if things had been different with the people in my life, maybe I wouldn't be so adamant about leaving this town. When I think of Miscruz Hills, I think of nothing. Nothing good, at least. No friends are begging me to stay. Even if the people I grew up with were my friends, many of them are off living their lives at college, shrinking the population of this town in their absence.

For me, moving to the other side of the property was the start of my getaway. I'd spent two years living alone in the farmhouse, fully emancipated from Mack while he was in prison. I couldn't have afforded to leave even if I wanted to. Though the land was peaceful with him gone. It was my escape. Once I graduated high school, I had enough money saved to fix up the old camping trailer to make it a temporary home. I'd been in the trailer nearly ten months by the time Mack was released and moved back home to the farmhouse. We were separated by trees and tall grass fields, but the sheer thought of even being on the same property enraged me.

When I look at him, all I see is the family who suffered at the drunken foot of my father and his truck. I don't know if they forgave him.

But I know I wouldn't. I haven't.

If that makes me a bad person, then so be it. I don't know how to come to terms with the person Mack has become.

I don't remember my mama. She died from terminal sickness when I was only two years old. I only know that Mack loved her more than he loved anyone, even me. He tried to be a good father for as long as he could. Most days, it feels like a light switch. One minute, I'm eight years old, being read bedtime stories by a single father who was rough but cared for me in his own way; the next, he's involved me in an accident that rattled our small town and left a boy in my town paralyzed.

My throat grows tight as I scrape a stone against the boulder I'm sitting on. Mack's never a welcome guest in my head, but it seems like he always has a way of sticking like glue.

What hurts the most isn't the nasty words hurled at me by my peers after that night. It's what wasn't said, what *Mack* never said. There was never a "sorry" or acknowledgment of the accident that changed our lives. I sometimes think that maybe Mack knew there was no going back, that he'd never regain my trust, which is why he never tried. Mack simply gave up on being a father to me.

So I gave up on him.

"Opie, come here!" My voice echoes among the tall trees. Opie's big head bounces up from the bent grass along the creek. As he nears, he drops a slobbery stone at my feet, nudging it toward me when I don't pick it up. He's always been odd, carrying stones around like tennis balls. "Good boy," I scratch his head, tossing him a stick instead.

As Opie chases it downstream, I pull off my boots, tucking my socks carefully inside and stretching my legs out in front of me, sitting on the smooth rock that's been a staple in my life for as long as I can remember. The creek rushes by slowly, the water clear and cool.

This spot is special. I've never brought anyone out here. Well, only one person: Darren Peters, my first and only boyfriend.

Darren is classically handsome, a talented football player, and well-liked. I still don't understand why he dated me, other than maybe me being a sophomore and him being a senior made it easier for him to manipulate me. When he asked me on a date, I thought it was a joke, but when it kept happening, I finally gave in, flattered that someone was paying attention to me. He isn't the kind of guy you say no to anyway.

One date turned into many, and though we had little in common, it was, for the most part, nice to be with him. Or maybe it was just nice to not be alone. He didn't mind that I was quiet. He said he preferred to keep our relationship between us. He told me he loved me, and I loved him, too, so I let him take my virginity. I thought maybe, after nearly a year of being together, that meant I wouldn't live my life as a quiet person in the shadows. Because Darren saw me. But that was so naive.

The day after the accident, once word had spread around town of what happened, Darren Peters waited on my front porch for me to get home from the hospital just to tell me he couldn't be with me anymore. I was broken and lost, hoping he, of all people, wouldn't blame me. But the first words out of his mouth were, "How could you?"

He made it clear there was no more *us*. Nothing I said mattered, and frankly, I had no fight left in me.

I had been in the truck with Mack, after all. I *was* gripping the wheel when my father drunkenly hit Everett Calloway, the football captain, golden boy of the town, Darren's friend.

That day, Darren confirmed something I feared was true.

Life would never be the same. I was forever, and always going to be, the girl in the car that night. I was Mack Hayes's daughter and forever responsible for the tragedy.

The cries of a hawk soaring overhead rip me from my memory and bring me back to the rock. I see Opie through hazy eyes, and I stand up, dipping my feet into the cold creek, whisking away the thoughts.

There's nothing left for you in this town but reminders of everything that was and everything that could've been. Let it go, Callie.

Chapter Five

Three knocks on my trailer door startle me from sleep. Rubbing my eyes, I pull back the navy-blue sheet hanging over my bedroom window, and my stomach drops. It's not Mack's truck out there this time but another car I've come to know.

Opie startles and lets out a howl big enough to scare off even the angriest black bear.

Three more knocks, gentler this time. I whip off the blankets.

"One moment! Coming!" I yell out, shushing Opie and pulling my shorts off the heap on the floor. I work the dinner shift, five to eleven tonight at the diner, and my midday nap is *essential*. So whatever my *visitor* needs, it better be imperative.

I nearly trip over the overturned basket of dog toys, rush past a sink full of dishes that still smell like breakfast, and unlock the door before pushing it open. I shield my eyes against the looming sun as I take in the person standing tall in front of the trailer door.

"Good afternoon, Callie," Officer Williams addresses me, tipping his head slightly.

His uniform looks neatly pressed and spotless, like his squad car, which is parked next to my piece of junk. Opie shoves into the back of my knees, bolting outside. Officer Williams smiles wide, squatting down to pet his head. Opie sniffs all over, quickly getting bored, and goes to check out the strange car. Over Officer Williams's shoulder, I catch Opie lifting a leg to pee on the tire, but I don't attempt to deter him. That's what he gets for disrupting our peaceful slumber.

"Um, what can I do for you?" I cross my arms abruptly over my chest, realizing I may have put shorts on, but I never put my bra back on under my oversized T-shirt.

"I'm here to check in on your dad. I stopped down at the house but didn't see him there. He isn't returning his probation officer's calls, so I thought maybe you had an idea where he could be." He looks up earnestly at me, and it takes everything in me not to roll my eyes.

Officer Williams is young and one of four officers in Miscruz Hills. He's only been here about three years, which is long enough to know my father *and,* subsequently, me.

"Yesterday, Mack asked for gas money so he could make his probation meeting. That's the last I saw of him."

Williams chews his lip pensively. We both know what that means.

"Well, see, the issue is he didn't actually show up to the meeting." He pauses, rubbing the stubble growing along his jawline. "And you haven't texted him or know where he might be today?"

A small chuckle breaks through my tight smile. Mack hasn't asked for my new number since returning from prison. It's not like I'd give it to him anyway. "I have no idea where he is." I just want to return to my nap, so I offer him a bone. "Have you checked his usual spots? He's dating a woman. Winnie . . . maybe it's Wendy?" I suggest, then push past him.

"Opie!" I call out, and he comes barreling out of the woods. He never strays far, but that's because I don't let him out of my sight for long.

"Okay, got it. Well, thank you, Ms. Hayes." His eyes waver as he chews his lip, surely hoping I'm holding back vital information.

I don't know where Mack is, and I don't care, I want to scream. He is a grown man, and it's not my job to keep track of him. He has barely kept track of me all these years.

"If you hear from him, will you give me a call?"

My eyes meet his outstretched hand, which is holding a business card with his info. I nod. "Uh-huh. Will do," I reply, not taking the card. I've had his number in my phone for three years now, and it's not something I need or want to be reminded of.

I push Opie inside and shut the door behind me, then wait until the sound of tires fades before I lay back down and close my eyes to the world.

Behind my eyelids, I can pretend I'm anywhere but here.

Chapter Six

I pull into the diner parking lot with only a few moments to spare. My old tennis shoes rub uncomfortably against my heel as I get out and lean down to look in the car window, using it as a mirror to loop my hair into a messy bun on top of my head. I swipe on a little mascara and ChapStick before tying my apron tight around my waist.

It doesn't take long after arriving at Peg's Diner for my tables to nearly fill up. The steam from the fryers clogs up the air of the kitchen as we grow busy, and greasy food smells cling to my hair and clothes. Between refilling sodas and badgering the cook for more French fries, I don't have a chance to even notice the group of college-aged guys sitting in my corner booth. I squint, trying to see who's there, hoping they'll cause me no trouble.

Peg pushes the kitchen door open. "Callie, can you take this order up? It's a take-out order for the foxy young officer." Peg winks at me, placing a heavy bag and four to-go cups in my arms. Peg sways away with an extra pep in her step, her four-foot-nine frame seemingly taller, and leaves a stream of heavy floral perfume.

Leave it to Peg to have a crush on the officer young enough to be her grandson. Meanwhile, I hold my anxiety about seeing Officer Williams at bay.

It's another tip. Another dollar toward the great escape jar.

The diner is crowded, which makes the lights feel brighter to me, and people wait impatiently in the entrance, hoping for a table. Officer Williams's stocky frame and short blond hair stick out in the crowd of teenagers. He smiles cordially at me as I approach him with his food.

"It's all here." The heavy bag thuds on the counter next to the register, and I don't look up as he hands me three twenty-dollar bills.

"How's Opie tonight?"

I can't help but narrow my eyebrows at him. "Probably at home chewing something he shouldn't be," I add dryly as the cash drawer whooshes open.

Officer Williams leans in, his face so close to mine I can smell his musky cologne. My shoulders tense, and I forget how much change I'm supposed to give him.

"We found Mack. He was at his girlfriend's house. Thanks for the tip."

I peer up as he smiles and shrugs at me. I don't acknowledge what he said. My fingers hover above the cash, frozen in time.

"And I mean it, Callie. If you need anything—anything at all—I'm here to help." He pats the countertop beside my hand, and I pull back. "And keep the change."

I expel my breath and slam the drawer shut. I'll figure out the difference after he leaves. "Enjoy your dinner," I say robotically, turning on my heel.

"It's for the whole crew. I'm not eating this all myself." He laughs as he scoops up the heavy bag in one arm.

I offer him a tight-lipped grin and nod, immediately turning my attention to the table in the corner. Officer Williams says no more, leaving.

The corner booth is usually reserved for groups, but tonight, it's just three large guys, taking up space with both their bodies and voices.

Boisterous laughter fills the diner as I walk near them, pen and pad in hand. As I scan the faces, my stomach flips.

Inky dark hair and eyes like ice. Square shoulders and lips that can cut.

The thought of dashing into the back and telling Peg I'm sick and need to leave wafts into my head but is gone in a poof when Darren makes eye contact with me. His blue eyes pierce mine. His lips twitch as my mouth falls open slightly. It's too late. If I give my table away now, he will know that merely his glance can make my heart feel shredded all over again.

I'll act completely unbothered. Simple enough. It's been three years. *Three whole years*, I remind myself.

"Hey. Can I start you all with something to drink?" I ask, my lips turned in a tight smile that doesn't match my eyes.

The guy to Darren's left starts, telling me he wants a coke. I focus on the emblem on his pocket as he speaks. Darren leans back, his muscular arms crossed over his chest, and smirks. His gaze bores into me, right through my layer of armor. I wish my hair wasn't pulled back and was instead unraveled in front of my face to hide the torment I know is written all over it.

I glance over, my pen leaving a pool of blue ink on my pad. "One coke. And for you?" I ask my ex-boyfriend.

He doesn't stop staring. An amused smirk is plastered to his full lips, making me want to crawl out of my skin.

"Callie, how've you been?" He smacks his lips, feigning care as his eyes drag the length of my body. His friends take the queue to back off, leaning into the booth.

"I'm good. Thanks." My throat quickly goes dry. I turn to the guy on Darren's other side, smiling and hoping he will tell me his damn drink order, but I'm not that lucky.

"I'm away for a few years, and everything's changed, huh?" Darren teases.

This time, I look him dead in the eye, genuinely clueless. "Sorry, I don't know what—"

"The officer. That's adorable, Cal." He winks and continues. "Ah, come on, baby. I saw the way he was looking at you. I know you like strong guys. He's not as big as me, but you know."

He winks again, and I want nothing more than to disintegrate into the air.

"Kinda hypocritical though, isn't it? Dating a cop, when you should be in prison," the guy next to Darren chimes in. His tone edges on joking, but it's clear enough to cut.

A wave of nausea rolls through me.

"Oh, Jeff. Come on . . . be nice to our girl Callie," Darren fakely protests, covering his mouth to stifle a laugh.

"Okay, three waters. I'll be back." I slip my pad and pen into my apron and walk through the swinging door, ignoring a woman motioning me from my other table.

Breathe, Callie. You're stronger now. What they say isn't true. It doesn't matter.

Minutes later, I deliver water to the table, and Darren seems pleased that I'm shaken up. After all, I haven't seen him since he graduated high school and went to university in South Carolina.

My tables stay full, with an endless stream of diners, giving me the chance to rightfully avoid Darren for long periods of time. When they finish eating, I flit by their table, drop the check, and ignore Darren's calling of my name.

"Peg, I'm taking five!" I call out, bustling through the kitchen to grab a drink.

The back door opens into the dark overflowing parking lot. I lean against the brick wall, shutting my eyes to the world. The smell of trash invades my senses, but I keep my eyes closed, mentally counting the tips I've made tonight.

Photography. Charleston. Opie. You're so close, Cal.

"Callie?"

Darren's voice jolts my eyelids open. "What do you want?" I croak dryly.

The parking lot lights shine brightly on the asphalt, glaring off the slick oil near the dumpster. Suddenly, the air feels chillier knowing Darren Peters is here in my space. He pushes his hands into his sweatpants pockets, his black hair falling over his eyebrows as he condescendingly leans down to talk to me. My chest rises rapidly with each passing second.

"You know I don't give a fuck who you're dating, right?" he starts.

I scoff, kicking the pebbles near my feet. I don't know where he's going with this, but I doubt it's anywhere good.

"Okay," I reply curtly, feeling the brick against my back. Darren leans in, shoving a toothpick between his lips, leaving only inches between us.

Please just leave.

"So you're still here?" His eyes scan the diner.

For a moment, I look at his face and think about the brief, naive time in my life when I thought we loved each other.

"Working? Yes, I still have a job," I push out through a dry throat, my arms tight across my chest.

"And still a wiseass, I see. I just thought you hated this town. Figured you'd be gone by now." He laughs loudly, and I can feel his breath on me.

I can't laugh, though. Not about him, not about us, and not about the situation I'm in.

Another waitress opens the door as my eyes start to well.

"Table six is asking for you, hon," she informs me while narrowing her eyes skeptically at Darren.

"Thanks, Carla." I bob under Darren's arm to follow her inside, pausing to look back over my shoulder at my past. "And don't worry about me. I *will* be gone soon." Darren's expression goes blank as I let the door slam behind me.

The noise of clinking silverware, babbling diners, and sizzling griddles drown out the thoughts manifesting in my head. Darren's words stung, but I'm not going to let them fester. Maybe they are the fire I need to push myself, to get out of here for good, one more piece of ammunition.

As I'm getting ready to clock out, I stop by Peg's small office. It's more of a closet, really, with wood-paneled walls and just enough room for a small desk and a large clock on the wall. Papers are piled all over the desk, and sometimes I worry that Peg's small frame will get buried if they ever come crashing down.

"Hey, sweet pea. Thanks for working tonight." She smiles at me, and the skin crinkles around her soft brown eyes.

A pool of warmth fills my heart when she stands to pat me on the arm. Peg's always been sweet to me, never once saying anything about my father or the accident. She treats me like everyone else, if not more special. I know she misses Memaw, too. They grew up together. I can't imagine losing a friend after all that time.

"Peg, I was wondering if I could pick up an extra shift or two this week." I chew my cheek, needlessly worried. I'm the hardest-working waitress she has, and we both know it.

"Of course! I'll get you added to a few breakfast shifts. How 'bout that?"

"That'd be great. Good night." I tap on the door and offer her a tired smile before yanking the string of my apron, letting it fall into my hand as I head to the car.

Chapter Seven

July

"It's really coming down out there, ain't it?" the old man in the booth remarks, whistling as he peers out the diner window.

I nod, half-listening, looking at the evening sky as the humidity builds and anxiety bubbles in my stomach. July is the wettest month in Southwestern North Carolina, but this storm is nastier than any we've seen yet. It has scared half the diners away tonight. More than anything, I hate that I'm not at home right now for Opie. It's only dinnertime, but the sky is dark as coal, making the lights in the diner feel glaringly bright.

I worked the morning shift, came home to get Opie out, rested a few hours, and returned for the expected dinner rush, but the rush never happened. I made out decently this morning, though.

Peg catches me on my way to grab the coffeepot. "Callie, you okay?"

No, I'm not. I'm barely holding on right now. The picture of the letter crumpled on my bed holds fast in my head. I almost called off from this shift—something I've never done—but I couldn't be in the trailer either. No place feels safe. Everything here in this town reminds me of *everything*. I didn't know what was next; I hadn't had time to process it yet.

Actually, I didn't want to process it.

When I went home for my break, Mack flagged me down as I drove past the farmhouse. He had an envelope in his hand, and immediately, a sinking feeling came over me, followed by cold chills. Mack handed me the mail through the passenger's side window, and I found out that he had the letter in his house for *a while*. He forgot to give it to me. Anger flashed before my eyes, but it was quickly overcome by the realization that this single piece of mail held my future—late or not.

However, it wasn't the thick packet I had been manifesting in my mind. No. It was a single, small, dirt-smeared envelope. Like it was nothing. Like the ink letters on the stamped stationery didn't hold the weight of my future.

With shaky hands, I opened the letter once I was home with Opie, who sat expectantly at my feet, his toes tapping in anticipation. Of course, he didn't know why, but he could sense I was on edge. He always knows.

The words I'd read next were enough to shatter me:

Callie Hayes,

Thank you for applying to Charleston Photography Co. It's humbling every year to see how many applicants we have from all over the nation who dream of partaking in our intensive and award-winning photography program. Your portfolio is impressive, and your ability to capture a story in a single shot really caught our attention.

However, we regret to inform you that you have not been selected for the fall program. We received a record-breaking number of applicants and had to be incredibly selective. As you know, we can only accept twenty students to study with us every fall.

Each year, we move a select number of applicants to a waitlist. This works like a standby. For several reasons, there may be students who cannot attend the fall session. Applicants accepted must monetarily commit by the second week in July. If, for any reason, there is a student who does not make this timeline and backs out of the program, we will contact you, as you are the first contender on our waitlist.

Regardless of our decision, we hope you have an excellent summer and continue with your photography studies.

Best,

Trisha Davenport
Director of Admissions
Charleston Photography Program

A clang of dishes brings me back to the diner, and I swallow hard, focusing on Peg. She looks concerned, so I wave toward the window.

"I'm okay. The storm just makes me uneasy. Opie hates storms." That part *is* true.

Peg looks around the diner before settling her soft gaze on me. "It's slow tonight, hon. Why don't you take the evening off? You can cover breakfast tomorrow morning if you want." Peg leans on the counter, her eyes heavy.

"Okay," I say, feeling both defeated and relieved to be going home.

Driving up the hill to the farm, I'm met with nothing but pelting rain that outpaces my windshield wipers. My mind flashes back to the nasty storm we had a while ago, where I was sure the water and wind would collapse my old tin roof. That night, Opie and I curled up in bed while I played a movie as loud as I could to drown out the storm for him. He wiggled his trembling body under the covers until he found his spot next to me, his head resting in the crook of my neck.

I comforted him the same way Memaw would comfort me as a little girl, rubbing my back while my head leaned on her chest.

As I pull into the driveway and pass the farmhouse, I can barely make out anything, except for Mack's rusty blob of a truck along with a red car I've seen here every day over the last week. I'm guessing it belongs to Mack's on-again, off-again girlfriend, Wendy. He only introduced us once. I came in through the back door to retrieve some things I stored in the attic, and she freaked out, thinking I was another woman. I guess having a nineteen-year-old daughter isn't something worth mentioning to him.

The farmhouse is in the rearview now, and all I can do is pray the blue tarp I tied over one side of the roof hasn't blown off. I preventatively placed a bucket inside before I left for work, right under the spot that always leaks. However, Opie has a bad habit of treating it as a second water bowl, pushing it along the door as he drinks from it. It's innocent but results in a puddle in a trailer that's already barely hanging on.

The sound of the rain is deafening, and taking two looks at the umbrella on the passenger seat, I know it's pointless. So I run for it. As my legs kick up mud behind me and I shield my face as best I can, I see it: the dented front door is banging wildly against the side of the trailer, leaving it wide open. Beyond it, all I see is a lake of water accumulating inside my home.

"Fuck!" I scream, abandoning all hope of keeping an inch of me dry.

How did this happen? When did this happen? Why, of all days, does this have to happen today?

Memaw's voice plays in my head: "When it rains, it pours honey!" I want to cry. But as I leap inside, my shoes sloshing in the inches of water on the trailer floor, a sinking feeling overcomes me.

"Opie! Opie!" I call, falsely chipper so I don't scare him away. Rushing toward the back of the trailer where my bedroom is, I throw myself through the doorway.

"Opie! Where are you, buddy?"

With each unanswered call, my heart pushes harder into my rib cage, threatening to burst. In a sweeping motion, I push the clothes and blankets off my bed, hoping my arm collides with a warm body, but my clothes fall onto a water-soaked bedroom floor. Falling to my knees, I dip my head to peer under the bed.

Thunder and lightning crack across the sky, and I curse at Mother Nature as I rush to the living space. Pulling on my wet hair, I spin in circles, scanning every inch of the trailer and praying Opie is camouflaging himself, that I'm just losing my mind. It's nearly eight p.m., and this storm doesn't look like it's letting up anytime soon.

Then I notice it.

The big pot I positioned under the leak isn't here. Peering up, I see a glint of silver right outside the front door. Opie must've pushed it right into the door, triggering the weak latch to open.

"Fuck, fuck, fuck! You're so stupid, Callie!"

My voice cracks, and a small sob releases from my tight chest. My clothes are already soaked through. My tears blend in.

You can't cry.

I have to keep it together and find Opie. It's not time to have a meltdown.

I push aside all the emotions that bubble up when I think about how scared Opie gets during storms. I can't think about that. I need to stay strong and focused. I need to go find my dog. He usually curls in a ball, tight, under something that makes him feel safe.

"Oh my God..." I whisper, grabbing the waterproof flashlight and bag of treats near the door. He's probably under the trailer. *Poor thing.*

Rain pelts my back as I step outside into the cold, wet air with a new sense of hope in my veins. Kneeling beside the trailer, my knees sink into nothing but pure mud. The old flashlight flickers as I scan the length of the trailer.

"Opie! It's okay, boy. Come on, Opie!" I call, slowly scanning the length of my home. There's nothing underneath but soggy cardboard boxes and a few tennis balls Opie stashes away for safekeeping.

Cold rainwater collects heavily on my eyelashes as I approach the harrowing woods. The trees that are beautiful and green in the morning now look frightening under the sagging weight of water and darkened skies. There are a million directions Opie could've run.

"Okay, think, Callie. *Think.*" A deep breath rattles my lungs. If he didn't run back into the trailer or hide under it, he probably would have gone to seek another shelter.

The darkroom shed! I run back inside, slipping off my soaked tennis shoes and sliding on rain boots and a rain jacket. The shed is a minute's walk through the field.

"Opie! Please be here. I have treats!" I shake the treat bag and dash into the shed, circling the small interior twice.

Empty.

He always comes, bounding across a field, if he hears my voice. *Always.*

There's a possibility Mack was creating a ruckus earlier, like usual, and Opie might have run down the hill to his house to investigate. It's not the first time he would've done it.

My feet slosh inside my boots, and mascara stings my eyes, but I jog through the field to my car, glad I left the keys in the ignition for once. I drive slowly to the farmhouse, my window cracked, as I call for Opie, praying I'll see a white dog run out of the woods.

As the farmhouse comes into view, I spot something white under the porch near the back door. My breath hitches in my chest, and I slam the brakes, jumping out of the car and running toward the farmhouse.

"Opie! Opie!" I scream the whole way, the ground so muddy and slippery that I have to walk with extreme caution.

The back door whips open, startling me. Mack leans out, wearing a faded flannel that's unevenly buttoned. A beer is clutched in one hand while smoke plumes from his mouth.

"What the hell is going on, Carolina?" he hollers through the rain, but I ignore him. The white ball comes clearly into view. It's just an old cooler.

"No! Dammit, no!" I fall to my knees at the base of the porch, running the palms of my hands down my cheeks.

"You going to tell me what the hell you're doing?" Mack slurs his words but stays under the protection of the porch roof.

Running my hand over the white cooler, I claw down the sides until I let my arms fall into the mud near my knees.

Hold it together.

I stand up, my limbs muddied with earth. The rain hasn't let up in volume, but the winds have died down, no longer blowing droplets sideways.

"Opie ran out into the storm while I was at work, and I can't find him," I speak, my voice breaking as the truth settles over my tired, shivering body.

Mack stares at me, his eyes blank but glassy, as he puffs another smoke, then tosses the cigarette into the yard, where it's swallowed by the puddles forming around the house. We stare at each other momentarily, a beat longer than we've looked at each other in a long time. My heart's racing, and my skin feels tight at my throat. Mack pushes himself forward. The slightest bit toward me. I want to fall on the ground, crying, begging my *father* to help me.

His mouth twitches, and his jaw hangs open before he speaks. "He'll come back, Carolina. Dogs ain't that dumb, you know? You wait and see. He'll be back once all this shit clears up." He nods at me like he's offered me a message from God himself.

I stare right past him, unblinking. Whatever small string of hope I once held for Mack, whatever comfort I craved from a father who once held me in times of need, died in this moment.

"Now get on home. It's dark, and I don't need your car stuck in my yard and blocking Wendy." He guzzles the rest of the beer, tossing the empty can into an overflowing bin. The clanging noise of the metal is marked by the silence that comes after he shuts the back door, leaving me standing there in the rain alone.

A chill settles into my bones.

Some people probably assume I feel lonely, living in the trailer by myself. Only child, no family. After Memaw died, I did feel alone for the first time. But then I got used to it. It still gnawed at me, but I made it through. I made it to eighteen without her by my side. And when the creeping feeling of loneliness crept back in, Opie found me.

With Opie, I never felt alone. I felt complete. He's my companion, my other half. We have a way of speaking to each other that no one would understand; dare I ever mention it to anyone anyway. He knows when I need him. He knows how to find me when my world is crumbling. He's my home.

And now you've lost him, Callie. Now you are alone.

More than the night sky and the violent rain, more than my father's denial of my call for help, standing here in the world not knowing where my boy is—*this* feels like my darkest hour.

Chapter Eight

At the sharp sound of snapping branches, I whip my body around, shining the flashlight behind me. The moonlight is gone, and it's nearly pitch black, leaving me to squint through the raindrops. Adrenaline pumps through my body, and my heart pounds in my throat, but there's nothing there.

Without warning, my leg is pierced with searing pain, and I frantically point the beam of light on my leg. Blood barely has time to puddle on my skin, with the rain washing it off my shins instantaneously. A vine of thorns has hooked itself into my leg, and I painfully grit my teeth as I pull it from my skin.

I *should* go home and clean this cut. I've been calling for Opie for hours now, circling the property, trekking every route, every single trail he knows. My muscles ache for rest, and my head pounds in the rhythm of my erratic heartbeat. Forget that I've been soaked to my bones for two hours now.

If I curled up on the mossy floor, would anyone find me? Would anyone even come looking for me?

No. Of course they wouldn't.

With eyes squeezed shut, I inhale deeply, trying to take my focus off my stinging leg and shivering limbs. But the pain, cold, and exhaustion rip through me viciously, and I know I must go home.

I trudge to the trailer, calling out Opie's name, shaking the bag of treats that have become useless wet crumbs. I desperately fight the tears stinging behind my eyes. Crying feels like I've succumbed to defeat, and I haven't.

I am not giving up. I can fix this.

Maybe he returned home. I've been gone for over three hours, and the thunder has stopped; now it's a misting of rain at midnight. Perhaps he missed his bed and the warmth of my body next to his. Maybe he thought about breakfast and how I put an extra fried egg on his kibble. Perhaps he can sense the fear in my body as I whisper his name into the night for no one but me to hear.

Maybe *he's* the one waiting for *me*.

The solar lantern hanging by the door glows in the distance. It appears even the stars have abandoned me out here, the night inky black, but I know these grounds like the back of my hand, and as I come over the hill, the outline of the trailer comes into view.

"Opie! I'm home! You here, boy?" I stop in my tracks, holding my breath to hear any noise that could be my boy. I try again. "Opie, come here!" I attempt to whistle, but my mouth is dry despite everything else being drenched.

I'm met with nothing but silence.

I round the trailer one more time, scanning the bushes and ditches for Opie, who, at this point, I'm accepting could be hurt or have strayed very, very far away. But my search comes up empty.

"Okay. Okay. Okay."

Maybe Mack is right. Dogs come back on their own. I can't search for him in the dark any longer. I'll have to continue in the morning. And the dog shelter isn't open yet *if* someone finds Opie and brings him in. There is nothing else to do right now. A golden glow comes from inside the trailer, a beacon of light in this darkness that surrounds me.

I swallow my fears and strip off my wet clothes, leaving them in a pile outside the front door. Stepping inside, I hesitate to latch the door, wondering if he might return. Would he bark to let me know? I decided, yes, Opie will bark. He'll let me know he is home.

Inside, the trailer is damp, and I spend the next hour using every towel I own to dry it with shaky arms and bloodshot eyes. I toss the towels in the shower stall and then throw on a long shirt that hangs to my thighs and fall onto my bed. The quilt feels damp, but my eyes are like steel weights. I curl up under the heavy quilt, clutching Opie's favorite plush dinosaur toy tightly to my chest.

Only five hours later, I stir awake. The leaves and grass drip with dew, and soon, the yolky sun will rise outside my window, but inside, I find anything but peace. I had a dream I was falling, the pit of my stomach tumbling inside me until I sprang up in a panic, sweat slickly coating my head and chest. My eyes cast downward to the faded plush toy still gripped tightly against my chest.

This isn't a dream, Callie.

The raised bloody welts on my legs and the bruises on my arms remind me that last night was very real indeed.

The sun has barely risen over the mountains, but it's enough light that I'll be able to see, so I roll off the bed, ignoring the pounding in my head and the bed that's still cold and damp. I slip on sweatpants and a sweatshirt and slide my bare feet into boots, giving up on finding socks. It was taking too long, and time isn't something I have to spare.

My voice is hoarse, but I fight through it, calling for Opie with all my might. With puffy eyes, I trace the ground outside, praying to see paw prints in the thick mud, but there's nothing but my boot tracks. They go in every direction, a million times over, making it appear like fifty people were searching for Opie.

Back inside, I fall onto the stiff sofa, which is still damp, when the familiar feeling of sickening adrenaline returns to my body.

Time is critical. I know enough about animal behavior to understand that the first forty-eight hours yield the highest results when searching for a missing pet.

When I close my eyes, all I see is the skin and bones that made up Opie's young body last summer. I will not let him endure that kind of suffering again. The thought of it makes my heart feel like a thousand knives are carving away, and I have to physically shake myself to clear the invading dread.

Grabbing my laptop, I start searching. *What to do when your dog goes missing. How to find a runaway dog.*

An overwhelming number of articles populate, but I read through each one, scribbling tip after tip on the back of a receipt. After an hour, my body is stiff from not moving, hunched over my laptop, but I have a list of things I can do.

I'll call Opie's vet and the dog shelter the minute they open. And the ones in the towns surrounding me. I will leave Opie's favorite things outside the trailer and around his favorite places on the property. My eyes skim over a point I've seen made in every article.

Gather your family, friends, and community to help you.

Well, you can't do it all. Everything else on this list will have to be enough. If this community has made anything clear, it's that nobody is interested in me and my dog.

However, there is *one* person who pops into my head. As I stand to dress, I try to dismiss the idea, but it keeps returning with a gnawing feeling that gets stronger and stronger.

Fine. I'll do it. I have to try for Opie.

CHAPTER NINE

I'm the first to open the police station door at seven a.m. The entrance chime is unnervingly loud and is mirrored by the hardened expression of the older woman behind the front desk. Her eyes peer over the desk at me. My sandals squeak on the tile floor as I approach the counter, and I tuck my T-shirt into my patched-up jean shorts, suddenly nervous to be here, unsure what to do with my hands or my thoughts.

A Hayes seeking help from the police. It's almost laughable.

"Can I help you?" she asks in an uninterested voice, pushing thick glasses up the bridge of her nose.

Every muscle in my body begs me to turn around and run. I don't want to ask for help from him, but I speak up before I can doubt my instincts.

"I wanted to talk with an officer. Is, um, Owen Williams in this morning?" The offices of the cops are behind the half wall, lined with dying houseplants.

"Are you here to report a crime? Because there's a sheet I need you to fill out." She looks up at me, her arms strewn across her chest.

"Well, no. I'm not sure, really. I just . . ."

"Officer Williams is busy this morning, ma'am, so if it's a personal thing—" she starts but is cut off when he pops above the wall. His eyes meet mine, and his eyebrows pinch together for a moment.

"Sharon, I have a moment," he says sweetly to her in a thick accent, and she rolls her eyes, returning to clicking ferociously on her ancient computer. "Callie, please come back."

I walk around, following him into his cubicle. He smells like soap and is freshly shaven, which makes me feel even more of a mess as I pull my braid over my shoulder and smooth the wrinkles in my faded shirt. Officer Williams points to the chair beside his desk, and I reluctantly sit on the edge. I don't *want* to sit. Sitting feels inactive. It feels like pausing when all I want to do is walk the streets and run through the woods and call out for Opie until I can no longer speak.

I pile my phone and keys onto my lap while an old box fan buzzes next to us, circulating warm air.

"It's a bit warm in here. Sorry 'bout that. Our AC went out this week." Officer Williams leans forward on his desk, turning pointedly toward me. He places his phone on his desk and turns it upside down, giving me his full attention. I know he is doing this to make me feel more comfortable, but what he doesn't know is I'm screaming inside. The lights are too bright, the coffee machine spitting coffee is too noisy, I can hear Sharon talking loudly to someone on the phone, and the chair is too cold on my bare legs. I can feel everything right now, and I just want to cry.

"Is everything okay, Callie?" His voice is laden with concern.

"It's kind of time-sensitive. I mean, I don't know if you can even help me . . . or why I came here. I didn't know what to do . . ." I ramble quickly and pinch the bridge of my nose, squeezing my eyes shut for a minute. I dig my fingernails into my legs.

"Okay. Slow down." He places a hand on his desk, then pulls it back. "Start at the beginning and tell me what happened."

My feet bounce on the speckled linoleum floor, my eyes suddenly heavy under the yellowing fluorescent light, but I manage to tell him everything.

I tell him how I got home last night and how my door was wide open. I tell him shamefully about the latch I never got fixed, wanting him to blame me for this entire mess. Lord knows I blame myself right now.

I tell him about searching for hours last night. And the whole time I talk, my eyes never leave his desk until I pause, and he clears his throat, so I peer up at him. His green eyes look dark, his brow furrowed low.

Officer Williams shakes his head slowly, rubbing his eyes, and pushes back from the desk, stretching his legs before him. The beats of silence between us make me start to squirm.

This may be a stupid mistake. What can he do?

"And you've checked in with Mack, made sure Opie didn't end up down at the house?" His fingers tap his chin, and I want to slap them away, push him back, and shake him. He *knows* my father. He knows everything.

"Of course, I did. He doesn't give a shit about me or my dog," I spit out, agitated with this man sitting calmly in front of me while I crumble.

He nods slowly.

I grip my phone harder in my hands, feeling my knuckles turn white, waiting on the cusp of his words, hoping for one tiny inkling of *help*.

"What about the neighbors? Have you checked with any of them?"

Scrunching my eyebrows, I shake my head. "There aren't any neighbors up there. Far as I've ever known, we own the land all around. If there are other houses, they aren't close by."

"Callie, I—"

We get interrupted by a call coming through on the radio. It's a code I don't understand, and Williams responds, grabbing keys off his desk and standing. So I stand, too.

"You have to go," I state matter-of-factly, and a sinking feeling returns, the same one I walked in here with. He can't help me. Because when he said if I needed anything, he didn't really mean *anything*.

"I do. Um, why don't you walk out with me?"

I oblige because there's only one way out of this building. We walk past Sharon, and I feel her eyes following us, judging me. Officer Williams walks briskly, and I have to nearly jog to keep up, but he holds the door open for me, and I walk by, eyes purposely avoiding him. Once outside, he turns to me on the sidewalk, the hazy fog making the morning feel like night. My feet beg me to turn away and rid myself of this embarrassment.

"So there's nothing you can do to help me?" I ask him one last time, saving him the trouble of saying it himself, fully aware of the desperation lacing my voice.

He rubs the back of his neck as he blows his breath toward the sky. "Callie . . ." His eyes meet mine as he pauses, and tension sits heavily between us.

"Sorry for wasting your time this morning, *Officer*," I snap.

"If I hear anything, I'll contact you. Officially, there is nothing we can do. I wish there was more I could do," he offers quickly, stepping toward me, arm outreached to offer a comforting touch.

But as I step back and out of his arm's reach, his radio sounds again. I respond by turning sharply away toward my car in the lot.

Officer Williams walks to the squad car, parked a few down from mine but stops before getting in, peering over the roof at me. "My dog ran away once."

I stop to listen, keeping my hand tightly on my door handle, ready to bolt.

"Me and my siblings all freaked out. We searched the neighborhood for hours. Had our whole street out looking for our dog. Everyone loved her. My parents had to distract us that night with pizza and movies just so we'd stop crying. But she came back, all on her own, the next day."

He waits momentarily for a response I simply can't give him. Instead, I duck into the driver's seat, pushing my face against the steering wheel, willing the tears to disappear. His story was meant to give me hope, I'm sure. But all I see is the cruelty, the dark juxtaposition to my current situation.

His story of a family searching together, with comfort and reassurance, when I spent the night searching the woods alone for a dog no one but me cares about.

But I won't let Opie down. I'm all he has.

I sit in the police station parking lot longer than I intend to because I can't get my head clear enough to drive. The article I read this morning keeps repeating like a bad headline: "After twenty-four hours, the chances of finding your dog drop significantly. Dogs can survive a few days without food and water, but damage can happen afterward." *Etc. etc. etc.*

Callie, stop. You can do this. Just focus. Opie needs you.

I squeeze my eyes shut, take a deep breath, and pull out my list. *Animal shelter and vet. That's what's next.* I decide to go in person to both.

I'm sure a phone call would be as efficient, but when I'm panicking like this, action feels better. Memaw used to tell me that when you're anxious, action is better than inaction. So I start the car and head to the vet.

I pass the diner, its parking lot overflowing with the breakfast rush.

Shit!

My tires squeal as I turn sharply into the parking lot. I rush inside, leaving my car running in the lot, but don't see anyone as I pass the host stand.

"Callie, where have you—oh my God, child. What in the world?" Peg sets the coffeepot down and pulls me out of the dining room by my elbow and into the kitchen. The revolving door swooshes behind us.

"I'm *so sorry,* Peg! I don't normally work breakfast, so I forgot . . . and—"

Peg cuts me off, smacking her lined pink lips and gripping my shoulders with surprising strength for her small frame. "Honey, what is going on? Is everything okay? You look like you spent the night in the woods." She scans me up and down, and her eyes widen when they land on my torn-up leg. "Oh my, Callie! Your leg!"

Biting my lip, I can't think of any excuse, so I tell her the truth. "Opie got out during the storm last night while I was here, and I haven't been able to find him. I've been searching for him since." I speak low enough for only her to hear.

"Oh, Callie," Peg starts, pulling me out of the way of a frantic waiter bustling past me. I look at Peg, feeling horrible about the situation I left her in. They needed me this morning, clearly. But I can't stay, and I start to rack my brain, hoping she doesn't fire me over this.

"I'm sorry. I just . . . I have to find him."

"Shh, you stop right now, sweet pea. I know that dog's important to you." She turns to grab a Styrofoam cup from the shelf and hands it to me.

"Go get some coffee and grab a muffin. We just finished making a new, fresh batch. Get out of here, find Opie today, and I'll see you tomorrow for your dinner shift. Okay, honey?" She smiles at me, triggering the tears I've expertly kept at bay until now. They burn like hell against my tired eyes.

"Thank you," I squeak as I'm pulled into a hug, my cheek brushing against her permed white hair. I start pouring coffee, wanting to guzzle it straight from the carafe.

"Chin up. You'll find your dog." Peg winks at me, and I watch her walk back through the doors to the dining room.

For a moment, everything stops spinning. With some food in my hands and a clear list of what to do next, I feel better. Every nerve in my body is still plagued with anxiety over where in the world my Opie boy could be, but for the first time since I arrived home last night, I feel a glimmer of something other than despair.

Chapter Ten

"We haven't had any dogs turn up in the last twenty-four hours," the middle-aged man replies.

I keep my face composed, but his words are a knife to the gut. The small pound is a cinder block building in need of paint and a cleaning. Varying levels of barks sound from the wall behind the man, and a corkboard with pictures of lost dogs is to my left. Some of the flyers are from spring, and I try to push that from my head. The man isn't looking at me but at a clipboard on the counter in front of him.

"What about calls? Did y'all get any calls about a lost dog on anyone's property or . . ." I let my voice trail off, unable to ask the other part of that question. *Reports of dead dogs.* The way my voice cracked gave it away, though the man behind the desk grows no more compassionate.

"There was a call about a dog, but it was small, a beagle mix, early this morning out by Lima Pond Road. That's it." He doesn't look at me as he crosses off something on the clipboard. Drops of water plop into a bucket next to me that's ready to spill over. I want to kick it just to get his attention.

Please, someone care. Just care for a moment about Opie.

I swallow hard and muster a reply. "Okay, thanks."

The phone rings, and the man picks it up, turning his back to me completely. I step away from the desk and walk over to the grimy glass window that peers into the pound. There are rows of half-full kennels. Many lost dogs come here after getting picked up by the animal warden, only to be reunited with their families hours later. I would give anything to see Opie's white face and honey eyes looking back at me from the other side of the glass.

The man slams the phone into the receiver harder than necessary, and I turn back to him. He shrugs and turns to grab a leash from the wall behind him before pausing and sighing loudly.

"Ma'am, there is *really* nothing we can do. You can call once a day to check if he turns up. Most lost dogs don't stray far."

He looks frazzled but nods and leaves the small lobby while I stand there, feet frozen. The little glimmer of hope Peg instilled in my heart this morning slowly slips through my fingers like sand, and I can't grip even a single grain.

I pull my legs up to my chest once I'm back in the safety of my car. A large, black coffee cup sits empty beside me, along with a muffin wrapper.

I stopped at the vet before the shelter, and I recall what the vet tech told me. She said to put out tasty foods to draw Opie home. She said to keep looking, but if he is hurt, he might run, even from me. When she said that, a sickening tickle crept up my throat.

I smooth out my crumpled list on my steering wheel. I'm getting toward the bottom of the list, but I buckle up anyway and drive back toward the trailer, stopping at the convenience store to get hot dogs, knowing damn well there's a fifty-fifty chance that I'll either attract Opie home or the wildlife that calls our land home too.

It's eerily quiet when I arrive home. *I never knew silence could be so loud.*

It hasn't even been twenty-four hours, and I feel closer to losing my mind than finding Opie.

The first twenty-four hours of anything are the hardest, though. That, I know.

The first twenty-four hours after Memaw died, I faltered between being utterly gutted and sobbing until I threw up on my bedroom floor to sitting frozen in absolute silence on the front steps. And after Mack got arrested, the first twenty-four hours were a blur. I pretended it didn't happen, pushing away the reality I knew would hit me like a freight train.

And now, looking around the tiny home I created for myself, it hits me. I've never been here without Opie. This place is *because* of Opie. He was here from the beginning. The first hot day I stumbled into this mess of a trailer, claiming it as mine, is also the first day Opie claimed me. One can't exist without the other.

Sitting at the table with a sandwich in front of me, I barely recollect how I even made it. Nothing makes sense to me. Why would Opie run away and not come back? How far did he go, and *why*? He hates it when I go to work or when we are hiking and I walk out of his sight. So what would make him run off, far away, and not come back? The what-ifs are relentless in the silence of the trailer.

My stomach begins to twist, and my head grows dizzy. What if a bear got him or someone on the side of the road saw him and decided to take him as their own?

I put down my sandwich. I'm no longer hungry.

The day goes by in a blur. A messy, frantic blur. I took a large trap from the dilapidated garage behind the farmhouse and set it up early the previous day. It's humane, only used to catch and relocate animals. I think Mack got it to catch a pesky coyote one year. Either way, it doesn't work, because when I check it at noon, all that's in it is a raccoon that isn't too happy. No Opie.

Reluctantly, I drive around, still in my clothes from the day before, my stomach growling but my body unable to eat. Officer Williams asked about neighbors, and I told him we had none. None close by, and no one I'd ever met, as small as this town was. Mack didn't make friends, and when Memaw was still alive, she wasn't one to stray from her usual routine, meaning I didn't meet anyone out here in these hills.

In the late afternoon, I decide to get in the car and drive along the road that borders our land. About a mile down the road, a driveway comes into view with a no trespassing sign hanging on the chain going across it. The overgrowth tells me it has been a while since anyone has been here, but I park the car anyway. There's an old house that he could've hidden in.

I don't fully get out of the car, leaving one leg on the ground and one inside, my fingers gripping the door as it hangs open. Then I call for him, his name beginning to feel like a broken record on my tongue.

It doesn't matter if I called him for one minute or fifty. It never seemed like long enough. It was a game of tug-of-war with my heart and mind. Because what if, the moment I get in the car and leave, he finally comes out?

I'm terrified I'll miss him just by a hair, terrified that a split second could be the difference between being reunited and him being lost forever. Split-second accidents have defined my life up until this moment. The incessant worry is what has kept me driving down the dirt road for two more hours, back and forth, calling his name until my body has nothing left to give, my throat excruciatingly raw.

Until now, I don't think I understood how easily someone could go mad. All it takes is losing something you know you can't live without.

CHAPTER ELEVEN

I lace up my apron and pull my face in different directions, hoping that pinching my cheeks will distract people from the purple circles making residency under my eyes. I promised Peg I'd be at the diner tonight. I know she'll understand if I don't show, but I dread looking her in the face and telling her Opie hasn't come home yet. She'll say to me something like, "Dogs stay gone for a week," or "He'll return. Don't you worry, sweet pea." And I'll smile out of politeness, replying with a false hope I don't actually embody, keeping secret the true hell the last forty-eight hours have been.

I didn't know you could go through such ups and downs of emotion, from hope to despair, desperation to determination. It's as if I can't regulate my body, like my limbs are missing and my heart can't keep up with my mind.

A voice of reason tells me that working tonight will distract me, and when I do find Opie—because I will—I'll be happy I kept working and saving. I can't lose this job, after all; this is the only thing funding my great escape. No one else in town will hire me.

The diner is full, which comes as both a relief and a panic. Simple things, like remembering drink orders, are challenging, but I power through the first hour, staying as busy as possible. I am moving around as much as I can because the moment I stop, it will hit me.

The usual mantra that runs through my veins seems to weaken each hour.

I'm doing this for us. That's what I think every time I smile for the tip, knowing each dollar brings me closer to affording a new start somewhere else for me and Opie.

But tonight, it doesn't seem to matter. Nothing seems to matter.

It's nearly eight, with only two hours left in my shift, when the regulars leave, and the high school crews start noisily filling in booths with their big orders and stingy tips. A familiar face pops up among the crowd.

Between tables, I notice Levi smile at the host as she sits him at a two-seater table near the back. Seeing Levi snaps me out of my self-pity. He breaks away from the group at the entrance and sits alone in the back of the diner.

Maybe he is waiting for a date. That would make sense, given how perfectly put together he looks with a clean white shirt, blue jeans, and, of course, messy hair that's tucked behind his ears.

Either way, Carla sat him in my section, so I hurry over with the water pitcher. A big smile spreads across his face as I approach. His smile reaches his hazel eyes, and though I return the gesture, mine doesn't.

"Hey, Levi." I pour water for him, growing uncomfortable with his steady gaze. Even sitting, we are nearly at eye level, and it always feels like Levi is trying to read me like a book.

"How're you doing?" he asks. He asks not as a formality or habit, like most people, but actually waits for an answer as I stand there with the water pitcher sweating down my hand.

"It's going." I offer a tight-lipped smile, hoping he accepts that answer.

"I see that. Well, I finally decided to give this place a shot." He turns the menu over in his hands.

I can't hide the surprise in my voice. "Wait, what? You've never been *here* before?" Miscruz Hills is small. There are only a handful of restaurants to choose from, and it's almost unimaginable that someone hasn't been to Peg's Diner.

Levi shakes his head. "I had takeout from here maybe once or twice, but my parents are big health nuts. You remember that, yeah? So we didn't come here growing up."

I remember Levi always having healthy, packed lunches, while I ate the school lunch.

"Never really hung out with a crew who went here either," he adds.

I nod knowingly. As charming and handsome as Levi is, he is shy and studious, preferring books to people in high school. We are loners but for entirely different reasons.

Somehow, him being alone was accepted and cool. Me? I was pathetic and sad.

I change the subject, wanting to make his first experience a good one. I don't know why I care, but it feels nice to do something other than cry or scream or search the ground for paw prints.

"Okay. Well, can I make some suggestions, if you're up for it?" My eyes wander to the empty stool across from him. "Unless you're waiting on someone."

Levi chuckles, shaking his head. I grab the menu from him and flip it over, pointing to some of our most popular dishes.

"The burger is good. Oh, and the strawberry cheesecake milkshake is my favorite." I smile and show him a few more entrees.

He sets the menu down and runs a hand through his hair. "I'll take them all."

"Wait. You want all of my suggestions?" I laugh because that's enough food for at least a family.

"Yeah. I'll take home whatever I can't finish. My parents went to a wedding this weekend, and I'm sure this beats my version of cooking."

"I'm honestly concerned for you." I laugh, writing down all the food I suggested, and Levi laughs, too.

"Hey now. Don't you judge me. I'm still growing."

"Uh-huh." I roll my eyes and grab his menu. I'm surprised at how easy it feels to fall back into this comfortable banter with him. It doesn't make logical sense that I can joke like this during a time of crisis. But even as kids, Levi had a warm presence. He's just one of those people who emits light.

I put in the orders for Levi. As I continue working, my feelings begin to shift. Guilt riddles me for even smiling and laughing a few minutes ago. How could I when Opie might be in danger?

Twenty minutes later, Levi's table is full of sizzling food and a plate of fries big enough to feed a football team.

"Please don't have a heart attack," I joke, handing him his final item, a strawberry cheesecake milkshake.

Levi smirks, eyeing the food. Before he has a chance to say anything, I hear it. Two women, one with a baby on her hip, walk past Levi and I, heading toward the exit. But their attempt—or lack thereof—to keep their voices low is useless, and their words sink into my skin like daggers.

"Isn't that waitress back there the Hayes girl?"

"Shit, I think so. She looks awful."

"How could she not after the shit she's done? Serves her right."

I try to glance away, but Levi's eyes meet mine and are riddled with pure anger. He heard every last word, and we're left staring at each other, wondering in humiliating silence if either of us are going to acknowledge what they said.

My chest moves steadily up and down with each controlled breath I take. I wish I could tell him to not pay attention to them, that I'm used to it. But that would be a partial lie. The whispers, the rumors, the gossip about me and Mack—it all slowed for a bit. Until his release from prison this year. Then it seemed to have all picked back up.

"I'll be back."

"Callie . . ." he starts, moving to the edge of his seat. His eyes dart between me and the women, who are already on the sidewalk in front of the diner laughing about something else.

"It's not worth it." I pinch my lips together and turn around, gripping the pitcher of water tightly.

In the kitchen, I fill up the water, focusing on the stream as I will the tears away. I check on my other few diners, who barely acknowledge me. When I swing by Levi's table to refill his drink, he pauses, setting down his phone and looking up at me, his elbows resting on the table, his muscles flexed as he brings his hands to his chest.

"Hey, I meant to ask you. What's going on with the photography program in Charleston?"

My head slightly dips in reaction, and my eyes stay averted as I refill his water.

"Starts next month, right?"

"I didn't get in," I respond quickly in almost a whisper. To my surprise, Levi slides his hand across the table toward me, looking like he is going to offer comfort but pulls back instantly, resting his hand on his thigh when I clutch the water pitcher to my stomach.

"I'm sorry. If it means anything, I think you're talented, Callie."

His words, the kindest I've heard in a long time, spread like warmth through my veins. I walk away, leaving him hanging with all his food, unable to respond for fear of crying.

Why do you have to be like this, Callie?

I wish life was different. If Opie was home and safe, if my reputation didn't follow me like a cloud, if I didn't need to desperately escape the ghosts of this town, maybe Levi and I could be friends. *Again.* But in this universe, it doesn't work like that.

Growing up, all my friendships started and ended at the school's doors. Levi is the only one who ever invited me to his house. At home, I only had Mack and Memaw. Mack worked long days, and Memaw had physical limitations, resulting in me playing outside alone. My friends were the animals we once had on the farm—the ducklings in spring, the goats I helped feed. We even had piglets one spring when Mack won them in some contest at the fair. I preferred to talk to things that couldn't talk back. Animals can't call you names, they don't ignore you, and they don't care about your family or past.

As I thought, Levi ate only half of what I brought him, so I give him a few take-home containers and slip him the check, leaving him at the table as I quickly make my way out back. I need five minutes.

Yet minutes later, Levi walks around the building with large bags full of food hanging from his forearms. I try to stay quiet and slink into the shadows, but the cook opens the door and leans out to tell me a table's been sat in my section. That's when Levi turns his head in my direction, and though the darkness shadows his face, I can feel his gaze on me.

He takes a step toward me. "Callie, I'm sorry if I said something wrong. I—"

"You didn't," I respond sharply, flipping my hand in his direction dismissively, but Levi steps closer again, and now I can see his eyes clearly. They look hurt, and I feel like shit because I caused that.

"It's nothing you said." I inhale sharply. "How was your first diner experience?" I change the subject, and he nods, but his shoulder stays tense. A car starts up, and the lights shine on us for a moment.

"I mean, I'm semi-embarrassed about how much I ate, but the service was ten out of ten." He flashes me a crooked smile, and my heart does a skip.

"Good." I want him to leave. The more I talk, the more the truth will spill out.

"Hey . . . are you sure you're okay? What happened was—"

"Levi." I hold up my hand and close my eyes briefly. "It's not you or the horrible people who don't know how to whisper. Please believe me. Actually, serving a friendly face was the only good thing about my day."

"Oh, I'm sorry. Do you . . . do you want to talk about it?"

I genuinely raise my eyebrows, holding in a scoff as bitterness comes over me. It's a feeling I don't welcome, but it's been in my bones for some time now, and I resent that. Levi doesn't waver, though. He stands there, facing me squarely. I have someone's full attention, and I forgot how this feels. It's jarring.

And just like that, my walls crumble a bit.

"My dog ran away two nights ago, and I can't find him." The feeling of failure falls on my shoulders.

Levi drops his brown bags to the ground, his jaw jutting forward in reaction. "Opie ran away?" he asks, exasperated.

I nod, tears stinging at the mention of his name.

Levi places his hands on his head, breathing and looking around the parking lot. "Have you printed any posters to put around town? Do people still do that?"

"Yeah, they do . . . and no, I haven't. I thought he'd return home by now . . . but I—" The truth is if I do that, if I officially call him lost, it will sink in. It will become real.

"When are you off work?" Levi leans forward a bit, and I hesitate before answering.

"Um, I'm done in an hour. At ten. Why?" I ask, chewing my lip.

"Come by the print shop after. We'll get some posters printed." He picks up his leftovers bag and gives me a look of concern.

"You don't have to do that. I'll wait until tomorrow." I'm already calculating everything else I was going to do to find Opie tomorrow. I read about hanging clothes up on a line around your home, so I was going to string every piece of clothing I own all over the property.

"You'll save me from sitting around and binging a show I've already seen a million times. Let me help you."

I nod and meekly say, "Okay." Levi appeared happy with that answer, and we agreed to meet at the print shop in an hour.

I count down the minutes for the rest of my shift, eager to move along the search for Opie. Asking for help makes me uneasy, but I try to remind myself that Levi offered. He seemed like he genuinely wanted to do this.

That's different, right?

Chapter Twelve

Main Street is dark at ten, but as I pull up to the print shop, there's a single glow inside. Levi unlocks the door and holds it open for me. Walking inside, I want to apologize for smelling like greasy French fries and milkshakes, but I keep my mouth shut.

"Your mom won't be pissed you're helping me?" I joke to break the ice as Levi ushers me behind the counter. It's quiet in here besides the humming of the computer, and I feel like I have to hold my breath just so I don't take up more space.

Levi laughs, his shoulders shaking, and I gaze at his face. He pulls up a chair next to him at the computer desk and tells me to take a seat. "Her and my dad are currently getting wasted right now at their friend's wedding. She won't care."

I wait for him to say more, but he doesn't; he just motions toward the laptop screen.

"Okay. Let's put this flyer together and get it printed. Can you email me a photo of Opie?"

"Okay. Um, yes. Let me do that." I pull out my phone, scrolling for a photo of him. It hurts my heart to look at him, and I swallow hard against my throat as I select a photo where you can see his white fur with his perfect black patch of fur around his eye.

Levi whistles a little tune I recognize from the radio. It's so odd to sit here in a dimly lit print shop with Levi. His hoodie sits on the counter next to a water bottle with stickers on it. It reminds me how there's so much I don't know about him now, but there's also a history between us. Levi's the opposite of me right now. Relaxed shoulders, slightly slouched in his seat as I sit rigid and straight in mine. He still towers over me even so. I want him to be more on-guard, to be put off by helping me. He has reason to. He has reason to hate me after what happened to Everett Calloway. *His cousin.*

"All right. Got it." He clicks the photo, dragging it onto the flyer. "He looks so happy," he says so quietly that I'm not sure it was meant for me to hear.

I reply back softly, too. "He is always like that. He was happy even when he was skin and bones and near death."

Levi insists on printing a hundred flyers. When he hands me the stack and I give him my bank card, he shoves it back to me. "Callie, I'm not letting you pay for this."

"Levi, don't be stubborn. This is like a hundred colored copies. I'm not going to get you fired."

"First, I'm my parents' only employee, so they can't fire me. And second, think of this as a concerned citizen's act." He smirks.

"Huh?"

"I'm doing it for Opie. As a concerned community member, I want to help you find your dog."

"Why am I getting flashbacks of Miss Hanson's civics class right now?" I smirk.

Levi laughs, shaking his head. "I'm surprised you even knew I was in that class with you." Levi tosses his head back dramatically.

"Of course, I knew," I blurt out.

I awkwardly invite the conversation to end by grabbing the stack of posters. I spent all of tenth grade staring at the back of Levi's head and having to smell the same familiar scent of cologne. He always said hi to me with a smile in that class when everyone else whispered behind my back. As much as it was a reprieve to see that smile, it almost would've been better if he acted like I was tainted like everyone else did. Of all people, I never understood his kindness toward me.

"Thanks for this. It's really helpful," I say, starting toward the door, unsure how to end things. I've never been good at conversation beyond waitressing. What Levi is doing for me feels like a lot. I owe him tremendously, and though that makes me uneasy, when I glance at his face, he looks *happy*. I think he genuinely enjoys helping me.

"Wait, Callie. Will you put those up tomorrow morning?"

I turn around to see his brows furrow as he taps lightly on the counter. "Yeah. After checking the traps, I will probably come back to town to post these everywhere."

"That's a lot of work. You can't do that all by yourself." Levi looks confused.

I pause, little bits of electricity running down my arms, my grip tightening on the stack of paper. I don't look at Levi anymore. "No, no, it's fine. It won't take too long." But as I say it, I know it's a lie. It will take me hours, if not all morning and afternoon, to post this many flyers throughout town.

"All right. Well, that's a lie. It will take you forever. I'm helping," he asserts.

My heart stops a beat.

When he sees me freeze, he continues. "I've got nothing else to do tomorrow anyway, so you're actually *helping me* escape boredom."

I don't need a mirror to know my expression is one of resistance, but I fight against it. "Okay, thanks. I'll meet you here at nine a.m.," I oblige through a tight mouth.

"Aye, aye, captain."

I smile, quickly pushing open the door to leave. I suck at goodbyes. Maybe Opie knew that.

Chapter Thirteen

They say it takes thirty days to form a new habit. But I call bullshit, because it's day three, and this is all becoming a dreadful habit, checking the property, the traps, and the food bowls.

Nothing.

The rabbits don't scatter as I walk to the creek this morning. They have nothing to fear, no four-legged beast to chase them from their morning meal. The creek offers little comfort; the water rushes slowly, still high from the bouts of rain this week.

It dawns on me this morning, as I sit with my legs dangling and my toes in the cool water, that I haven't picked up my camera in three days. It sits unbothered in my disheveled trailer on the shelf. For the past two years, everything revolved around photography, but this week, I didn't think about it once. I didn't notice the sunrise or sunset, the swaying of the meadow grasses outside my window, or the cardinals that have been dependable visitors on my windowsill.

The world doesn't feel worth capturing without Opie. He is my ray of sunshine. He gives me a vision to see the world in a way that isn't so painful. Without him, it's all a little darker.

My pocket buzzes, breaking the spell of my spiraling. A number I don't have saved is displayed on the screen. I gave Levi my number, but I don't plan on adding his to my phone—not permanently. That would make him *permanent*, and he can't be.

> **I accidentally ordered an extra coffee this morning – hope you'll take one! See you at 9**

My lips twitch as I stare at my phone before sliding it into my pocket. I push my tired limbs off the rock, walking barefoot back to the trailer.

How does someone accidentally order two coffees?

Levi looks well-rested, which makes me remember how unrested I look and feel. My jean shorts are visibly dirty, and the flannel tied around my waist has an old hole from Opie's sharp puppy teeth. *I'm a mess.*

But Levi doesn't seem to notice. He pushes his sunglasses up on his head as he hands me a cup of coffee. I take it reluctantly, mumbling a thanks. I don't want to grow used to this. Being without my dog is already making the world seem like it's flipped upside down, but letting someone help me is more unnerving than anything.

"Sleep well?" I ask, hiding my sarcasm.

"Actually, not really." Levi takes a sip of what looks like black coffee and slaps a stapler in my hand. "But I'm ready when you are." He looks down at me, smiling sympathetically. "When we are done, everyone will know who Opie is."

Chuckling, I glance at the picture of Opie in my hands, hoping Levi is right. Posting these all over town feels so personal, like hanging a piece of my laundry on every telephone pole. I've tried so hard to blend into the background of this town, but doing *this* undoes that. Once these posters are out there with my name on them, it's a reminder that I'm still here. I have to keep reminding myself this is an essential step in finding my sweet boy.

Levi leads the way, divvying up the flyers. We take opposite sidewalks, stapling the posters to every telephone pole on the street and taping them to any surface we can find. Everyone greets Levi as they pass him on the sidewalk, asking how he is and how his parents are. Not one single person looks at me, even though I'm just a few feet away from him.

If Levi is a diamond, I'm a piece of coal. It's an abomination I'm even walking with him.

I remind myself that doesn't really matter right now; it can't matter right now.

When we reach the end of the street, the only place we haven't touched is the coffee shop. I stand in the middle of the sidewalk, staring at it as people bustle in and out of the doors. Levi crosses the street, stopping at my side where my feet are firmly planted.

My eyebrows crease as I stare at the propped-open door and hear pop music coming from the speakers within. People with smiles, friends, and moms with babies walk in and out. A stroller sits outside the front door, along with planters full of blooming flowers and a menu board promising sweets inside. It's somehow both picturesque and the place of my darkest nightmares.

A breeze blows by, fluttering the flyers in my hand and blowing my blonde hair in front of my face. I tuck the loose strands behind my ear and notice how clammy my hands are.

"Let's ask if we can put a flyer in the window or on their bulletin board, yeah?" Levi runs his fingers through his dark brown hair and bites his lip pensively.

My eyes linger too long on him, long enough that apparently he sees through my facade.

"Callie, you all right?"

"Yeah . . . I . . ." I can't finish my sentence. *Because I'm not all right.*

It's been three years since I was last inside that building. From the passenger seat, I tried to grab the wheel from Mack in a last-ditch effort to get the car to stop as we swerved down Main Street, but he forcefully shoved me away. When we crashed through the front window, everything went black. I promised myself I'd never go back in that building—physically or mentally.

Levi must've miraculously forgotten the event that rattled our town because he nudges my elbow gently. "Are you worried they'll say no? I promise they won't. The owner, Jane, comes to the print shop all the time. She'll want to help."

I'm jealous of how easy it is for Levi to forget about the accident. Of course, Jane won't say no to Levi. *No one would say no to Levi.*

I look again at the coffee shop as it grows busier. Out walks an older man I recognize instantly: the school janitor. My feet are glued to the cement as a memory rushes back to me, and with Levi standing right here, facing me, I wonder if he can sense the anxiety eating away at me.

A few weeks after the accident, a few girls started a trend of shoving my lunch tray off the table. Levi didn't have the same lunch schedule as me that year. One day, after weeks of whispers, and rumors, and tossed lunches, I broke down in tears. The janitor had kneeled down, cleaning up my spilled food beside me as people rushed around us. And one pair of hazel eyes met mine as they passed by the open cafeteria doors. I'll never forget the look on Levi's face. It's the same look he's giving me now: confusion and sorrow.

"I need to take a break. Can you please just go ask, since you know Jane?" I attempt a smile and, without waiting for his response, move to sit on the closest bench.

"Yeah, sure. I'll be right back." He walks toward the coffee shop.

A few minutes later, he's taping Opie's flyer to the front window. An older gentleman does a double take in front of the window, but he isn't looking at Levi. He is eyeing the flyer.

They start talking, but I'm too far away to hear, so I dash toward them, my lungs on fire.

"It's her dog actually." Levi gestures at me, and the old man starts speaking.

"I was bird-watching up at the Old Hunter Creek Trail. You know, past the bridge on the way out of town. And I swear I saw a white dog running around. Was a big thing. He didn't come close when I whistled, so I didn't get a good look, but maybe it's worth checking."

My heart does a somersault, and I want to shake every last detail out of this old man.

"Are you serious? When was this?" I ramble, desperate for any information.

"Around seven this morning. You know which trail I'm talking about?"

"Yeah. Yeah, I do." I nod vigorously, my heart in my throat. "Thank you, sir. Thank you," I spit out, nearly forgetting Levi as I turn to run to my car. Even if Opie was spotted two hours ago, it doesn't matter. I haven't had a sign my dog was even alive for nearly seventy-two hours now.

I'd find a way to reach the moon if that's where he was.

Levi chases after me, catching up in seconds. "He said he was less than a half mile into the trail when he spotted the dog," he relays the message, and I nod, rolling the rest of the flyers into my back pocket. "You heading there now?"

"Yeah!" I respond, halting at my car to fiddle in my side bag for my keys. Levi rounds the car at the passenger's side door, and I pause to look at him. "What . . . what are you doing?" I ask, shoving the key into the door.

"I-I'm coming w-with you."

He stumbles over his words, and I instantly regret pulling him into this.

I shake my head vigorously. "No, I need to do this alone."

"Why do you think you have to do this alone?"

"It's how it's always been. It's how I work best." My body turns to stone. My convictions run deep, and I know I'm hurting him, but I can't stop.

Levi backs away from the door. "If that's what you believe, Callie," he responds. As I open the car door, Levi motions for the remaining papers in my pocket. "How about I finish hanging the flyers around town?"

I'm numb as I slide them over the top of the car. There's less than a dozen left. We've worked tirelessly this morning. As he rounds them up in his hand, I smile quickly before he can probably even register it.

"Thanks, Levi." I may be completely lost inside, but my manners aren't dead too.

"Yeah, sure thing."

I slide fully into the car, but he bends down and peers nervously at me through the window. I release a breath.

"Callie, that trail is remote and pretty long. Are you sure you'll be okay out there alone?" he asks.

I stifle a laugh as I click in my seat belt. I guess he wouldn't know how often and for how long I've been wandering the woods alone. He may be right about it being long and remote, but I work better when I can think and not have to dedicate *thinking* to how I act in social interactions.

"I'll be fine!" I start the car as Levi steps onto the sidewalk. He watches me drive off. To avoid the droves of summer tourists, I have to take the long way around the block. A few minutes later, once I reach the end of the street, I see Levi stapling a poster to a tree in the park. He lifts his head and crinkles his brow, jogging over to the car while I idle at the stop sign. His hands are empty, and it's only been five minutes.

"You're all done?" I keep my eyes forward even though he's leaning on the open window.

"Yes, ma'am." He smiles, amused, and I have to believe he went fast on purpose.

I hesitate, pinching the steering wheel between my fists. "Okay. Well . . . the trail splits at the top; we could each go one direction. If you're willing to walk and shout for Opie and jiggle treats, that is." I eye him, waiting for him to decide this is too much, but he just turns his hat backward and crouches to gaze into my car.

"The shop is closed today, so I have nothing else to do," he comments.

I appreciate the lack of enthusiasm. It's better for me if he doesn't act like this is the best thing ever. Because it's not. And it'll be easier to break off whatever hopes of friendship he has blooming in his mind.

I gun it the moment he clicks his seat belt.

Chapter Fourteen

Old Hunter Creek Trail is nearly five miles from the farm. It's technically in the next town over, though it's all wilderness out here. Barely any tourists know it exists, which makes it a trail where wild animals, like black bears and coyotes, find refuge. But I push that out of my head and hold onto the fact that someone saw a white dog.

My heart races as we pull into the patch of gravel at the base of the trail. I'm not prepared for a hike, but I've walked the whole property at home barefoot, so I don't blink when it's time to trudge up the trail in sandals. The day quickly became hot, and humidity sticks to my skin, so I pile my hair on top of my head as I walk swiftly.

Levi keeps up, not speaking much, other than us both calling out Opie's name every fifty feet or so. Between our shouts, there's nothing but the sound of crunching and rustling leaves under our feet. A dense mix of tall pines and thick oak trees makes this trail feel like it stretches on forever. And in actuality, it does; it spills right into the wilderness. But surely, if Opie is in these woods, he will hear me, and he will come running or bark to tell me where he is. He's a willful and intelligent dog. Opie wouldn't give up; I know it.

We pass a few hikers and ask if they've seen a loose dog. I show them a picture of him on my phone, but they shake their heads, looking at me with sorrowful expressions. But I don't let their words discourage me; we aren't even at the spot where the old man said he saw Opie.

"You go left. I'll go right. Just keep calling for him, and if anything happens, holler for me," I instruct Levi. He cocks his head quizzically but does as I say, turning left and disappearing into the thick Carolina forest.

It's quiet out here, quiet enough I can hear my heart thumping in my chest. I can feel Opie out here.

After a few minutes of strenuous walking, I reach a section of the trail that's thick with tree roots, so I must slow my pace. It doesn't matter how cautious I am, though, because a grouping of rocks and roots catches my foot at the wrong angle, sending me forward to my hands and knees.

"Fuck!" I scream loud enough for anyone on the mountain to hear. My sandal rips at the seam, and the sharp rock slices the top of my foot like cake.

You've got to be kidding me.

Whenever I feel like I'm getting closer to my dog, my body betrays me. First, the thorns, which have formed raised scars on my calf, and now my foot's sliced open, gushing blood. All I have to stop the bleeding is the bandanna I grabbed from the car. Pulling Opie's bandanna from my back pocket, I wrap it around my foot.

Sitting down on the same root that tripped me, I curse again. I'll have to get a different item of Opie's to bring out with me. And maybe a first aid kit. But that hardly matters now because this mission is ruined.

"Callie! Callie, where are you?" Levi and his blue shirt come into view. His face is shiny, and his cheeks are flushed. I think he ran to find me.

His gaze instantly drops to my foot, then he dashes toward me, squatting inches in front of me.

"Holy shit, what happened? Are you okay?" His hands rest on my thighs, but the pain is too much for me to give any thought to his sudden physical touch.

"I tripped and sliced it. It's fine," I reply through gritted teeth. The bleeding is slowing, and I think I can fashion my sandal into a flip-flop so the straps don't push on the cut. There's only a little more trail to cover, and I can't let this stop me. I peer around Levi's head down the winding path.

"We've got to go back. I'm pretty sure you need stitches. That's deep." Levi pinches his lips together and inhales deeply.

"We *can't,* and I *don't* need stitches." I attempt to stand but fall back down as Levi's hands instinctively reach out to grab my arms and steady me. I pull them out of his reach.

"It's really fucking deep. My brother is a surgery tech and—"

"Levi, stop!" I yell a bit too loudly, clamping my eyes shut when I do. "My health insurance sucks. I can't afford stitches, okay? So I'm not getting stitches." I stand up, wincing.

Levi swallows as he also stands, eyes wide, like what I'm saying is inconceivable to him.

"Listen, I'm fine. I've had worse. Let's just finish the trail and head back down. I'll go home and clean this up after, and once I've rested, I'll come back here this evening." The pain *is* bad, but we are here, and I'm not leaving without trying.

Levi wrings his hands in front of him, tipping his head back as he stares at me with contemplation. "Fine. But get on my back."

"Absolutely not." I grimace as I pick up a stick to use as a crutch. There's no doubt that Levi could carry me up or down this mountain, but I have too much pride to let him try.

He lets out an exasperated huff beside me but zips his lips as he closely follows me farther down the trail. I know he's waiting for me to surrender and say I need his help.

I'm going slow, but I'm still moving.

We cross paths with another pair of hikers, who take one look at my foot, their mouths agape, but as soon as their eyes reach my face, they close them.

"We are out here looking for my dog. Have you seen a white one running around by chance or heard anything?" I ask, my voice audibly strained. I bite my cheek to bring my attention away from the pain in my foot.

The woman hesitantly shakes her head, eyeing her partner. "We have not."

I mumble "thanks" as we part ways.

"Hey . . . I think we should turn around, Callie." Levi speaks up a few minutes later.

I stop, happy to take a load off. The bleeding has stopped, but it's still throbbing. I glance down at the soaked bandanna. Levi isn't wrong; I *could* probably get stitches. But I can't afford that.

"Fine," I reply, and I hate the relief that washes over his face like he's won.

"I'll even come back with you tomorrow if you'd like."

Silence fills the space between us as I take calculated breaths, pivoting back toward the car's direction, silently wondering how I'm going to keep this up.

I pause after a few steps and face Levi. In the lighting of the woods, the shadows make patterns on him, and I can see how handsome he is. He always was—classically beautiful with a strong jaw, pretty eyes, and full hair. He is tall, strong, and kind. But he's wasting his time helping me.

I can't tell if he wants me to find Opie or just wants to spend time with me. Because right now, the only kind of time I have has to be dedicated to finding Opie and getting the hell out of this town.

"You know, I want to pay you back for the flyers."

"What are you talking about?"

"Levi . . . thank you for all your help. Really, I appreciate it. But I think tomorrow, and moving forward, I just need to do this on my own."

The words cut like ice through the air. His shoulders sag a bit in response.

The shitty part is, I don't have a logical reason, not a solid one at least, as to why he can't come with me. It's better to have more people help when searching for a lost dog. The articles say so. My brain says so. But my heart knows otherwise.

"Did I ever tell you I lost my dog when I was fifteen?"

God, here we go again with the sympathy stories. First Officer Williams, now Levi. But I'm huffing and biting my lips to keep from crying out in pain with every step I take down this rocky trail, so Levi continues.

"You remember Duke? He got hit by a car sophomore year."

My chest constricts, and I look up at Levi. I do remember Duke. He was Levi's Christmas present from his parents the year we turned ten. "Oh, that's so awful." I genuinely feel horrible, but I don't know what else to say. Along with goodbyes, add *incapable of saying sorry* to the list of things I suck at.

"All I'm saying, Callie, is I know how you're feeling right now. It truly sucks, and I'm sorry."

Opie isn't dead. Opie is lost. He is here. I know he is here.

My blood gets hot, and I get more angry than I should, my words spewing out with resentment as I confront Levi face-to-face.

"Opie isn't dead! And no, you don't know how I feel," I bark at him, unable to hold it back. Levi's eyes enlarge with each word. "You *do not* get it. I'm sorry about what happened to your dog; I am. Because you're right—it does fucking suck. But you don't know how I feel right now."

He stays quiet, just watches me unravel in the middle of the woods as the words burn a hole in my throat.

"When you lost your dog, you still had people, yeah? You had your brother and your parents. And friends." Our eyes meet under my furrowed brow, and he cocks his head to the side, trying to grasp what I'm laying out.

"Callie, I didn't mean it—"

I grimace, my hands forming fists by my side. "Stop, please, while you're ahead. I know you think you're helping, but you aren't." I hobble forward again, fighting the tears back. "My mama died when I was two, my papa right after, and then Memaw died when I was thirteen. They were the only people who ever truly looked out for me. My dad... Well, you know all about Mack, I'm sure. I'm good as dead to him. I can assure you I hate him more than everyone in this whole town combined. But naturally, as his daughter and *accomplice*, the town hates me. But I don't have to tell you that. You already know what people say about me."

My foot has turned totally numb.

"I have *no one*, Levi." My voice trembles, shame lacing every syllable as I choke on my words. "I only have Opie. My dog is my whole family. And I know it sounds pathetic that my family and friends begin and end with a stray dog, but it's my truth."

Levi's face is pale, his eyes far away, but I don't give him a chance to respond. Instead, I speed up my tempo, limping as fast as I can down the steep, rocky hill to the tiny, gravel parking lot.

The inside of me feels like a waterfall of tears, but nothing marks my sweat-stained face as I walk, eyes forward and heart thumping. Levi is only a few steps behind me. He stays silent.

I drop Levi off at his car in town, and I know he wants to say something, but I don't give him the chance. I hate myself as I drive away quickly, watching him stand on the sidewalk outside the print shop.

I barely hold it together on the way home. As I pull into the driveway and approach the farmhouse, I notice plumes of gray smoke rising from the backyard. A few beat-up cars are parked haphazardly in the yard. Memaw would turn in her grave seeing her beloved farmhouse like this.

Inhaling deeply, hoping it will propel me forward, I weave through the cars to get to the little lane to my trailer but not before I hear my name being called in the distance.

" 'Ey! 'Ey, Carolina!"

My temple throbs at the drunken sound of my name, and I barely gaze out the open passenger window to see Mack standing on the back porch with no shirt on, his arm draped around Wendy, as a few other people I don't recognize sit around a makeshift firepit. I don't make eye contact with them as I glare directly at my father.

I slow down and yell back. "What do you want, Mack?"

"That's no way to speak to your old man," he grumbles, but then his face grows serious. As serious as it can while beer courses through his body. "Find your dog yet?"

The question hits me like a bullet to the chest, making my breath hard to steady. Sometimes, I wonder if, under layers of alcohol, drugs, years in prison, and hardship, Mack still has a soft spot for me, for his daughter. But that's just hopeful thinking. And hope's never done me well. It's been an anchor, one that both holds me and sinks me all at the same time.

"No," I reply. I'm not even sure if it's loud enough for him to hear, but he nods ever so slightly and turns his attention back to the mess around him.

I keep driving home to the place I used to call home.

Chapter Fifteen

The last thing I want to do is housework, but I have one pair of clean underwear left after I strung up most of my clothes around the property, hoping to attract Opie. The refrigerator holds a half-empty jug of orange juice, and moldy bread sits on the counter. The only thing my body has energy for right now is to curl up on the bed, but I know the moment I sit, the silence and truth will become overbearing. I have enough wits about me to keep myself from going completely mad, so I scratch a messy to-do list onto the back of a receipt and round up my dirty clothes.

Usually, I wait for Mack to leave the house, then I do my laundry at the farmhouse. But his machines have been broken for weeks, and there's only so much handwashing you can do, so I'm off to the laundromat in town.

Before I leave, I quickly braid my hair, which has grown lighter in the sun like it does every summer. My fair skin has grown darker from all the time I've spent outside with Opie. But my once sky-blue eyes look dark and permanently red-rimmed.

As I walk to the car, arms full of laundry, my attention is drawn to my foot, where warmth puddles in my shoe. Setting the laundry basket down, I kneel in the dirt beside the car and gently pull my foot out of my boot to find my cut has reopened and bled through my sock. Hobbling into the trailer, I pull off my bloody sock, wincing at the sting. Last night, I cleaned it and wrapped it as well as I could, remembering everything Memaw taught me about first aid.

Hopping on one foot in front of the kitchen sink, I fumble around for the first aid kit I threw on the shelf, but in one clumsy swipe, my camera comes crashing down from the counter.

There's a sickening crack of glass.

I hold my breath and don't move a muscle, even as blood drips warmly from my foot to the floor. Bracing myself, I peer at the floor. The lens, the lens I worked months to save for, is shattered. It lies on the floor, staring back at me, mocking my misery.

"Fuck! Why? Why?" I scream to no one in particular, slamming my fist on the speckled yellow countertop.

If I can't take quality photos, I'll never make it into any program. If I get moved from the waitlist, I won't even be able to take photos.

As I draw in a deep breath, I shakily grab the first aid kit, wet a towel in the sink, and sit gingerly on the floor, pulling my knees to my chest. Tears sting my already dry eyes, but I continue to wipe the blood from my foot. I do it precisely like Memaw taught me with hydrogen peroxide on a cotton ball and a gentle rub on the broken skin. "*It hurts. That's how you know it's working, Callie,*" she'd say to me. If only that's how you knew life was working.

Once the bleeding stops and I let the skin dry, I take a bandage—the largest one and the last one left in this first aid kit—and wrap my foot gently.

The entire time, I avoid looking at the camera on the floor next to me. I can't even bring myself to pick it up before I slam the trailer door shut, leaving it behind on the dusty floor.

The laundromat sits directly across the street from Levi's family's print shop. Luckily, it's closed on Sundays, so I push the worry of running into him out of my head. I take a swig of my gas station coffee, that I bought with the crumpled-up dollars I found in my glove box, as I shove quarters into the ancient washing machine. Nobody in here seems to pay me any attention, which is a relief.

However, the rhythmic whirring of the laundry and the heat radiating from the dryers around me make me feel sleepier than I already am. The elderly woman who owns this place doesn't move from her perch near the door, an open crossword puzzle on the table in front of her. She eyes me, mumbling something about young people under her breath. Letting my body sink into a faded orange plastic chair, I tip my head back, closing my eyes slowly. *I'll rest for just a moment.*

A minute or so later, the door chimes, jolting me out of my quiet rest, and a familiar voice fills the space.

"Callie?" Officer Williams's voice hums an octave higher than the washing machines.

I use all my energy to open my eyes and turn my head toward him. His arms flex around a large bag of laundry.

"My washing machine decided it was a great day to stop working, and the landlord's on vacation, so here I am." He sounds oddly chipper for a guy who has to do laundry at a run-down laundromat. I don't remember asking him why he was here. But I'm so tired. Maybe I did?

"I see." I wait for him to step away, but as soon as I close my eyes again, I can feel his presence still standing there. I open my eyes a sliver, and he's still only a few feet from me.

"I saw the signs all over town for Opie," he begins, loading the washing machine next to mine even though ten more are open.

"Yep." I take another sip of now-lukewarm coffee from the Styrofoam cup.

"That was smart to put them all the way up on Hunter Creek Trail." He slams the door shut and jiggles the quarters in his pocket.

I nod, but then, like lightning to my chest, I sit up abruptly to look at him clearly.

"Did you say you saw the posters up by *Old Hunter Creek Trail*? The hiking trail past the railway bridge?"

"Yeah. I jog out there every morning. There were at least a dozen of them scattered on the map posts and the marker trees all over the trail. That was smart," he adds, turning toward me.

"Yeah, it was," I mutter, my eyes searching the speckled linoleum floor before I look out the window and rack my brain for answers. Am I so tired that I can't remember posting those? No, I certainly didn't. There's only one person who could have. *Or would have.* And he's walking into the print shop with his mother right now.

Levi and Mrs. Whitaker enter the print shop, but as the door shuts, they keep the closed sign facing out. It's not like that ever stopped me, though.

"I'll be right back," I mumble to Officer Williams, who glances at me with confusion and watches as I leave, against my better judgment, and hastily cross the street. Before I can even knock, Levi appears at the glass door with a furrowed brow, followed by a smirk when I wave apprehensively.

I should've let it go. It would've been done.

But I can't let sleeping dogs lie, so here I am, staring at him through an open doorway.

"Hey, why'd you do that?" I start, crossing my arms over my tank top.

Levi crosses his arms, too. "You're going to have to be more specific, Callie."

"Why'd you go back to the trail and put up signs?"

He rubs the back of his neck, and his lips turn down. "I wanted to help."

"You didn't have to do that," I reply snappily.

"Most people would just say thanks."

Dammit. He's right. Why is it so hard for me to be nice to Levi?

"Thank you." I'm still unsure of his motives.

"I mean, maybe someone will see them and call, yeah? He's got to turn up sometime." He flashes a small, but knowing, smile as his mom calls for him. Levi gazes over his shoulder.

I jut my thumb toward the laundromat. "I have to get back to my laundry. Just wanted to catch you and say thanks."

"A text suffices, too, you know," he jabs.

I could've, but I didn't have his number. I deleted our texts last night. I omit that detail, though. "Yeah. I hate texting," I add and turn to cross back before Mrs. Whitaker can see me standing there.

When I walk back into the laundromat, Williams quickly drops his face toward his phone, though I guarantee he was watching me. Ignoring him, I check on my laundry.

I have twenty minutes left, and it doesn't look like Williams will move anytime soon from his seat, so I set a timer on my phone and leave again without saying a word. My stomach is grumbling anyway. A few blocks away is a sub shop, and as I stand in line, the door chimes, and in walks Levi.

Just my luck.

"Are you everywhere? Or are you stalking me?" I'm mildly annoyed but genuinely curious.

"I'm not stalking you, Callie." Levi sucks in a breath, laughing. "I'm hungry. Is that a crime?" He smiles, and I feel my barrier lighten a bit.

What's wrong with this boy and his damn infectious smile?

"Fair enough." I awkwardly turn my gaze back to the menu, pretending to thoroughly read it even though I get the same thing every time. Levi doesn't even look at it.

"My mom is on another level today, so I needed to get out."

When I tip my head back, he is standing close enough for me to lean back on his chest. I wait for him to continue, feeling like there's more to it, and I'm right.

"I work with my parents daily at the shop, and I still live with them. It's a lot." He bites his cheek.

I don't know how to respond, so I quickly step forward to place my order, and the woman in front of me checks out.

In some way, I have sympathy for Levi, having to deal with parents who are less than ideal. His issues stem from overbearing parents, who keep him sheltered unnecessarily, while mine stem from lack of care. I don't mention that, of course.

We don't talk again until both of us place our orders. He steps off to the side with me to wait. It's now empty in here, besides the teenagers behind the counter who pay us no mind. So I turn to Levi. "You're not here to tell me you have more flyers to put up, I hope. Because every inch of this town has a picture of Opie's face. And even though that's great . . . I don't think it needs more," I force out a small, nervous laugh.

"No, I don't. Though I actually thought of something—or *someone*, who might be able to help you," Levi says, and for once, he is the one who looks nervous. His hazel eyes scan the floor in front of us instead of looking at me.

"Oh? I kinda prefer to work alone, which you know," I respond matter-of-factly.

Levi rolls his eyes at me. "It's day four, right?" he reminds me, but not in a mean way.

"Yes. It's day four."

I know every minute Opie's been missing. Every tortuous second.

"Just hear me out, then. I know *someone*. He's a close family friend. He has bloodhounds that are trained to track. He's a retired detective, but he's getting back into private investigation."

I narrow my eyes at Levi, confused.

First, I can't hire a private investigator. I don't even want to know what that would cost, but anything with *private* in the name can't be in the price range I can afford. My price range is buying beanie weenies from the gas station to bait my dog. And second, *why*?

"Why are you looking at me like that?" Levi asks as the teenage worker holds out both of our bags. We pause and snatch them, and then Levi follows me to grab napkins from the counter.

"Like what?" I feign dumb.

"Like I scare you."

I shove the napkins in my bag and squarely face Levi, who stops what he is doing. His hazel eyes flicker over me. "Why are you helping me?" I demand.

"Why can't I help you? I think this guy can actually help." He talks quickly, evading an answer.

"I don't know, Levi," I say, unsure how to rebut and too exhausted to fight so hard.

"Callie—" He places a hand on my shoulder, but instantly removes it when I tense. "—he's tracked missing people and hunted all his life. He grew up in this town. He knows these woods."

I grind my jaw, breaking eye contact as customers walk in the door. *This* is why I didn't want other people involved. This complicates shit. Why does Levi have to stick his nose where it doesn't belong? I know he is trying to help. He'd probably help a complete stranger this much, too, if I'm being honest. But he is scaling the walls I've expertly built around myself.

Walls I've built up for good reason.

Levi doesn't stop looking at me, his stance brooding.

I let out a small groan. "I don't want to rope anyone else into this mess."

"I know. I *know* you do things alone. I *get it*. But for a moment, just think. If this *person* could help you find Opie, isn't that worth it?"

Fuck you was on the tip of my tongue. Not because I meant it, but because he was right. I'd do anything for Opie, even go to the uncomfortable extremes of airing my troubles to a strange old man with hunting dogs.

"Okay, so where would I even find this *person*?"

Levi perks up but tries to act cool, running his hand through his hair. "How about we meet him later this afternoon if you're free?"

I should've known this was a package deal. Levi senses the hesitation as I look past him, internally struggling.

"I'll come with you, okay? Once you two meet, I'm out of this. I promise, Callie."

Our gazes meet, and I know he means it. Levi is nothing if not sincere. And I have no other choice. At least if this guy turns out to be some ax murderer, I'll have Levi with me.

"All right. That works," I reply dryly, knowing I should thank him, but I'm lost in my mind.

We part ways after getting our food, and Levi looks chapped with himself while I have one thought running through my head.

If this *person* has lived here his whole life, he knows Mack. He knows me. And there's nothing I can do to change that.

Chapter Sixteen

I wait by the end of the driveway, picking chipped paint off the faded blue mailbox that's leaning too far to the right. I remember the day Memaw said we should paint it. The mailbox stood out like a bluebird in the forest. She let me pick the color, of course—robin's-egg blue. But that was thirteen years ago, and the sun has done as it does best: faded it.

My thoughts are interrupted by the sound of gravel crunching under car tires. Levi stops, hopping out of the car to run around and open the passenger door. I chuckle as I narrow my eyes at him.

"I still don't understand why you won't let me pick you up at your front door like a normal person."

I shrug it off. "I need to stretch my legs," I bargain with him. It's not *entirely* a lie. The walk from my trailer to the mailbox is a pretty one with lush trees lining the driveway. There was no way I would let Levi see where I lived or drive past the farmhouse, where my father was passed out on the sofa on the front porch.

Some things are too hard to explain.

"So what did your friend say?" I ask, turning toward Levi.

"Callie, aka the queen of avoiding questions," Levi replies, shifting the vehicle into drive.

My face turns red.

"He knows we are coming."

"And you say I'm the queen of avoidance?"

Levi smirks, turning on the music.

Just a few miles down the road, we stop. A hidden, steep driveway peeks out from between the tree line.

"This is it," Levi states, leaning forward to get a look at the mailbox that is more dingy than my own.

I'm about to suggest we turn around and forgo this whole plan. I don't like meeting strangers to ask them for help; it opens up a world of vulnerabilities. And in this town, *no one* is a true stranger. Before I can speak, though, I nudge my phone screen, causing it to light up. A photo of Opie stares back at me. His tongue hangs sideways out of his big mouth. It's his famous smile. Famous to me.

You can do this for Opie.

We climb the steep, narrow driveway in silence, winding through trees until we come to a small clearing. A log cabin-style home sits peaceful and serene, like a postcard, with a red pickup truck parked out front.

Clearly, this private investigator has money, and I have none. Everything I have is holed up in the local bank's savings account. If I'm miraculously un-waitlisted by the Charleston Photography Co., it will take every cent of that.

I've already made up my mind that right now, that money has to be used to find Opie, though. Without him, there is no Charleston. Without him, photography won't even matter.

Levi smiles at me reassuringly, opening my door again. I sit there, unmoving.

"Callie, he won't bite."

Looking up slowly, Levi's stretched-out hand awaits me. His honeyed eyes are gentle, encouraging me to take his hand. He pulls me out, and I drop my hand back into the safety of my jean short pockets.

Levi leads the way to the front door. If he wasn't with me, I'd probably dash into the woods and not stop until I was back at the trailer. The front door opens after the first knock, a screen door separating us from the man on the other side. Two bloodhounds come rushing up beside him, sniffling loudly. My mouth tugs into a tiny smile when I see them. I can't *not* smile when a dog is near, granted two.

"Foster, hey. Thanks for meeting with us." Levi smiles.

The name *Foster* sounds so familiar. It didn't even occur to me to ask for his name beforehand. Too many nerves. I stay still behind Levi, and it brings me back to being a child with him. Because when I was with Levi, the other kids didn't bother me. He protected me without even knowing it.

Foster grunts, his arm reaching over his head as he leans on the doorway. It's dark in the house behind him despite it being the middle of the day. His eyes scan my face, and I smile weakly.

"Hi. I'm, um, I'm Callie." I would offer my hand, but he hasn't moved, the screen door still dividing us. Levi tenses beside me suddenly.

Dammit, Levi. This was a mistake.

"Come in," he mumbles, unlatching the door and turning around, disappearing into the house.

Levi doesn't hesitate to open the door, motioning for me to walk in first.

I can't help but feel like I'm walking into a trap. We follow him silently to the back of the house, where expansive windows overlook the back of the property and flood the kitchen with sunlight. The dogs have their entire noses shoved all around me. I reach down, lazily scratching their soft heads. I miss the feel of velvety ears under my fingers. I'd do anything to hold Opie's sweet face in my hands.

I can now see Foster more clearly, though he's still not looking at us as he pulls a chair out at the kitchen table and drops into it. An empty mug sits on the table in front of him.

He can't be much older than my father because his dark hair is peppered with gray. His eyes are as blue, but unlike Mack, Foster is clean-shaven and alert.

He looks very familiar. He could be a customer at the diner. I'm sure I've served most of the town by this point in my life.

Levi and I sit, the wood feeling shockingly cold on my legs. The two bloodhounds follow me, sitting by my side, and I silently thank them. Their presence is the only comfort in this moment.

"So I told you a little about Callie's situation with her lost dog, Opie. Dad said you've gotten back into business with PI and search, right?"

Levi speaks like he is my manager, and I have to intervene. The last thing I want to seem is weak, *even if I do feel faint.*

"Really, I am just looking for some advice. My dog ran away four days ago, and I'm growing a bit desperate to find him. I've had no leads." I spit it all out quickly, and silence befalls the room as Foster keeps his eyes on the coffee mug before him. The only audible noise is the whirring of the ceiling fan above us and the dogs' loud panting.

I shoot a nervous glance at Levi, but he's watching Foster.

Foster stands and walks to the counter, grabbing the coffee mug to refill his cup. I'm starting to hate him. This might have been his strategy to get bad guys to speak in the station, but I'm here for help. I'm not a criminal.

"Dog's name is Opie?" Foster asks, his voice gravelly.

"Yes." I twiddle my thumbs, uneasy.

"He ran away four days ago . . . and you've been searching for him?"

I nod in response.

"Tell me what you've done so far." He retakes a seat, and his full attention is on me, making my heart race.

I swallow hard, suddenly embarrassed by how little it feels like I've done. I tell Foster everything, from the list I found online on what to do in the first forty-eight hours to calling the vet and shelter every few hours, so much so that I swear they will block my number. I tell him about Officer Williams and how he was no help.

He breaks eye contact and chuckles to himself. "Those rookies don't know what the hell they are doing down there. They couldn't find a damn elephant if it went missing in their own building." Foster tips his head back, amused.

Levi laughs too, but I don't find anything funny about it. It only fills me with more self-doubt. Has everything been a waste of time? Could I have found Opie if I knew what the hell I was doing? Worries ticks away in my veins as Foster slowly sits up straight in his chair.

"I was a detective for twenty years for the county. I've solved a lot of crimes and worked on a lot of missing people cases. Now, this ain't no big city, but don't be fooled by that. People out here think they can get away with things just because they have the false cover of the trees. And it was just me—well, me and the little boys they call officers down at the station." He scoffs and continues as Levi and I listen to his every word. "I retired three years ago."

His right hand rubs against his empty ring finger. It's like he's expecting something to be there. I pull my eyes back to his face before he notices me watching.

He hesitates and exhales a deep breath before continuing. "I'm a PI now, like Levi said. Daisy and May are my two girls here. They've spent years training to search for missing people and animals. We go all over the state now. They're big cases, lots of money, lots of hush if you get what I mean."

He looks pointedly at Levi, and I want to cry. What kind of fool am I to think he'd have time for someone like me? No one cares about Callie Hayes, and no one fucking cares about Opie, alone and scared out there in the world. I have no idea where my dog is, and I can't do a damn thing about it, and now Levi's brought me here, and this guy is basically telling me to my face that I'm not *big enough* for him. That my life isn't significant enough for him.

Levi's large hand encompasses mine under the table, and he gives it a quick squeeze. The gesture is so simple but feels like a hug.

"So what exactly does that mean for Callie and Opie?" Levi asks skeptically.

I don't understand why he thought this was a good idea.

Foster smirks at both of us. "Well, it means I'm pretty damn confident we can find your dog."

My heart hitches in my chest, and I nearly choke as I look up at him. His returning stare is sharp.

Daisy and May readjust under my feet, their wrinkly fur soft on my leg, offering comfort I'm sure they sense I need. That's what's so great about dogs. They just know. They don't need to be told like people do.

"Oh, really?" I'm unable to hide the surprise in my voice.

"There's no guarantee, but you say he's a young dog that's healthy and smart. And my girls can track just about anything. There are papers to sign. And a fee, of course."

I nod, my stomach going queasy.

The phone rings, and Foster stands up, excusing himself to the other room. I take that moment to check in with Levi, but as I glance over at him, I see the wall covered in family photos I hadn't noticed when we sat down.

"Levi, why does that person look so familiar?" I ask.

He turns in his seat, looking at the photo of a boy fishing with Foster. He turns back to me, gnawing on his bottom lip. "That's my cousin . . . Everett."

All the oxygen is sucked from my chest. I bend forward in my seat, feeling Levi's hand on my back, but before I can think of what to say, I leap from the chair, startling Daisy and May.

"Callie, what's wrong?" Levi stands with me, his hands gripping the edge of the table.

"You brought me to Everett Calloway's house, and you're asking me *what's wrong*? You brought me to meet his father?" I hiss at him, and the walls in the kitchen feel like they are closing in on me.

This is a sick joke. This is why Levi was friendly to me. Just to get close, just to torment me!

Levi stares at me, confused, a flash of hurt on his face, but then it's like he came to. His eyebrows shoot up, his shoulders arched back. "I wasn't even thinking about *that*, Callie, I swear. All that was on my mind was helping you, and my uncle is the best. He can help."

His uncle.

It must be nice to not have a family reputation and trauma following you around, because it's *all* I think about. I'm so flustered that I can't reply as I spin around to see where Foster has wandered.

"I promise you, no one is worried about the past right now. I wouldn't have brought you here if he wasn't willing to help."

I shake my head in disbelief, unsure if I want to cry or use my fists. All I can manage is to mumble that we are leaving *now*.

"Callie, wait! Think of Opie!"

All I do is think of Opie.

Foster intercepts us in the hallway. "Everything all right?" His eyes dart between me and Levi.

I'm sick of people asking me that question when nothing is all right.

"I'm sorry. We have to go! But thank you for your time," I add quickly, ducking my head as I motion for Levi to follow me.

"I'm sorry, Foster. I . . ." Levi says as I dash to the truck, where I've already buckled myself in. Levi says something inaudible to Foster on the porch. I peel my eyes away, sick to my stomach. With a tight chest, my eyes stay trained on the car's dash.

Levi climbs into the cab, looking frazzled. "Look, I'm truly sorry. I didn't know this would be a big deal. I should have told you who he was, but I knew you wouldn't give him a chance if you knew."

"Please, can we just go?" I beg in defeat, eyes on the floorboard.

"Yeah, of course," Levi responds flatly.

I know Levi is upset. And I'm mad at myself.

We ride in silence until he drops me off at the end of my driveway. With my hand still gripping the car door, I turn to face him.

"I told you I'm better off on my own," I voice solemnly, watching his face as my words sink in.

With eyes straight ahead, his hand pulls through his hair, and he nods.

It breaks my heart for a moment. It takes a lot to dull Levi's light, but if anyone can do it, it's me. And I think I just have.

Foster and Levi can rectify their relationship, whatever it is. But I don't have that privilege. My father ruined all of that. Not many people can see beyond the shadow of my father looming over me. My face is a spitting image of his. It's like an evil joke.

And the people who do see beyond it see me, Callie, as just me, *Callie*. They either take pity on me, or I push them away. Just look at Levi, driving away, jaw clenched and shoulders tense. *I did that.*

That's why I have to get out of this town. To a place where I can start new, where Opie and Callie won't be forgotten coal but diamonds instead.

I kick up the dust outside the trailer and squat when a yellow ball catches my eye.

Opie's tennis ball.

I didn't notice it before. Picking it up, I bring it to my nose, smelling the rubber and the faint scent of slobber. I want to hold it and bring it inside, but I know it could help him find his way back, so I put it back on the ground.

After doing my daily rounds on the property, I go inside to make the daily phone calls to the animal shelters and vets that make my heart pound outside my chest. Then I check all the online forums for lost-and-found pets. It was actually Levi's idea to join these forums. *I forgot to thank him for that tip.*

The afternoon drags on, and while it feels like I'm doing a lot, it somehow feels like I've done nothing by the time I have to go to work. As I get my uniform on for the diner, I scroll through photos of lost-and-found dogs on local websites. Each new image and post sends a new roll of emotions. *A glimmer of hope, sadness, then sickness.*

Dropping my phone on the counter, I reach for Opie's purple dinosaur stuffie with the cotton still halfway sticking out. If I could grant one wish right now, I'd go back in time. I'd stay home the night of the storm. I'd never let him out of my sight ever again.

As I make this outlandish wish, I'm met with a deafening silence in the trailer. Then three little words slip from my mouth.

"I'm sorry, boy."

Chapter Seventeen

The moment he enters the diner, I quickly look up from the coffee machine, and recognition sets in. A faded baseball cap hangs low over his eyes, and a pocketknife dangles from his belt. There's nothing unusual about him, but he scans the diner like he is looking for someone. I'm guessing me. But then again, maybe that's how all ex-detectives are: extra weary of their surroundings.

I'm on counter duty tonight, which means I primarily serve people who are eating alone. A lot of them come in, hoping for both a meal and someone to chat with. That someone is the waiter. But tonight, no one has tried to strike up small talk with me; it's been strictly business. I even tried to look halfway decent, braiding my hair and putting on a little makeup, but only so Peg wouldn't comment again on how tired I look.

There's been no Levi or Officer Williams tonight, but I would've welcomed either of them over Foster, who just sat at the very end of the bar next to the old jukebox that hasn't worked a day in my lifetime.

Either way, I keep my head ducked, refilling drinks and walking back into the kitchen, taking way too long to fiddle with a stack of dinner plates. It's not like I can ask another server to take him; I only have two other customers now. It's slow tonight, and I need the tips.

On the other hand, I can't imagine the tip he leaves will be anything other than a hate-filled note.

Or nothing at all, which would somehow be worse.

I can't stall any longer, I decide, so I wander back into the dining room, and immediately, his hand lazily waves in the air, eyes glued to the menu.

I walk toward Foster, knowing it would be a damn miracle if he doesn't hear the thumping in my chest. It's overpowering my senses, taking control of my body, to the point where I swear the next thing that happens won't be me scribbling an order on the greasy notepad but my head hitting the ground after I pass out.

"How's the Reuben?" Foster's voice is calm and collected as he points at the sandwich on the plastic menu. His gaze remains there.

My body stiffens. "People seem to like it." I squeeze the words out of my lungs. It's agony. He's either going to say something to torment me or act like nothing happened. I'm waiting for him to look up and see me, *really see me.*

"Okay, well, that's as good as any, then. And I'll take an iced tea. Thanks."

He slides the menu toward me as I scribble, aware of my unsteady hand. I snatch the menu, shoving it under my arm, and turn away before we can make eye contact.

Carla approaches me as I slide my order onto the wire. "Callie, are those dog posters yours? I remember seeing you one day with a big dog like that." She's Peg's newest hire—a sixteen-year-old who's overly eager to be here. We haven't talked much, and I'm sure, at this point, she thinks I hate her.

"Um, yeah. They are," I respond. It literally says my name on the poster, but I don't bother pointing that out.

"Aw, I can't believe you lost your pup. Did you find him yet?" she asks, her mouth exaggeratedly pouting.

I want to scream no, but instead, I fill a glass with iced tea and shake my head. "Not yet."

I flash her a pursed-lipped look, pushing the swinging door open back into the dining room. She doesn't follow, thank God.

My heart pounds as I walk toward Foster. He's squinting at his phone screen, so I try to slip the drink onto the counter in front of him and slink away like a fox, but as I turn, he catches me.

"You going to tell me why you ran out of my house today like you were fleeing a crime scene?" Foster's sharp eyes bore right into mine. His gaze is intense but not mean. Not like Mack's.

I falter over the answer to his question. The last thing I want to do is discuss my trauma with a diner. But his gaze holds me, my feet unable to move from the tile floor.

"I'm really sorry about that. I realized your services weren't what I was looking for, so I didn't want to waste any more of your time." The polite lie rolls off my tongue with shaky confidence.

At first, it seems like he buys it, nodding and putting the drink to his lips, but he lowers his glass too soon, swallowing quickly.

"Listen, I need you to know one thing, okay?"

The blood drains from my face. I can feel the other diners looking at me. I inch closer to Foster, wishing he would have done this anywhere but *here*.

"Okay," I say, looking Foster in the eyes, keeping my face composed.

"I knew *exactly* who you were before you even got to my house." He narrows his eyes slightly at me, tapping his index finger on the counter. "I agreed to meet with you and Levi *after* I knew who you were," he responds, driving home the point. A point I can't really comprehend.

"Oh. I'm . . . I'm sorry."

Sorry for running away. Sorry for making a fool of myself. Sorry for being in the car that night. Sorry for letting Mack drive. Sorry for not being old enough or strong enough to get him to listen to me when I realized he was too drunk to drive. Sorry, your son will never walk again.

Foster's jaw tenses. He nods to himself slightly, and a beat of silence goes by, where I forget I'm working. Instead, I'm here, with Foster, in the corner of this diner, both of us reliving things we'd rather never think about again.

He clears his throat, and I clear mine.

"I'm not sure this is a good idea," I say.

His demeanor doesn't change. "I take a deposit of $250. From there, I charge seventy an hour."

Rocking back and forth ever so slightly, we lock eyes. I don't know if I can trust him, I don't know if he can find Opie, and I don't know if this man simply wants revenge.

But I know one thing. I have to try. For Opie.

"When can you start?" I respond without thinking if I even have the money.

Foster looks surprised but quickly hides it, extending a hand toward me. "Seven a.m. sharp, tomorrow. I'll meet you at your house. The hounds do their best work in the morning," he explains firmly, shaking my hand once.

I drop it to my side but nearly jump out of my skin when I realize what this means.

"My house? You'll be at my house at seven a.m.?" *Of course,* he'd have to start there. But that also means he will be near Mack.

"Where else would I start? And don't clean up. We need the scene as it is."

I nod, not really listening. "Okay. Um, it's just . . . you should know I live on my father's property. Far up from the farmhouse, but still, you'll have to pass it when you come to mine."

He pauses, his mouth pulling down slightly for a moment before he speaks and takes a swig of tea. "I'm a grown man, Miss Hayes, but thanks for the warning."

I smile out of politeness. "I'll check on your food," I mumble, rushing to the kitchen. I lean against the chilly cooler doors, hoping it steadies my racing heart.

Breathe in . . . out . . . in . . . out.

All I've wanted from the moment I left the hospital was to escape this town . . . to escape that night. I squeeze my eyes shut.

It's all for Opie. Everything is for him.

Chapter Eighteen

At seven a.m. on Monday morning, I'm woken by the sound of tires on gravel. My mind shoots awake from grogginess as I jump up, still half-asleep, and pull on some clean clothes, splashing water on my face. The humidity is already seeping through the thin walls, and my stomach rumbles, but I have no time to think about food.

Foster is parking out front, so I take a few shallow breaths, attempting to calm the nerves spidering up my arms. I quickly pray that Mack stays far away today, holed up in the house or out causing shit anywhere but here.

Foster only gets in one knock on the door before I swing it open, offering an awkward hello. His eyes roam past me, scanning the inside of my place immediately. I want to close the door and hide the truth, but it's too late. If I ever want to be reunited with Opie, I must let Foster in.

Into the trailer, at least.

"Good morning, Miss Hayes," he starts.

My eyes trail to the large dogs sitting obediently beside him, then back to his outfit. He's in blue jeans, a khaki shirt with lots of pockets, and hiking boots that look brand new. At least it appears like he's dressed for the job. Unlike me.

"Morning. You can come in." I move aside as he steps inside, Daisy and May following suit. The tiny trailer quickly becomes overcrowded. It's a mess, something I overlook when I'm alone, but as Foster looks to the banquette to sit, a folder in his hand, I realize he's the *only* person besides myself who's stepped foot in here since I moved in. Even Officer Williams knew my boundaries, never inviting himself inside.

This feels like a new era, like a line has literally been crossed, and I don't know how to feel about it. Though I don't have a choice either.

"We just have a few papers to sign and a deposit to collect, and then we can begin," he starts, pulling reading glasses from one of his shirt pockets and sliding them on his face. The tabletop is cluttered with half-folded laundry and photographs, but he doesn't seem to notice or mind. I take this opportunity to grab a glass of water, suddenly thirsty.

"Would you like some water?" I ask with my back to him.

"No, thank you."

I gulp an entire glass before turning to look at him. He doesn't look up from the papers he's organizing. I cautiously step over the large bloodhounds and sit across from him, feeling out of body in my own place. No longer my *home*.

He reads the first few lines of the contract aloud and slides it toward me to see. My eyes quickly trace the words, but all that sticks in my head is "no guarantees."

"Last thing you should know is that if you agree to work with me, Miss Hayes, you have to let me do things my way. No interference, no going behind my back, and no playing with, or distracting, the hounds."

Biting my lip, I look at the two dogs, panting and drooling on the floor.

Yeah, sure, but there's no guarantee I won't be petting your dogs.

I sign it, eyeing the thick cash envelope on my kitchen counter. I hand it to him and sign the bottom of the paper. He slips the envelope into his shirt and taps the table.

"You ready, then?" His eyes crinkle, forming lines around his eyes as he looks at me.

"Ready as I'll ever be," I enthuse with no idea what was about to happen, even though he explained it to me. *Twice.*

He tells me this could take days or weeks. It depends on how far Opie has strayed or if he is hurt and stuck somewhere close by. He says something else, something I haven't been willing to consider.

Opie could've been picked up and taken somewhere.

And the worst, which he doesn't have to say, sits in our silence.

Opie could be dead.

That thought makes me dizzy, my insides twisting at merely the notion of it. My whole life's been preparing me for moments like this, moments of absolute desperation and despair. It seems like that is what I do best, so I saddle up, mustering the strength I somehow almost find.

I've found something to be true about my own strength. It doesn't come from choice, but when there is *no other* choice.

I back myself up into my "bedroom," trying to give them all the space they need. Leaning against my hastily made bed, I watch as Daisy and May sniff around the tiny trailer and Foster spreads Opie's things on the ground in front of them. This situation *should* calm my nerves; I should feel less anxious and more hopeful right now, but I can't stop staring at Foster and thinking about Everett.

There was no criminal court after the accident. Mack pled guilty immediately, so I never had to face Everett or his family. As a minor, I'm not sure I would've had to anyway, but it was pretty easy to stay away from the Calloway family, holing myself up at the farm or making myself invisible at school as best I could. I had started the process to be an emancipated minor months before the accident. It was the last legal step to separate myself from my father, though I'd been taking care of myself for years at that point anyway. The judge granted me it without question just days after Mack's arrest.

You would've thought during that time, in a town as small as Miscruz Hills, that running into the Calloway family would be inescapable, but Everett didn't return to school his senior year, and his parents stayed in the shadows, too, busy with their newly disabled son. The incident was like a ghost haunting everyone in town. There's so much from that time in my life I've blocked out. With or without meaning to, I had to do it. It's what you do to survive.

"I need to take these with me." Foster's voice breaks me out of my thoughts as he stands in front of me holding one of Opie's blankets and a toy.

"Yeah, yeah, of course," I say quickly. My cheeks flush as if he could read my mind and know I'm anywhere but *here* right now. I almost apologize, but I bite my tongue hard. It's something I've been wanting to say for three years. After the accident, once Mack was out of my life, I wanted to reach out. I wanted to say sorry, but it felt pointless. Everyone had already made up their mind about him and me. So instead of facing the people he hurt, trying to prove that I was not my father's daughter, I went deeper into seclusion. I let no one in. I let them think what they wanted.

Now I stand here at the mercy of Foster and his dogs, and I feel like I've stepped back into the shoes of sixteen-year-old Callie, *helpless*.

"We will do a perimeter search today." Foster breaks the silence, and I jerk my head up toward him.

"I've searched every inch of this land for four days. I don't think Opie is here," I reckon, but Foster's face remains stone. He licks his lips before staring out beyond the meadow.

"I understand you've been *thorough*, but this is protocol, Miss Hayes. The hounds will search the property today and lock in Opie's scent. I'll see where it takes them. This part is all a guessing game right now."

"Okay, got it. What about the trail, the one I mentioned with the possible lead? Will they go there today?"

He hangs his head, shaking it back and forth. "No, that will be tomorrow. This work here's exhausting. It might take all day to do a perimeter search here on your property. We will see what we turn up, and that will determine what happens next. You understand?"

"Yeah," I reply dryly. I hired him, and he's costing me a lot. And not just money. Emotional baggage.

I know I need to set aside my pride and put my trust in him. But that's asking a lot, considering I barely trust myself. Opie wouldn't be gone if I had fixed the leak and the latch and provided a better home for him.

He starts walking, following Daisy and May as their ears drag along the ground and they work, trotting down the trail. *Our* trail to the creek.

A sad smile tugs on the corner of my lips. Opie would lose his mind if he saw these two dogs walking his trail. He'd think I brought him friends to play with.

I need him back. God, I need him back.

Momentarily, I stay put, but the silence of the trailer hits me like a truck. Pushing off the door, I bolt after Foster. "Wait, Foster. Can I come with you? I'd like to see them work."

His face scrunches up, and he uncomfortably adjusts his hat to shield himself from the sun. "No, ma'am. I'm sorry. I can't have that. We work best alone. And it looks like you have an injury." He nods to my wrapped foot.

Tears well in my eyes, but I keep my mouth shut. Foster turns back, following his dogs. I'm left standing there, my bare feet on the cool earth.

It's ironic, isn't it, searching for someone? All the while insisting we're best alone.

I'm not dying to be in Foster's presence, but I can't hide the fact that Daisy and May bring a calmness to me. They are working hard; I know it. And I want to be there working, too. I need to be useful.

Instead, I tread back home and decide to use the time to clean up. I don't have the mental energy to do so, but I can't go back to bed, and my shift isn't until five, so I clean to keep my mind busy. As I start picking things up, my foot accidentally kicks my camera. I realize Foster didn't say anything about it. Surely, though, he saw it. *He must think I'm a total train wreck.*

The thought of even picking it up brings a lump to my throat. It seems so feeble now—the thing that was once my escape, my only reprieve, offers me no comfort today. It's more than disheartening; it feels like the clouds have permanently covered the sun.

There are towels on the floor, dried in the position I left them in on the day of the storm. I pick them up to shake them out, then set them in the laundry basket. Five days seems like a lifetime ago. The towels cover water damage on the trailer floor, but it's the least of my worries right now.

My phone rings, making me jump. The only person who calls me is Peg when she needs me for a shift. If it's her, I'll have to tell her I'm busy. I'm not leaving this property until Foster and the girls return and give me an update.

Levi's number lights up my screen, and my finger hovers over the red "X." I ignore the call, tossing my phone onto my bed.

I don't have the capacity for this right now.

He doesn't text or call back.

After two hours, the entire camper is cleaned up, floor to ceiling. All Opie's toys are in a box, as Foster requested, except for the purple dinosaur. That's staying on my bed.

It's nearly an hour later when I hear trotting outside the trailer, and I step outside hastily to greet them, eager for news. I can't read the expression on Foster's face as he looks at me, his skin sun-worn from the morning that's quickly gotten warm. I search the dogs for clues, for *anything* indicating there was a success.

I go to talk, but he speaks first.

"The rain, mixed with the heat this week, has made any scent here weak. They didn't pick up on Opie's scent."

"What does that mean?" I ask as a chill runs down my spine.

Foster shifts his weight from one foot to the other. "Well, it means a few things. It's rural land out here, Miss Hayes, but you know that. It's like searching for a needle in a haystack. Opie could've run any direction, though you have neighbors not far east of here. But they claim they haven't seen—"

"You already spoke to them?" I ask, dumbfounded.

"Yes, I did. It's part of the investigation," he says matter-of-factly. "As I was saying, due to your diligent baiting, I don't believe Opie stayed near the property, or he would've come back. So there are two probable situations here if we are banking on him being alive beyond the night of the disappearance."

Foster stops as I let out a small involuntary whimper. My palm slaps to my mouth. I don't want to break down in front of this man. I don't know what he thinks of me. Sure, he agreed to work with me, but he could really need the money. I don't want to cry, but it's too late to mask how I feel as his cold, logical words slice me to the core.

His tone softens up as he sucks in his cheeks and looks at me. "Listen, Miss Hayes. I need you to be realistic. I know this is difficult. Right now, I'm considering the two theories that rely on Opie being alive and out there. Okay?" His lips twitch into what I'm assuming is supposed to be a reassuring smile.

"Okay. What are the two options we have?" I pull my arms protectively across my chest.

"He could've run far. You said he can be a timid dog when he's not near you. With everything I know about dogs who've run away, the more fearful he is, the more likely he is to run far during something like a storm. I believe he could've covered a lot of ground. Dogs Opie's size can travel miles in a day, *though* it's not likely he would've gone miles without someone spotting him or being picked up. Unless he is that good at being elusive, then that's another issue."

"And what if he *is* elusive?" I hesitantly ask.

"Then I'll need you to come with me when we search. We will use you as the lure."

I nod, processing this information. I want to be there every step of the way. I want to be the one to find Opie. Even if Daisy and May are the heroes who lead me to him, I want to be the one to lay eyes on him.

To say I'm sorry first.

"Wait. Then what is the other theory?"

"Tell me, did Opie have a collar on?" Foster asks.

I want to nod. I want to scream yes. But I can't.

"No, I take it off when he's inside. He has hated wearing it ever since he was a puppy," I whisper. It's a detail that's already crossed my mind, but it has agonized me. "But he is microchipped. To this address," I add.

"That's something." Foster nods, rubbing his stubble. "We need to consider the very real possibility that the night he fled, he reached the street, and someone driving by stopped and grabbed him."

My heart rate elevates rapidly. "Hold on. Are you implying someone could've stolen him *five days ago*?" I spit out, rage coursing through my bloodstream.

"I did not say *steal*. Many people see a wet dog on the side of the road, one with no collar, especially a mutt like Opie, and assume he is a stray. Someone could've picked him up, thinking they were doing the right thing, saving him during a storm. It's a genuine possibility."

As scary as that thought is, I know he's right. If I saw a dog out in a storm, seemingly lost, I wouldn't hesitate to take it to safety.

"And what do we do in that case?" I ask, though I'm unsure I want to hear the answer.

"You've been already doing it. Put up flyers. Call shelters and rescues, vet offices. Typically, someone will take a dog to the vet, have it scanned, or it will turn up on an adoption page. We will chase both routes. We will meet tomorrow to put up trail cameras. I am going to see what I can find out about any found dogs, any stray sightings, and we will set up cameras where we need to."

"Okay. What should I do for the rest of the day? I can't just sit here," I object, looking for something, for someone to tell me what to do.

"We're already doing it all, Miss Hayes," he responds pointedly.

I nod, not satisfied with the answer but knowing it's all I will get from him.

As the bloodhounds jump into Foster's truck, I stop at the trailer door and turn to thank him, but his door is already shut.

Chapter Nineteen

I manage to keep myself busy after Foster leaves. On the way to work that evening, I wonder if anyone has caught wind yet that I'm working with him. As much as people love Everett, and with how his injury rattled this town, Foster has majorly stayed in the shadows—or tried to. I guess we have that in common.

As I pull into the familiar parking spot at the diner, I try to dispel the worry about it. But anxiety doesn't completely leave my body as my mind moves on to the next thing: checking the online forums for lost dog listings. For the hundredth time today. Admittedly, I know, even if I checked them four times a minute, it still wouldn't be enough to quiet my mind.

It's hot and humid out, and the smell of burgers greets me as soon as I meander through the kitchen. No one seems to notice I'm here, so I take my time gathering myself, tying my apron and throwing my hair up messily, before I make it to the front where the dinner crowd is starting to gather. The top of my foot is still tender, so I kneel down to loosen the laces when Carla sneaks up beside me, smacking her gum and twirling her hair.

"Hey, girl. I sat you at table ten." She giggles, wiggling her eyebrows, which makes me stand up and peer over at table ten. A guy with perfectly tousled hair and arms that have no right to be in a T-shirt is waiting there.

"Carla, that booth is supposed to be reserved for parties of six or more."

She shrugs nonchalantly. "He said he wanted to sit in your section, so . . ."

"It's fine." I wave her off and grab a menu. By the time I'm walking over, Levi's already smirking at me, a look that gives me butterflies, much to my surprise. Butterflies . . . I don't deserve to feel them after how I treated him the last time we were together.

"I begged Carla," Levi admits, holding up the menu in front of his face.

I bite my cheeks to hold back a grin I don't want him to see. I glance at Carla over my shoulder, who turns red when I catch her checking out Levi. *Her and every other teenage girl in here.*

"Well, since you have the whole booth to yourself, are you going to order the whole menu again, or are you going to try to eat a normal serving? You know . . . to stay alive to see twenty and all," I say, attempting to crack a joke. This makes Levi put down his menu.

"Wait a minute. Is Callie Hayes attempting to make fun of me?"

My mouth twitches as Levi says my full name. "Don't get used to it," I snap.

"Ah, there's the girl I'm used to."

I offer a sarcastic smile and point toward the menu in his hands.

"Right. I will have the slam burger and fries." He doesn't even look at the menu.

When I reach to grab the menu from his outstretched arm, he doesn't let go. Our gazes meet, and a look of concern crosses his hazel eyes. I wait for him to say something in the uncomfortable silence as our eyes stay locked.

"How did it go today with Foster?"

"Excuse me?" I reply, confused. *Since when did Levi keep tabs on my life?*

"Didn't he come out to start the search today?"

I take the chance to pull the menu from his hand a bit too aggressively. I pause before replying. "Yeah, he did. But how did you know that?"

"We're close," he says, running a hand through his unruly hair.

I peer at him suspiciously. "Well, I don't appreciate you two talking about me."

"Ah, come on now. I just wanted to make sure he kept his word."

"Why wouldn't he?" My heart hitches in my chest, and Levi hesitates, looking like he regrets talking.

"Never mind." He swallows. "I just feel really crappy about the whole situation. It wasn't right how I did it. I should've told you who he was and let you decide."

"Yes, you should've," I reply pointedly. Though as he talks, I'm having a hard time being upset with him. Before I can keep talking to Levi, Carla calls for me. "I'll be back with your food," I add, walking away.

"You have a call." She leans against the wall near the door to the kitchen, holding the yellowed phone in one hand while her other covers the mouthpiece. I want to tell her that doing that doesn't really mute it, but I'm more concerned about who would be trying to reach me at the diner.

"Who is it?" I whisper, but Carla shrugs, pushing the phone into my chest, and bounces away without a care in the world. The voices in the diner jumble into background noise as I turn my back to Levi, who I can feel is watching me. Luckily, the music is louder than usual since Peg's not working tonight, so I stay put, shifting my weight to my uninjured foot.

"Hello?" I make my voice as confident sounding as possible.

"Callie Hayes?" A familiar voice fills my ears.

"This is Callie."

"It's Officer Williams," he replies, his voice low.

I want to sigh and say I know, but my heart is pounding through my chest.

Oh no . . . Did someone find Opie?

"What's going on?" I rush my words out.

"I'm sorry to call you at work. I tried your cell, and it went to voicemail. I'm calling about your father." He takes a deep breath and continues. "First, I want you to know he's okay, or going to be okay, but he will be spending the night in the ER."

My heart drops. Not because I'm worried about Mack, though. I'm sure whatever he did, he brought it upon himself.

I'm angry it's news about *him*. It's *him* taking up time and space. It's him and not Opie.

"Okay," I reply curtly. Radio silence fills the line, and I'm sure Officer Williams is waiting for me to ask what happened, but I can't bring myself to care.

"He fell from a ladder earlier today and has a broken collarbone and rib, along with a mild concussion. He wasn't up for making phone calls, so I told him I'd let you know. He should be released and back home tomorrow or the day after."

My leg bounces, annoyed with this conversation. "Can I ask why you're the one calling me and not the hospital?"

A pregnant pause again. I hear a car door open and keys jingling, and then it gets quiet again. I look around the diner, but no one's paying me much mind.

"Well, Callie, it's because his girlfriend intentionally caused this. It's currently an ongoing investigation. We are unclear if he will be bringing charges, but that's all I'm at liberty to say right now. And the hospital didn't have you listed as a person to call, but I felt you should know."

Of course, they didn't. Why would Mack want me to know any of this?

"When Mack gets home, you can speak to him more about it," Williams adds, and I almost laugh, but bitterness beats me to it.

"Okay. Thank you so much for the info," I respond sarcastically, not waiting for his response. I place the phone on the receiver and regain my wits.

Walking to the back with heavy legs, my eyes stay trained straight ahead. I do what I do best. I push this info into my mental folder full of Mack's bullshit—it's nearly full.

I've lost count of times Mack's gone to jail in my lifetime or been hospitalized for injuries incurred from alcohol. I was over it before, but now I'm beyond over it because none of it makes a difference in my life. He wouldn't have notified me himself, and I wouldn't have noticed him gone.

The only thing that's upsetting me is that Wendy got to push the ladder out from under him and not me.

The white plate clangs loudly on the tabletop in front of Levi, and he looks up from his phone, eyes wide. I want to ask him why he never comes here with his friends, parents, or a date. But I don't ask. Instead, I ask something else.

"Do you want to come with us tomorrow?" I blurt, anger unintentionally lacing my voice as I hold my notepad tightly in my hands.

Levi sits up, noticeably taller, pushing his shoulders back, while the corner of his lips tug to the side in a small smile. It makes my heart flutter, seeing him consider my horrendously presented olive branch. The one I will most likely regret extending when I'm an emotional wreck tomorrow. And there Levi will be to witness it—*again*.

Warmth pools in his honey eyes as he looks to me. "Come with you and Foster?"

I shrug like it's no big deal. "Yeah. He is setting up trail cams where there's been some sightings of a stray dog on the edge of town. I'm going to help him *lure* Opie, as he puts it. He's hopeful it's him." I added the last little bit for myself.

"Wouldn't want to be anywhere else," Levi replies.

I nod, fighting back a smile, and turn to get him ketchup, which I've learned he loves. When I return with it, though, he's watching me closely.

"Hey, I know this is cliché, or whatever, but I feel like you need to hear it. Don't lose hope, okay?" he says.

I try to catch my breath as a moment of stillness rides between us, and I shift back and forth on my feet, suddenly aware of how vulnerable I feel in front of him.

"Hope has never been my friend." I offer a smile, followed by an exaggerated breath. "*But* I'm not giving up, if that's what you're saying. I will exhaust myself for him. I love him more than anything."

Levi nods. "I know you do, Callie."

Our eyes meet, and the world around us stops spinning for a minute. My chest tightens as Levi's words sink in. For the first time in a long time, I want to hang on to someone else's words.

Chapter Twenty

It's dark by the time I leave the diner, and I'm tired as hell. My mind is already preoccupied with tomorrow, until I approach the farmhouse and see the yellow glow near the front door. The truck is parked out front, and Mack's standing slouched on the front porch, the screen door resting on his back.

Is he seriously back already? He's like a cockroach.

He wasn't supposed to be home until tomorrow, but I doubt he listened to the doctor's orders. I drive past him, catching a closer glimpse of him leaning against the front door, eyes shut and hand on the doorknob. I peel my eyes away as a pit forms in my stomach halfway up the drive to my trailer. Slamming on the brakes, I palm the steering wheel, whipping the car around before I can think better of my actions.

"Dammit!" I scream out in the safety of my car as my headlights illuminate the front yard. I put the car in park, silently turning it off. My hands hesitate on the buckle, but I bite my lip and step out.

You never learn, do you, Cal?

Sure enough, Mack's still standing there, struggling to get the front door open with one arm in a sling.

Questioning my sanity, I approach the porch with haste. Mack spins around. His eyes narrow as they meet mine. Surely, I'm the last person he's expecting.

There's an uneasiness in my stomach where the feelings about my father live. The years of resentment have built up a fortress. That happens when your father repeatedly abandons you when you need him.

Mack and I had never, not once, talked about the night of the accident. There's nothing he could say now, three years later, that would take away the pain. The consequences have already played out. Sometimes, though, I fantasize about how it would feel to hear him say sorry—and actually mean it.

"Here, let me," I offer, keeping my voice emotionless as I shimmy between him and the front door, jiggling the front door open. It's an old door and nearly impossible to open without two hands and a good shoulder shove. The door opens wide, and I keep my eyes on the floor, not wanting to peer into the living room I once loved, knowing the home's soul is no longer there.

It's not like there was nice furniture or a spotless space to begin with; it's always been a mash-up of stuff. Stuff I loved. But Memaw kept it clean to the best of her ability, and she made it a home. The walls provided a feeling of safety and comfort.

I wait for Mack to step inside or say something, but out of my peripherals, I see Mack looking at me. When I don't return the stare, he steps over the threshold, wincing. He smells of cigarettes and sweat as he passes me.

Now that the door is open, it would be appropriate to leave. But I can't; my feet are frozen to the uneven porch floor, and the darkness feels like a veil. Mack limps into the kitchen, switching on the light and setting down the white paper bag from the hospital pharmacy. Mack walks with his shoulders slumped, and his limp is more exaggerated than I remember. Sometimes I wonder what my mama ever saw in him and if he's even the same man that made her fall in love twenty years ago.

"You're gonna let the mosquitos in. Shut the door, Carolina," he barks, but I don't shut the door. Mack dumps the pharmacy bag on the counter, and two pill bottles roll toward him. He turns to face me, mouth hanging open, but I cut him off.

"Why can't you call me Callie like everyone else?"

He pauses, fists balancing himself on the counter.

I wait patiently, knowing I just nudged a hibernating bear. But Mack shakes his head slightly and turns toward the cupboard to reach for a glass. He lets out a pained groan as his hand extends.

"You know why," he retorts gruffly and begins to fill his glass with water.

"If you wanted to respect Mama's wishes, you would've been a real father."

"I'm not in the mood for this," Mack bites out, slamming the cabinet shut.

My muscles jump in response, but I don't move. "Calling me by her name won't bring her back, Mack! All she wanted was for you to be kind to me. That's all she asked of you. Or did all the liquor make you forget your wife's dying wish?" Tears stream down my face regardless of the anger and hurt spewing from my mouth.

"Damnit, I don't have time for your shit!" His voice bellows loudly, shaking the house to the core.

The words slice through my skin, reaching into a place I thought I had long closed off.

Losing Opie has reopened so much. Too much.

Stepping backward, I turn around, running straight to my car without shutting the front door of the house.

Chapter Twenty-One

It's day six. Six days without Opie. That's what I think about as I follow Levi and Foster through the forest.

"So these cameras send video straight to your phone in real-time?" Levi asks as he positions a trail camera on a pine tree.

It's dewy this Tuesday morning, and I'm still unsure if Foster is happy that I invited Levi, even if he is his nephew. To be fair, though, I think only a psychic would know what Foster is genuinely feeling. He hides behind a stone-walled face.

Foster grunts something that sounds like yes, and Levi shoots me an amused look. He thinks Foster's stubborn hostility toward talking is humorous.

We fall behind a few paces from Foster, and Levi leans toward me.

"He's kinda like an older, male version of you, you know?"

I turn and playfully punch him in the arm, making us both laugh. "I take great offense to that!" I respond.

"Okay, kids. Settle down back there," Foster says sarcastically.

Levi and I both straighten as we exchange more playful side glances.

The only reason we are on this trail is because a power-line worker saw my sign on a telephone pole on the way out of town and called me to tell me he saw a dog out by the same trail the first lead did. Said the dog ran before he could get a good look, but it appeared to be a large, short-haired white dog.

Foster thought we should set up a few trail cameras to see if we can get a glimpse of what he hopes is Opie. He says it casually as if we are looking for a raccoon. As if my future, my state of life, isn't riding on locating my dog. But I heed Levi's words and try with all my might to trust Foster.

After a mile in, and three cameras set up, I pause to sit on a downed tree trunk and pull off my shoe. The bandage on my foot has come loose, though it's healing up nicely. For an at-home-first-aid-kit version of healing, that is.

Foster doesn't stop what he's doing as he barely turns to look at my shoe. "What happened?" he asks.

Levi and I make eye contact, considering Foster hasn't spoken a complete sentence aloud for nearly fifteen minutes.

"I sliced my foot open on a rock a few days ago," I say, gingerly undoing the bandage. "We were on this trail actually," I add, keeping my eyes averted from Levi.

Back when I made an absolute ass of myself.

Foster clips the final camera into place as I rewrap my foot, keeping it tight.

"You get it checked out?" he asks, opening his water to take a drink.

I shake my head no.

"I told her she should. It was pretty bad when it happened," Levi exclaims.

I glare at him. "It's fine. I'm walking, I'm working. No one needs to be concerned." I grin fakely at both of them, and Levi flashes me a real grin.

Talk about a million-dollar smile.

"I tried to carry her down the trail, but as you can imagine, that didn't go over well," Levi adds, nudging me with a wink.

"Opie and I hike seven miles out and back, some days with equipment. So no, I wasn't going to let you *carry* me to my car." I scoff and stand up.

"What kind of equipment?" Fosters prods.

I pause, pursing my lips, surprised by this sudden inquisition. We've all been on this trail for an hour, so maybe he's just bored. "Camera stuff," I reply quietly, trekking down the hill with the guys directly behind me.

"Callie's a really talented photographer. Best I've seen," Levi adds.

I'm glad I'm in front of them because a grin tugs at the corner of my lips, but I force it away, whipping my head back around to face them. "Okay, enough about me. Levi, why are you still here?" I ask.

Levi gives me a dumbfounded look. Foster seems amused, though his mouth is still in a tight line. We continue to walk and talk in a triangle formation, the sound of pine needles crunching beneath our feet.

"You invited me?" Levi asks, hurt lacing his tone.

"No, I mean *here* in Miscruz Hills. You were like second in our class, if I remember. Didn't you want to go to college?"

"Yeah, I did . . . I still do. I'm unsure yet what I want to do, so I figured I wouldn't waste money. Plus, believe it or not, I actually kind of like this town," he protests mockingly.

I want to say I don't believe him. But then again, Levi's someone who sees the good in everything, in everyone. So it makes sense he likes it here.

And why he can tolerate me.

Foster and Levi make small talk as we descend to the parking lot. Before we go our separate ways, Foster gives me the rundown of the next steps.

"We'll monitor the cameras and keep doing what we're doing," he instructs vaguely, and his loose guidance feels like a cop-out, but I agreed to follow his lead. I signed on to it. He also reminds me where we are hours-wise, and I make a mental note to pull money from my savings.

Levi walks me to my car and pauses at the door. "Thanks for letting me come today."

"There's something I still don't get," I admit, and he leans on my car, coming closer to me.

"What's that?"

"Why are you so invested in finding Opie?" I add sheepishly, staring at the keys in my hands.

"I'm invested in helping *you*, Callie. Believe it or not, I want you to be happy."

Our eyes meet. My mouth is dry, and no words form in my head. There are only foreign feelings in my heart. Ones I swore I wouldn't feel again after Darren shredded what was left of me.

"See you around, yeah?" Levi asks, drumming his fingers on the hood of my car.

"Yeah," I replied before slinking down into my car.

CHAPTER TWENTY-TWO

I could sense the impending storm before I could see or hear it. The smell of the rain, the chill of the wind on my skin, and the distant sound of thunder all signaled its impending arrival. I couldn't help but think of Memaw's words about the angels washing the floors, but it's hard to find peace in the midst of a storm that reminds me of the tragic reality of Opie's disappearance.

It only took about thirty seconds for me to decide, without much debate, that I need to go back to Hunter Creek Trail. Tomorrow marks one week. The chances of finding Opie seem to be getting closer with Foster's help, but time is the devil. My worry intensifies with every passing minute. He is alone, cold, scared, and hungry, and the thought of Opie being lost drives me insane. If he is going to be lost, I will lose my mind finding him.

Find him, or die trying.

Memaw also used to say I didn't think rationally when I was emotional. But there's no time to think rationally right now.

Rustling through my clothes, I find old rain boots and a rain jacket three sizes too big that I pull on over my hoodie. I tuck my hair into the hood before I beeline to my car, wasting no time as I peel out of the dirt patch and onto the winding road with storm clouds in my rearview mirror. I have to beat the storm, and I have to get to the cell tower before the lightning starts. It's where the worker initially said he saw a dog.

My heart pounds in my chest as my knuckles turn white on my steering wheel. I know I promised Foster I wouldn't do anything to interfere, but this is a promise I can't keep tonight. When I was lying in bed this evening, every nerve in my body buzzed, begging me to get up.

What if that's Opie calling to me? Maybe it's just me losing my mind, but either way, I give in.

I'm so deep in thought, in fear, that I almost miss the turn and pull the wheel at the last minute, peeling into the parking lot. My car loses traction against the loose gravel, but when the car skids to a stop, I park and leave it there. Time is of the essence, and my heart is racing too fast to care. There's not a soul here anyway, so I take off up the trail, running.

I might be the only one crazy enough to hike this trail tonight, but it doesn't matter if there are any people out here. Because maybe, nearby, there is a dog. Maybe *my dog*. And that is all I need to carry my legs up the trail, straight to his last sighting.

My pulse picks up with the tempo of my legs; the faster I am, the more adrenaline courses through me. My lungs burn, and my arms swing, holding Opie's items, hoping the scent will pull him in. The clouds loom overhead, covering the last of the nighttime summer sun, as I pull out my flashlight. When the Keep Out signs appear, I quickly dart off the trail. I don't want Foster's cameras to pick up on me. I have a feeling he wouldn't be too happy to learn I am out here right now.

The steepness starts to level, and I know a meadow is up ahead, right where the cell tower is, but as that relief settles over me, a distant rumble shakes me. I peer over my shoulder to see the storm is on my heel.

Hurry up, hurry up, hurry up.

I've learned from Foster not to call out to Opie because, at this point, it could scare him away. He told me he could smell me from far distances, so I brought his purple dinosaur. It's swinging from my right arm, while foil-wrapped hot dogs sit in my left pocket.

A few minutes later, with burning legs to match my lungs, I reach the cell tower and stop right below it, figuring out my next course of action. Frantically, I twirl around in my dirty rubber boots, scanning the dim tree line, looking for any sign that a dog has been here.

I had it in my head that I'll just know. It defies all logic and all reason, and I know that as I stand here, wanting to scream his name. But the connection I have with Opie defies all odds, too.

"I wish Daisy and May were with me," I whisper as I stumble away from the cell tower toward the closest trail and see a large patch of freshly trampled-down grass. It could be from a white-tailed deer or a dog, so I follow the trail a bit further, hoping to make it to a spot to sit still long enough to spot something.

I don't know what else to do. I don't know what I was thinking.

But I didn't climb this high to give up this quickly.

The warning signs of an impending storm roar overhead, and I gaze up, only to realize I'm near a trail camera we set up earlier. I quickly duck, trying to get out of view. A few feet away is a hidden spot under a tall pine, so I crawl over to take refuge under it. The temperature is at least fifteen degrees cooler up here than it was at home, and I pull my jacket tighter to me, wrapping my arms in front of my legs.

If Opie is around, he will take shelter too, somewhere under these pines. A white dog is not hard to spot in a lush green forest. So I settle in, ready to wait, but lightning cracks above, followed shortly by thunder that's so loud the hair on my neck stands up. My mind pinballs between huddling deeper into this tree's safety and making a mad dash back to my car, but before I can decide, the sky opens with a vengeance. It's the kind of rain that's deafeningly loud, the kind that reaches the forest floor and instantly creates puddles as big as lakes. I pull Opie's dinosaur into the safety of my jacket, not wanting water to soak the scent out.

What was left of the daylight is quickly diminished by rain clouds, and I find myself in darkness, bringing an overwhelming sense of déjà vu from the night Opie went missing. That night, I wished for all the pain to go away, and as I sit here under the tree, I can't fight that feeling from creeping back into my bones.

The thunder booms, and the lightning cracks while the rain falls sideways. The forest comes alive with the storm, and I make myself as small as possible, closing my eyes and resting my forehead on my knees. Time eludes me here in the woods, and I don't know how long I stay half-huddled under the pine tree, but I know it only takes minutes for my body to become soaked through to the bone. There's even water inside my rubber boots.

So much for coming prepared.

The purple dinosaur inside my coat is drenched too. I start to shiver as water flows down my face along with tears. I can't differentiate them from the icy rain. There's no use trying to find Opie now. My vision is so obscured that I can't see just a few feet in front of me. My mission tonight is over.

That's when a flash of light catches my eye. I wipe the water from my face to clear my vision. The dome of light pointing through the wall of rain appears to be getting rapidly closer. Leaning out on my knees from under the sagging tree limbs above me, I see two eyes staring at me. Before I can stand or make a sound, Daisy comes barreling into me, shoving her long, wet nose into my face.

I let out a small scream as she lets out a low howl, and my cold, stiff fingers find her face. Daisy nudges my arm, and I rest a hand on her back, using her frame to pull myself up. Foster arrives right behind her. His green raincoat and boots are as drenched as mine, and his face is dripping with water as he furrows his dark brows at me.

Shame washes over me like a flame. I didn't come out here intending to be rescued. Nor was I expecting it. I did this by choice; I came out here. And now Foster is saving me.

By choice.

"You going to explain why you're huddled under a tree on a mountaintop . . . in a storm . . . at night?" Foster yells out over the drumming of rain, sounding exasperated.

I open and close my mouth, unsure how to answer. He waits patiently before I finally choke out a response that's simply the truth. "I had to look for him," I admit pitifully, expecting him to scold me.

Foster stares at me for a long time. His blue eyes aren't angry, and I want him to say something, anything, as his dog circles my legs. He doesn't though. He just looks at me knowingly.

"How'd you find me anyway?" I question, feeling uneasy.

"The cameras picked up a lot of activity. When I saw a small woman carrying a food bag and a teddy bear, I figured it had to be you," he jokes, and it's the first time I think he's made light of something. A trace of a smile lines his lips.

"It's a dinosaur. It's Opie's favorite," I reply quietly, pulling the soaking toy from my jacket.

"Of course, it is, Miss Hayes."

We both let out the tiniest chuckle.

"Please call me Callie," I reply.

Foster nods. "All right, Callie. I'm not a fan of standing in the rain. Let's get off this mountain."

I nod silently and follow Foster as he starts walking down the winding path. It's cold and damp and dark, and we both stay quiet, with flashlights pointed in front of us, cautiously trekking down the muddy trail. Daisy tromps alongside me, looking up at me every few minutes. Seeing her soaked, brown fur, I feel horrible that she is out here in this storm because of me. And then I think of Opie out here, cold and alone, and it hurts too much to think about. It hurts in places I didn't know could feel pain.

"I tried, buddy," I whisper sorrowfully to the trees, praying they will carry my message to him.

Foster's truck sits next to my green piece of junk in the lot, which was once gravel but is now riddled with deep pockets of water and mud. My eyes linger too long on the slick ground beneath my car, and I feel Foster's eyes on the back of my head. The rain has now turned to a mist but left everything in its path a wreck.

"I'll drive you home, but toss your coat in the back before you get in." My eyes dart between him and my car. Even if I wanted to argue and be stubborn—which I do—I could potentially be stuck here all night. My car won't make it out of this lot until it dries up. So I do as he says, peeling the wet raincoat from my skin and tossing it in the back. Opie's toy rests safely inside it as I climb up into Foster's truck. Daisy perches herself in the back seat, her face leaning between the front seats.

Foster's eyes are focused on the road as we leave, and I wonder what he's thinking right now. We don't talk, but he blasts the heat, directing the vents toward me, even though I didn't ask for that.

"Thank you. For rescuing me." I keep my voice even, my eyes out the window at the dark night.

"Let's not make a habit of going off-course. I don't need to exhaust the dogs looking for you *and* your missing dog. Okay?"

I slump in my seat, biting my lip. A lump forms in my throat, so I nod and whisper, "Deal." I feel like a complete idiot. I don't think Foster would tell Levi about this, but as I sit here, I pray he doesn't.

I point out the window at my driveway, which is hard to find in the dark, and he slows down, turning into it and passing the crooked blue mailbox.

When we drive past the farmhouse, I instinctively hold my breath, waiting for Foster to bring up my father. The light is on in Mack's bedroom, and I wonder how he's fairing with a broken arm. For a moment, I think about checking in on him. But then I remember all the reasons I shouldn't.

"Can I ask you something?"

Foster's voice breaks my train of thought and instantly sends me into a mini panic. I say yes anyway.

"How long have you lived in the trailer alone?"

There is something about Foster that is oddly disarming, like he's the kind of person who would know right away if I was lying. Maybe it's the detective in him. Maybe it's him being a dad.

"For a year. Since graduation."

Foster pulls in front of my place. The headlights shine off the dulled metal trailer.

"I see." He nods, his jaw tense.

I turn to pet Daisy goodbye when he speaks again, catching me completely off guard.

"He never hurt you, did he?" he questions.

I freeze, my hand on Daisy's back. "Not in the way you need to worry about," I reply. There's a look in his eyes that makes me quickly look away. "Let me know what I owe you for this," I add.

"I'm not *charging* you for this. Next time, if you think it's a good idea to do *this*, call me first," he demands.

"Right. Okay. Thanks again." I smile weakly and turn to pet Daisy, whose face has puddled around her paws. I'm jealous Foster gets to go home with his dog tonight.

I grab my jacket and head to the door, turning to wave quickly before disappearing into the camper. Quietness encompasses me again.

Except for one thought.

For the first time since Memaw died, I feel like there is maybe someone out there who cares about me after all.

Chapter
Twenty-Three

I force myself to eat something for breakfast, but as usual, the toast tastes bland. Even the coffee does nothing to warm me. The warmness I felt after Foster brought me home last night dissipated as I woke up alone this morning.

I'm reminded when I go outside and see the empty spot in front of the trailer where my car usually sits that last night I hit bottom. This is saying a lot, given I've felt like I've hit bottom many times in my short life.

I don't like being without my car, and it's too early to bother anyone to drive me to it. Plus, I'd never ask. I got myself into this mess, and I can get myself out of it. The trailhead parking lot is about a five-mile walk from the end of the driveway, which shouldn't take more than an hour and a half if I walk really fast.

With the decision made, I gear up and start heading that way. After Foster's reality check, or suggestion of allocating resources, I don't check the property. He told me *if* Opie did come back this way, he'd seek me out. I don't need to search for him here, but it still feels wrong to not spend every moment scouring this earth for him. But I'm trying to listen to Foster's *seventy-dollar-an-hour* advice.

My heart rate is up as I trek down the gentle slope, and the back of the farmhouse comes into view. The grass grows tall around it. Mack hasn't cut it for months. Opie loves weaving through the tall meadow grasses, hopping like a jackrabbit as I race him to the creek. He always beat me, circling back to jump on me, covering my laughing face in wet dog kisses.

As I round the corner of the house, I nearly jump, startled by Mack's back to me as he leans over the open hood of his truck. Tools rest in the pockets of his stained jeans.

Slowing my pace, I realize he doesn't even know I'm here, so I observe him tinkering with his right hand as the left arm hangs in a sling. Watching his hunched form causes my chest to constrict as memories from childhood flood my mind. My bedroom in the farmhouse faced the front yard, where a tire swing still hangs from the maple tree I'd lean against every day after school.

There were so many times I'd watch from the window as Mack would work on something—the lawn mower, the car, a piece of junk he brought home. I'd observe him with such curiosity, wondering how he knew how to fix anything and everything; he was amazing to me. People always said my father was dumb, but as a little girl, I thought he was the smartest person I knew. Though we were only divided by the walls of a house when I watched him from my window, it felt like he was hundreds of miles away, always too far to touch. I was always too far to be seen by him.

The only thing that's different now is I'm older. And with age comes wisdom. I'm far too wise now to ever think that man will turn around, look up in the window, and smile at the little girl who never could quite call him *dad* long before she understood why.

I quicken my stride, hoping he won't say anything as I walk by, but it's not me who causes him to swear and lift his head from his work.

It's the red pickup truck slowly creeping toward us both that also stops me in my tracks.

Foster's truck pulls up next to me, acting as a barrier between Mack and me. Dumbfounded, I yank out my earbuds and rush to the driver's side, aware of Mack's wandering gaze. I bite my lip, a rush of nerves bouncing in my stomach as I meet not only Foster's steely gaze but Levi's unfairly handsome face.

"What are you two doing here?" I ask breathily.

"I tried calling you, but it went to voicemail. Figured you needed a ride to your car this morning," Foster answers nonchalantly, his arm hanging out of the window. He adjusts his baseball cap.

"Oh!" I try to hide the pleasant surprise in my voice. That doesn't answer why Levi is with him, but I don't ask any more questions as I make my way around the side of the truck and hop in as Levi scoots awkwardly to the middle seat.

Mack stays silent but slams the hood of his truck down aggressively, making me flinch in my seat, and Foster clocks my sudden unease. Foster gazes out the window at him, his stare intense as Mack hobbles into the house. Foster shifts into drive, his face unreadable as we start to move.

"What happened to Mack?" Levi nods toward the farmhouse.

"He fell off a ladder," I respond casually.

"Heard he got pushed," Foster pipes up.

I can't help but snap my head in his direction, but he doesn't look back at me. I notice his stubble is growing in, and he seems more gruff than usual.

"How did you know that?" Levi's eyes toggle between us as his bare arm brushes against mine.

"I know people," Foster retorts so seriously that Levi and I glance at each other, breaking into a laugh.

Foster's lips falter as he glares at us from the side of his eye. "You two making fun of the old man?"

"No, sir," Levi answers sternly, and I bite my lip to stop laughing again. But then I realize Foster isn't turning around but heading up my narrow driveway toward the trailer. Panic rises in my chest, burning my throat as it does.

Only Foster knows where I live, which is entirely out of necessity for Opie. But I don't want Levi to see it. Not yet. Maybe not ever. It's bad enough they already witnessed Mack in all his glory.

"We can just turn around here," I blurt a little too loudly as I point to the field to the right.

"I need you to grab another blanket or toy of Opie's for Daisy and May. Do you have something else?"

I close my eyes as dread overtakes my body when my blue, tarp-covered trailer comes into view. As soon as he stops the truck, I hop out without looking back at either of them. Once inside, I rush to retrieve Opie's blanket from my bed. It's covered in white fur, and nothing could make me wash it. The fur is a reminder that he is real.

"I can't believe you've been keeping this from me."

I whip my body around, startled by Levi's voice in my kitchen. My heart jumps into my throat, but I exhale a shaky breath and pretend all is well. "Well, now you see it," I respond dryly, balling up the blanket and placing my hand on his waist to turn him around and out of the trailer, but he doesn't budge.

"It's cool, Callie."

"Ha! Okay. You can keep the bullshit for someone else," I blurt, but he doesn't laugh. His face and smile fade into a straight line. My hand slowly drops from his waist as he traces his eyes to the spot where my hand was.

"It's nice to finally get an inside look at you."

I roll my eyes, but Levi continues.

"It's retro in here. I like all the string lights you have." He touches the twinkle lights I have strewn across the ceiling. Seeing him touch them so delicately pulls on my heartstrings.

Maybe this isn't the worst thing in the world.

"My favorite thing to do on a cloudy night is lay on my bed and look up at the lights with Opie. It's like our own galaxy in here," I whisper as my eyes mist over, thinking about those simple things I took for granted, thinking he'd always be here.

We both scan the maze of twinkle lights, but when I look away, Levi is looking at me. No, not *at* me. Looking in me. If that is even a thing. My face flushes and my heart squeezes in my chest in response.

"I know you desperately want to say goodbye to this town, but you've created your own sanctuary here. You should give yourself credit, yeah?"

We all do what we need to do to survive.

I smile sheepishly.

"Is this why you never let me come past your driveway?" Levi probes, and I catch the hint of disappointment in his voice. I don't like it.

"No, I just didn't—" I stumble over my words. "Yes. It is. This isn't exactly a home to be proud of." I look him directly in the eye because there's nowhere to hide in this trailer. Nowhere to hide with Levi. And frankly, I'm sick of hiding everything.

Levi scoffs, looking around. "If you ask me, it's pretty badass how independent you are, Callie. I mean, you have your own place. You don't rely on anyone. That's something to be proud of."

Choosing to be self-reliant and being abandoned are two different things. But I don't say anything like that because he means it as a compliment.

"Well, you saw my father. He isn't exactly the most charming person to live with." I wink, deflecting the shame rooted in me and shimmy past Levi, who turns to follow me out. He lingers in the doorway, taking up the whole frame with his broad shoulders and larger-than-life smirk.

"Just to be clear, you know you're nothing like him, right?"

I crinkle my brow, my throat growing hot. "What? Why did you say that?" I stutter breathily.

Levi takes a calculated pause, biting his lip before he speaks. "Everyone knows who Mack is and what he's done. And I know some people have mistreated you because of it, but I want you to know I never thought any differently of you. You've always been the same Callie to me. Not just *Mack's daughter*."

He stops talking, and I stare at him, unsure how to respond verbally and physically. My hands grow clammy around the fleece blanket in my arms. After standing awkwardly for more than acceptably long, Levi nods and smiles slightly, walks to me, and places a hand on my back, guiding me toward Foster's truck.

Always saving the day.

"Thanks. For not judging me," I whisper to him as he walks beside me.

"We can't control who our parents are. But that doesn't mean it has to define us."

I smile sadly at him because I know. At that moment, I know he sees me.

Chapter Twenty-Four

"Ouch!" I scream, waking up to a throbbing in my head.

I had another nightmare, one that resulted in me flailing my arms and sitting straight up, knocking my head against the cabinet above my head. Tears stain my cheeks, and my chest hurts. The dream was so real. Opie was there. It was so vivid. I could smell the pine trees, feel the dampness on my skin. I was in the woods, following Opie. He started walking faster until he was running, and I was too, chasing him until he entered a fog and everything disappeared in it.

It's the third time I've had that same dream, and I'm sick of waking up in a cold sweat.

Quickly showering, I let the water wash away the feeling of dread over today. Before leaving, I add my tips from last night to the envelope labeled with Foster's name on it. I've counted the tips from my savings jar three times already today. Every dollar and quarter are accounted for. All the tips I've been squirreling away in the glass jar labeled *Callie & Opie's Great Escape*.

I find myself, still with wet hair from my shower, sitting in my car, ready to go. It's early, but I can't sit idle. I text Foster and ask him if I can come now, though I know the answer is yes. He is up with the sun, he says.

My emotions about Opie have been as tumultuous as the ocean the last two days. Today marks day eight since he's been missing. I thought by now he'd be spotted, and every minute that passes adds to my anxious heart and angry mind.

I even stayed up last night considering adding a reward for his safe-finding, but then I broke down in tears, realizing that's impossible. *I don't have a single cent to my name that's not already being siphoned into finding him.*

When Foster told me last night that he needed to talk to me, I assumed the worst. But now that the time has come, the idea of going to his house alone to talk terrifies me. With my fingers hovering over my phone screen, I open my messages, then close my phone. Only to repeat it, but this time, I quickly type out a message to Levi and hit send before I can come to terms with the truth about how I feel about him.

Because it's snuck up on me.

They say in times of crisis, you cling to an anchor, and somewhere along the way this past week, Levi's became my anchor.

So I asked him if he would come with me to Foster's. I don't go into why I asked him because going into that house does nothing but stir up guilt, and I need a buffer. I need a ray of sunshine for the clouds I'm about to walk into. But *why* doesn't apparently seem to matter to Levi because he texts me back a few minutes later saying, "Of course. I'll pick you up in fifteen." And I smile to myself, then physically pinch my mouth to wipe the smile away.

When Levi arrives, I hop into the passenger seat, and I already know what music to expect on the radio. Levi likes nineties rock. The two coffee cups in the center console also don't come as a surprise. Mine black. Because he knows that about me. And part of me feels optimistic. Not happy per se, but positive. Like there's a tiny glimmer of hope because maybe I'm not destined to have zero friends forever. Levi's given me hope that maybe one day, I could have a friend, one who isn't bothered by my quietness or my love for Opie.

That dreamy glimmer of thought is quickly replaced by remembering *why* Levi and I became friends again in the first place. If Opie hadn't run away, I would've never had a reason to talk to Levi. I would've left town with no thought to him.

The realization reminds me I can never be friends with Levi, not really. I still plan on getting far away from here and never coming back. I won't mention this to him as he asks me if the air is too cold. I mumble it's good and thank him before drinking coffee, which I don't deserve.

Levi distracts me from the impending feeling of doom as we inch closer to Foster's house by telling me about his late night at the print shop yesterday. He said the school is printing all new banners this year, and he worked all week designing them and coordinating with the school admin. He talks about school like it wasn't an awful place. Outside of art class, it was never a place I wanted to be, especially after my sixteenth birthday. Levi was quiet in school, too, but he was respected. To my knowledge, he was never bullied, the girls had crushes on him, and he graduated with perfect grades.

"Hey, so have you heard anything about the waitlist?" Levi asks.

My throat tightens. In the chaos of everything, I've pushed it from my mind. "No, I haven't. If I was let in, I would've heard by yesterday."

"Shit, Callie, I'm sorry—" he starts, but I cut him off.

"It's fine. It doesn't matter anyway," I lie straight through my teeth.

"What do you mean it doesn't matter? It's your passion! I was convinced senior year that you actually lived in the darkroom in high school."

"I pretty much did." I smile wistfully, thinking how I dove in, spending every moment of my last year of school learning how to develop film photography.

"You were known as the photography girl."

I laugh and turn to Levi, whose expression implies he is making this up. "I *never* heard that one. I only heard *low-life* and *fuck-up*." I cringe as the words leave my lips, the air between us growing cold instantly. I have tried to push the list of names I heard whispered not so discreetly behind my back.

Levi's face goes flat, and I grow annoyed with myself for yet again dragging down the mood with my blast to the fucking past.

"Only assholes who don't matter said that shit. You know they were all just jealous of you, Cal."

"Jealous of me? Ha! What in the world is there to be jealous of?" I inquire, but it's rhetorical. I don't want Levi to answer.

"Because you're brave, Callie. You know who you are, and you're just you. Not many people can say that." Levi reaches his arm around the back of my seat while his gaze lingers on me.

"I could've used these pep talks about three years ago," I nearly whisper, swallowing hard and turning to gaze out the window. I bring my hand to my mouth, hoping that will somehow deter me from saying more. Levi sighs, and it sounds guttural.

We park in Foster's driveway, but neither of us move.

"I should've been there," he utters, breaking the heavy silence between us.

"I wouldn't have let you in anyway. You know that." I turn to him, and I have to look away after a few seconds. There's too much honesty in his eyes, too much knowing. Levi knows who I was *before*. Even if we stopped talking three years before the accident, he was still the closest friend I had growing up.

"I still should've tried harder. Smiling in the hallway doesn't count. I was scared, Callie, and I didn't know what to say to you. It's my biggest regret."

I consider what he's saying. High school feels like a distant memory, but the wounds still lay under my skin.

Reaching across the seat, my hand rests on Levi's forearm, still strewn across the steering wheel. "I don't hold it against you. We are friends now, yeah?"

Levi sniffs, nodding as his hazel eyes find mine under his thick eyelashes. I know he has more to say, but it will come out when he's ready. And I'll respond when *I'm* ready.

"Friends, yeah," he mimics.

I catch a glimpse of sadness that flickers across his eyes. I quickly pull myself back to the situation we are in *now*. And right now, part of me considers begging Levi to just take my money inside and let me hide under the car's dash. But Daisy and May come bounding out of the house toward the car, and I give into my weakness, opening the door to give them my love.

We walk to Foster's front door side by side, which is propped open, and I knock on the doorframe. Foster hollers from the kitchen to come in. The windows of the house are open, and I can't help but notice the peacefulness of the home as I walk through the large living room to the kitchen.

The dogs follow us in, running ahead to find a spot on the floor where the sun floods in from the windows. Foster looks up from the kitchen island, but he doesn't seem surprised to see Levi with me. If anything, he looks relieved.

Thank God!

A box of pancake mix sits on the counter next to a slab of bacon and a carton of eggs while country music streams from a speaker in the corner. It looks like he was about to host a brunch for ten.

I exhale. This is good: an excuse to get out of his hair quickly. *I hope he has forgotten that he has to tell me something.*

"Here is everything I owe you. It's in cash. Hope that's okay." I set the envelope on the counter, and he puts his hand over it but says nothing.

Everything is silent for a moment before Foster gazes up at both Levi and me, standing there expectantly. "Y'all want breakfast?" Foster poses, a hopeful expression in his eyes.

I nervously look at Levi, hoping he says no for the both of us so we can leave, but of course, a crooked grin takes over his face.

"Hell yeah, we do!"

I feel my face grow red but remember I'm at his mercy. I didn't drive here.

And what nineteen-year-old boy will say no to a free home-cooked meal?

Was this the plan all along? Is Foster going to butter me up before dropping bad news?

I watch him place the envelope of cash in a kitchen drawer, then grab mixing bowls before pointing to the cabinet.

"Grab some plates, will you?" he asks.

When I don't move, feeling disoriented, Levi jumps to it, furrowing his brow at me behind Foster's back. I shrug, playing it off.

"How's your dad doing, Levi? Haven't seen him around much," Foster says.

Levi tenses. It's so slight that if I wasn't attuned to his body language, I wouldn't have noticed.

"He's good. He's been spending a lot of time with Robbie. They golf together in Charlotte almost every weekend, as you know."

I sense Foster also picks up on the bitterness of his answer. Levi mentioned his parents obsess over his older brother Robbie all the time. Robbie is a successful architect who lives in Charlotte. His parents seem to disappear there a lot, which leaves Levi to single-handedly run the family business. He acts like it's okay, but from what I've gathered, he feels like the black sheep of his family. And from what I've seen of his parents, they don't appreciate his sacrifices.

"I see." This is all Foster says as he mindlessly adds oil to the griddle.

To break the tension and change subjects, though I don't know if it's for mine or Levi's sake, I ask something safe. "Do you always make a big breakfast on Friday mornings?"

Foster's lips pull up, but the smile seems sad. "Breakfast is my son's favorite meal. I was always busy working when he was growing up, but on Sunday mornings, I'd make a big breakfast for the family. Pancakes, eggs, and bacon, whatever he wanted."

He sets bacon on the sizzling griddle, and I feel like I can't breathe.

For his family that is no longer together.

Levi looks at me, eyes searching my face, then he faces Foster and hesitates, mouth open. Then he asks. He asks what I never had the guts to ask, what is not my right to ask.

"Speaking of Everett, it's been forever since we caught up. How's he doing?"

I brace for impact, my shoulders tensed, visibly so, I'm sure. But Foster doesn't twitch. He doesn't lunge at my neck or throw a plate or anything I imagined he would do. He smiles for real this time, the kind that crinkles your eyes, and pours batter on the griddle like a natural.

"He misses you, I know that. He's doing real well actually. His internship is going well."

Levi interrupts and looks at me. "Everett's working for a sports media company in Atlanta."

I silently thank him, feeling the air in my lungs slightly give.

Foster nods, continuing to watch the pancakes. "I couldn't tell you what he is doing, but he loves it. He's got two more years of school at Clemson and is on track to graduate on time."

Foster's face lights up the way I imagine a father's face lights up when they are proud. I've seen the expression on other fathers' faces, just never directed at me.

"Damn, he always was the smart cousin," Levi jokes, and I know it's all for me. He's trying to lighten the mood, the mood I invited because of my question.

Foster says nothing else about Everett but asks Levi if he can whip the eggs in the bowl on the counter. He does so, and at the same time, Foster turns the dial on the old radio playing country music.

I stand there, feeling helpless, wishing I was the one whipping eggs just so my mind didn't wander away from me. Because right now, my feelings terrify me. Feelings I don't know how to discern.

I feel relief *and* sadness over learning about Everett. Because his wheelchair-bound life is more complicated than either of them let on. It's the elephant in the room.

There's also another feeling I'm not used to. I'm about to sit down to eat breakfast in a house that used to hold a loving family, a family that's shattered because of me.

And now, it holds three unlikely people sitting around a table, eating a meal that is Everett's favorite. And it's Opie who's missing. It's everything stirring in me like a tornado.

Everything, everything, everything.

"This is really good. Thank you." I flash a smile at Foster and quickly place my gaze back on my plate of stacked pancakes and syrup.

And I mean it. It tastes really good. It's not instant oatmeal made in my microwave or a granola bar eaten by the creek with Opie as I snap a photo of a hawk. This meal feels nourishing in more ways than one.

"So I need to talk to you, Callie," Foster says, sipping coffee.

There it is. I don't look at Levi, though I know he has stopped eating and is looking at me. I maintain my gaze on Foster, trying to gain an advantage, studying his face to see if I can beat him to the punch. The wooden chair beneath me feels like it's made of paper mâché and I'm about to collapse through it to the floor.

"Okay," I manage.

Foster clears his throat and sets down his fork. If he doesn't speak soon, I swear my heart will leap out of my chest, or I will hit the floor after passing out. Either are welcome to this excruciating anticipation.

"Callie, it's been over a week, as you know. We have had no leads outside of the trail lead, and as I told you, I spent all day over there. Covered nearly the whole mountainside. The hounds aren't catching any scent of him."

My throat grows tight, and my hands tremble slightly in my lap, but no tears come. He continues, his words slow and calculated, like the wrong word could cause a bomb to explode.

"There have been no calls, no shelters in the county that have checked him in, and I've been checking with shelters and rescues within hundreds of miles in every direction of here. Everyone in this town is aware of his disappearance. And we need to consider the reality here." He pauses, and I know by the look on his scrunched face that it pains him to say all this. But I also know it's not the first time he's had to deliver news like this to people who put their hope in him. Tell them the *reality* and watch the last little glimmer of hope fade from their eyes.

I push myself up abruptly, nearly knocking the wooden chair down behind me. I grip the table's edge, my mouth hanging open. Before I can croak a word, Levi stands too, reaching out to place his hand over mine, but his eyes are trained on Foster, who remains seated.

"*Or* let's consider the reality that Opie could've been stolen," Levi speaks steadily, addressing us both.

Foster's face changes as he looks at Levi. They stare at each other, and the exchange of glances makes me feel like everyone is speaking a language I don't know.

"He is out there. I know he is. Opie is not gone," I say sternly, breaking their tension.

I know who Foster is. He is logical, and he knows how to detach his emotions from a task, but that's not who I am. Not when it comes to Opie.

"You said *you* work for *me*." I point at him. "And *I* am not done. We are not giving up. We *cannot* give up. Do you understand me?"

Foster stares at me in disbelief, and I know my whole body is shaking, but he nods, expelling an exhausted breath.

"And he was not stolen." I peer at Levi out of the corner of my eye, who, in turn, throws his palms up as a white flag.

"Both of you, sit back down. Finish your meal," Foster demands, and I scoff because he's not my father, and Levi and I are not children. But I'm still hungry, so I let him win this one.

"So you won't give up, correct?" I say.

Foster tips his chin back and studies me before answering. "No, ma'am. You have the facts now, and if you say we keep looking, that's what we will do."

I nod. "Thank you."

"I'm pretty sure Callie would have flipped this table if you said no," Levi comments under his breath, grabbing another pancake from the stack, and I bite my cheeks until Foster starts laughing. Then we all burst out laughing, and it feels good.

Because for a moment in time, I'm sitting around the table, looking at Foster and Levi, and despite the way this started, despite the news I just got, *this* feels nice, being with these two.

Once we wrap up breakfast, Foster insists we leave the plates where they are, and I walk toward the door.

"Business as usual?" I offer my hand. I don't mean it as a question though. More as a demand.

Foster smirks and offers a solid shake. "I'll be in touch, Callie." His voice is soft, and I feel accomplished.

On the front porch, the hounds are lounging in the morning sunbeams like lazy cats. "Don't give up yet, ladies. We are going to prove him wrong. We are going to find my Opie." Tears form in my eyes as my walls crumble near the animals. They always make my defenses utterly collapse. Kneeling down next to them, I give them belly rubs. Hushed tones come from inside the cabin where Levi and Foster stand facing each other in the hallway.

Steadying my breath and slowing my petting of May's head, I turn my head toward the open door.

"You told her things like this could take weeks, if not months."

Levi's voice is more severe than I've ever heard. It causes the hair on my arms to stand up. May lifts her head and looks at me.

"Levi, I can't pretend there is a lot of hope left here. No one has seen him. It's like he vanished, and the longer this goes on, the harder it might be for her to accept the truth. He is more than likely long gone, and I don't want to be the one to run her out of money or, worse, give her false hope."

My chest constricts, and I wish I had not paused on these steps and heard the words that were not meant for me. A rush of anger and hurt rise inside me.

"Foster, you told me you weren't giving up," Levi rebuts and, after a beat of silence on both ends, adds, "If you didn't mean it, tell her now. She isn't a fragile person, but her heart is broken right now."

"I know you want to protect her—"

"She's been through enough; can't you agree? Do not abandon her now. And don't pretend for a moment you don't want to protect her too."

At the sound of Levi's gravely and demanding tone, I sit very still, my hand hovering over the dogs. I can't make out the rest of their words; it's merely garbling, and then, moments later, Levi appears on the front porch, offering me a smile.

"Ready?" he asks, and I nod, standing up to follow him.

His chest is physically puffed, and as we walk to the car, he stands close behind me. I turn to look over my shoulder, but Foster's not on the front porch waving goodbye like I've grown to expect.

Levi swings open my door, and I hop in. His hazel eyes are a shade darker, and the muscles under his shirt restrict against the fabric, but as soon as we turn out of the driveway, he relaxes, going back to his calm self.

I want to thank him for fighting for me, but my heart is still broken by Foster's words.

Words I absolutely cannot choose to believe.

I look out the window on the way back, watching the beautiful shadows through the canopy of trees. Levi releases the steering wheel, his right hand reaching to hold mine.

The small but intimate gesture causes me to shutter my eyes. I feel the weight of his hand on mine as his thumb strokes the back of my hand. Holding myself still under his touch, silence stretching between us, I'm left reeling in the truth about my feelings for Levi.

How can I be who Levi deserves, and who I want him to have, when I'm merely a shell of myself without Opie?

Levi stops at the driveway's edge and looks to me for permission.

"It's okay. You can drive me all the way back," I add. But as we turn in, I lunge forward, slamming my hands onto the dash. "Wait, stop!"

My fingers frantically grasp the door handle. Levi's left in a bout of confusion as I jump out, rushing toward the mailbox, where a thick envelope sticks out of the crooked blue box.

I read the name first, *Charleston Photography Co.*, and I swear the earth trembles beneath me.

Chapter Twenty-Five

I don't let Levi stay, even though I know his cat-like curiosity was getting the best of him. He dropped me off, and I rushed our goodbye, as the thick envelope burned a metaphorical hole in my side. As he drove away, waving with a concerned pout on his lips, I returned the wave and then dashed inside, seeking solitude for what I knew was about to be shattering news.

Sitting at the kitchen table, my forearms stick to the top, and humidity causes sweat to roll down my forehead, but I rip open the envelope with shaky hands and am barely able to read past the first paragraph before the tears start streaming down my cheeks.

Carolina Hayes,

Due to unexpected circumstances, a spot has opened up on our fall roster, meaning we are thrilled to offer you the twentieth spot at Charleston Photography Co.

As mentioned before, your work is exquisitely beautiful, and you show promising talent that we know will thrive under our direction. The program starts on Monday, August 15th. We need to hear back from you no later than August seventh, from which the first installment payment will be due.

We understand being waitlisted means you have less time than the other students in the program to prepare. However, we've attached all that you need inside this packet.

I can't continue to read on. I scan the outside of the package, which is dusty and a bit worn. Bringing my elbows to the tabletop, with my face in my palms, I shake my head back and forth, trying to make sense of this.

This is not how it was supposed to be. Not at all.

All those days, weeks, months, fucking years spent trying to carve out a path for myself. Watching every video and reading every book I could get my hands on, trying to become better every single day at photography. I saved and made my own darkroom from an old shed. Opie and I spent a whole weekend doing it together. I woke up at the crack of dawn, dragging him on miles and miles of hikes through these mountains to just get a photo of the sunrise.

All of it for this. For the chance to get into one of the top programs in the country, and here I am holding the letter in my hand.

I got in.

Callie Hayes, from Miscruz Hills, got in.

I've imagined this moment a million times before. It always involved me crying with happy tears, jumping around my camper, running out into the meadow gripping the acceptance letter in my hands, gleaming with joy as Opie ran around barking, unsure of what we were celebrating but knowing it was good. I'd kiss his nose and tell him, "This is it! We are getting out! Callie and Opie are onto bigger, better adventures!"

I imagined us packing up the little green car together. I always planned on selling the camper and taking those profits to secure an apartment in Charleston. Something small, maybe a studio. Opie and I were used to living small anyway. I'd let him know it was only five months long. Just five months and then we'd move somewhere with expansive skies. Maybe out west, where Opie could see new horizons, and we'd meet new people, people who wouldn't whisper while averting their gaze. Instead, they would see me, a talented and successful photographer, and Opie, my irreplaceable sidekick. We are a team.

We'd make new friends, and Opie would tag along everywhere. I hear there are towns that are dog friendly, where Opie can come into restaurants and stores with me. *That's where we'd move.* And I'd get a sprinter van, so when I go photograph on assignment, he can tag along in our home on wheels.

That's what I imagined.

I never imagined this.

Leaving the packet on the table, my eyes wander over the broken camera lens on my shelf. Getting up, I swing open the door, not bothering to latch it shut on my way out. Nothing more can escape. Nothing more can be taken from me.

I run all the way to the creek.

Chapter Twenty-Six

I loved many things about my memaw. Her soft voice was like cotton on my skin. I loved the way her cheeks crinkled like tissue paper when she smiled, her face sweet but worn from a life of hard work.

My father was her only child, by her body's choice and not her own. She loved him in ways I couldn't understand, and he failed her in ways I would never forgive. I loved her deeply. I loved her cooking, which she taught me from a young age. Even then I think she knew I'd need to look after myself one day.

Memaw was also afraid to drive, or she never learned—both probably true. Papa used to drive before he passed, but not Memaw, which meant she didn't see many places unless someone else took her. She only saw the ocean a handful of times despite living in North Carolina her whole life.

As I sit here, my sandals off to the side, my feet dipping in the cool creek that rushes quickly by, the sun on my face, I wonder if this is how she felt—trapped by love. She couldn't go anywhere, not really. She barely had two nickels to rub together and had nowhere to really go. But even if she wanted to, she would've stayed here. Because I needed her. And in some ways, Mack needed her. He was better when she was around.

And now I just see the strings of my life, crisscrossed and knotted.

I've missed half my working shifts these past eight days and drained nearly all I had saved in my great escape fund to pay Foster to search for a dog who doesn't want to be found.

I'm here, trapped, by a love I wouldn't trade for the world.

This is not how it's supposed to be.

I remain by the creek for a while and am jostled out of my solitude by the sound of paws pattering along the grassy path. I hear them before I see them, which I think is the opposite of what they intend. Their ears drag on the ground until they look up, eyes droopy but excited, and I give them a small smile, unable to contain any love for an animal despite the circumstances.

Levi told me the other day about the TSA dogs at the airport and joked that I'd probably be detained, unable to *not* pet them. I've never been to the airport, but I laughed because I think he is right.

"Hey, Daisy. What are you doing here?" I call as she comes to rest at my side.

She licks my face, clearing the remnants of salty tears staining my cheeks. Her rusty-brown fur shines in the afternoon sun. As Foster's hat peeks over the tall grass, I jump from my place in the water, feeling like a child being caught in a moment of vulnerability.

"There she is," he says, scratching May's head.

"You searching for *me* now?" I joke, wiping my eyes before he gets too close. Daisy stands next to me, like a pillar of stability.

Foster comes to a stop in front of me, his steel eyes lingering on mine. "The girls have to train daily to keep sharp."

I tilt my head in confusion, wanting to ask, "On my property?"

He adds, "I stopped by the diner for lunch this afternoon."

My heart stammers, and my eyes dart toward the trail leading to the trailer. That means it's well past the one o'clock start time for my work shift, which I completely forgot.

Though I'm not sure that's entirely true. Somewhere in my mind I knew, along with work, there were things I was just letting go of. There are responsibilities I am letting fall to the wayside, but I can't bring myself to care.

I owe Peg the biggest apology and already know she'll accept it because that's the kind of person she is. But Peg doesn't deserve this, not after everything she's done for me.

"I didn't make it in today." My shoulders sag as I admit this to Foster.

"I see that."

The way Foster looks at me makes me squirm, unable to stay silent. "I've never missed a work shift in the nearly four years I've worked at the diner. I'm responsible to a fault. It's just been . . . Well, I don't have to tell you. And after we left your house this morning, I got some news that was hard to swallow."

Foster ponders my response for a moment, twirling his leather wristband in circles. He takes a step toward me, squinting against the sun. "What kind of news?"

"It's complicated." It's a total cop-out, and I know that.

Looking away, Foster laughs to himself. "Oh, I know complicated. Try me," he persists, which is the only reason I give in. He's talked more today than all of last week combined. And I get the idea it's not easy to get him to talk. You have to earn his trust.

"I got accepted into a photography program this fall."

"That's the complicated news, Callie? That sounds like good news to me."

"Yeah, it should've been," I bite out, bitterness leaching me.

Foster comes around, steadying his stance on the rock Opie used to sunbathe on and peers down the creek. "They always said Mack Hayes owned the nicest land out here in the hills." His voice was wistful, but I read between the lines.

The best land belonged to the worst man.

"Well, despite him, this land has been good to me." I bite my lip, holding back a smile as I stare beyond the pines lining the creek bank. "It's not there anymore, but up there—" I point, and Foster's eyes follow my invisible line to a tall pine beyond my throw. "—was an eagle's nest. I once waited for an entire day just to get a few photos of her. The photo ended up in the Western Carolina Audubon Society magazine." I smile to myself, remembering that day clearly. I still have a copy under my bed.

"So Levi wasn't lying. You're good at it."

I shrug. "It was a high school competition. I don't think many people even entered, so it's not like I was competing with a bunch of people. It's not a big deal."

Foster furrows his brow at me. "So when do you leave for school, then?"

"I'm not going." My whisper carries across the open space between us as pine needles rustle in the wind and the smell of the creek penetrates my senses.

Foster sucks in a breath, tilting his head back. I wrap my arms around myself, the air suddenly chilly.

"I've lived here almost my whole life, you know that?" he starts. "And I've seen a lot of people make dumb decisions. I'm not just talking about getting heated and committing crimes, Callie. I'm talking about decisions that go by unnoticed. Staying here for a girl or a guy, staying because the world *out there* seems scary. You know what's scarier than that bullshit, though?"

He pauses, and I realize he's waiting for me to answer. I bite my lip and shake my head.

"Looking back at life, seeing that if you weren't afraid, things could have been different. So damn different."

I stare at Foster, a bit dumbfounded. Who is this man standing in front of me with endless thoughts? I think I prefer the Foster who grunts answers and doesn't stare at me like he is right now, like he knows me. What we had going before worked for us—*I think*.

"Am I just supposed to walk away, leave my dog out there?" The wind rustles again, pulling my voice with it. I imagine it carrying my words into the forest, where the trees will pass my message along, finding my dog.

"You will survive, and Opie will survive. He lived alone before you, right?"

I scoff and turn, feeling the rough rock beneath my bare feet. "He was on the brink of *death* when he found me. And I was barely surviving before I found him." I rake my hand through my messy braid. "Take a look around, Foster. I don't exactly have people rallying around me." It comes out as a shout toward the end, taking me by surprise. "He *is* my life. When I find him, I will go," I voice more to myself than to him.

He rubs the stubble on his jaw with his palm, working out thoughts in his head I wish he'd keep to himself. But I seem to unravel him.

"Photography means a lot to you. That's clear."

"It *did*."

Foster goes to speak, but I cut him off. "Why did you agree to work with me, Foster?"

"Because, Callie." Foster crosses his arms across his chest, so I cross mine. Two can play this game.

"Because *why*?" I verbally push him.

He inhales a sharp breath. "You remind me of someone, okay? I feel responsible for you. Just because I haven't found Opie yet isn't a good enough reason for you to throw away your dreams."

"Well, don't. You're not responsible for me. I hired you to find my dog. I've been paying you, yeah? So keep searching. I'm *not* leaving without him. If you want me gone from this town so badly, maybe it's time to try harder."

Chapter
Twenty-Seven

Later that night, I got a call around ten. Foster's name lights up my phone in the same stride my heart starts racing. I pick up the phone quickly, fumbling to adjust my eyes to the darkness in the trailer.

"Hello?" I breathe out shakily.

"Callie, I got a call from Officer Williams."

There's an edge to Foster's voice, like someone lessening a blow. Bile rises up my throat as my free hand balls my quilt in my fist. I can't speak, and my tongue feels glued to my mouth, but he keeps talking.

"He got a call a few minutes ago about . . . about a dog that was hit off old State Highway 1. It's about ten minutes west of you. He agreed to let me check it out first . . . before he sends anyone else out there."

The string of lights overhead grows blurry, then dim. I gasp for air, but it does nothing to steady me as I teeter on the edge of my bed.

"Callie?" Foster's voice grows loud with concern for me.

I want to throw my phone. I want nothing more than to close my eyes and pretend this is all a dream. A *horrible* dream. My fingers dig deeper into the side of my mattress, and I'm sure, at any moment, my head is going to collide with the floor below. But Foster's voice cuts through the air, sharp and loud, bringing me back to the moment.

"Callie! Answer me! Are you okay?"

I don't know why the next words come out of my mouth, but they do. They come from a deep place within me, a reservoir of strength I thought was tapped dry long ago.

"I'm coming with you."

"You don't have to—"

"Foster." I sit up slowly, the nausea fighting and churning in my stomach. "Pick me up on the way. Please . . . I need to come with you."

The next five minutes are a blur. I turn on a single light above my kitchen sink, just lighting up the space enough so I can pull on warmer clothes and shoes. I take a sip of water, but it's hard to swallow. They say when you've experienced enough heartbreak, the brain learns to shut off as a mode of self-protection.

Maybe I could believe that's what's happening to me as I stand outside the trailer, my legs feeling numb. Foster is still a few minutes away, but I need air, so I stand under the trees and the veil of stars as the choking sensation of crying encases my throat. But no tears come to relieve me.

It doesn't feel like I am shutting down to protect myself.

It feels like I am holding on. Just holding on.

Foster's truck rumbles, a loud and jarring noise in the quiet of the night. He barely has a chance to slow to a halt before I run over, flinging open the door and climbing into the front seat. His hat is low, casting a shadow over his eyes, but I don't look at him long. I just click my seat belt into place.

I feel Foster's gaze on me though. I know he doesn't want me to come for one reason or another. Probably the same reason I like to work alone. But Opie is mine. He is my boy. If it's him lying alone on the side of the road, I need my arms to be the ones that wrap around him.

I owe him this much.

We pull out of the drive in silence, a low hum on the radio. It's turned down but not off. It's not until we are two miles down the road and about to turn onto the old highway, where it's somehow even darker, that I pull my braid out, letting my wavy hair feather down in front of my face.

One more wall of protection.

"People have been driving twenty over on this road since I was learning to drive," Foster remarks, breaking the silence.

I peek at him through my hair but don't say anything.

We don't pass another car the entire drive. The moon is thick in the sky, lighting up the bank of the road, and Foster slows to a roll, checking his rearview mirror. I don't ask him if he knows exactly where the dog was seen, but he seems to know.

When my eyes catch it first, I clasp my mouth so hard with my hand that I taste blood. In a flash, my fingers are frantically pulling the door handle, and I push it open before the truck is even in park.

"Careful, Callie!" he hollers.

I leap out of the cab, my ankles burning as I run down the side of the highway, the headlights bright on my back.

Breathe in, breathe out.

Every ounce of blood pumps through my body, my heart loud in my ears. I don't understand how my heart is still working, how it's still going, but it is.

Foster's boots sound behind me as an oblong, white body comes into view. A small whimper escapes my mouth before I collapse, gravel digging into my knees as my hands come down gently on the dog's torso.

"Callie . . . I'm . . ." Foster starts.

I turn to look up at him through blurry eyes. "It's not him," I mutter, my voice so small as he squats down, gingerly placing his hand on my shoulder, and I can see he doesn't believe me.

"Are you sure?" His voice is equally low.

"It's a female . . . and Opie has a patch over his left eye." My shoulders shake with relief, but my head hangs low. I pause before a ripple of emotion rushes through me, and a sob escapes my lungs.

It's not Opie. This dog is not Opie.

But my heart is still broken in two as I look down and hope with all my might she was loved and that this was painless. There's no collar on her bare neck.

Tipping my head to the sky, the stars shine brightly down on me, and my breath creates a haze around my face. Pushing myself from the ground, letting the gravel fall from my knees, I wipe my eyes, overwhelmed by the mix of grief and relief stirring inside me.

"Do you have a shovel?" I ask.

Foster's face is shaded by the headlights of his truck. I can't see his reaction, though there's a shift in the air.

"Wait here."

He walks to the truck bed. A few moments later, he reappears with a lantern in one hand and a shovel in the other. A tarp of sorts is folded under his arm. I stretch my arm toward him for the shovel, but he hands me the lantern instead.

"Please, let me dig," I say.

He hesitates, but my outstretched arm is unrelenting. I need to do this. I take the mud-covered lantern and shovel, saying nothing, and watch as Foster sets the tarp next to the female dog.

Fosters approaches me, hands in pockets. "If this is someone's dog, don't you think they'd want to bury her themselves?" he asks, peering down at me as mud begins to fleck onto my legs as I make the initial dig. I wipe at my eyes, smearing the lingering tears, feeling the heat wipe across my cheeks.

"This isn't someone's dog. You know that, and I know that," I state pointedly.

This area is known as a dumping ground for stray or unwanted pets, and by the condition of this dog, she wasn't in a home with love. The shovel hits another rock, and I slam my feet onto the metal head, causing my body to jolt with the kickback. I do it again and again, and it keeps getting harder, but I don't care. My glazed eyes meet Foster's. "No one is coming to get her, Foster. No one is wondering where she is tonight. No one cares. But I do. I'm not going to let her die in vain."

A huff leaves his chest, and he nods at me. Pulling off his baseball hat, he tosses it to the side and, with one stride, comes to my side, placing a large hand on the splintered wood shovel's handle.

"Let me help," he says.

My first instinct is to hold on tightly, to not let anyone take this shovel from me. Help is a convoluted word. It usually accompanies trust. And right now, I'm still upset with him over the words he said to Levi the other day, the words I wasn't meant to hear.

"Go unroll the tarp and wrap her in it," he instructs in a warm tone I've never heard from him before, but I stay with my hand tightly on the handle. Until our eyes meet. His steel-colored eyes are gentle. The wrinkles around his eyes soften too, and he nods ever so slightly at me, causing all my muscles to relax at once. I do what he says, returning my body to the dog's side, where I unroll the green plastic tarp and lay it over her, slowly rolling the small body in plastic.

The sound of shoveling begins again, and the thought that pops into my head catches me by surprise:

I'm thankful Foster is here.

I'm not sure I would've been able to do this without him. Not just the shoveling, but emotionally, I feel like he is holding me up.

"I'll be right back." I jot down the dark street. I return a minute later with a bunch of wildflowers grasped between my dirt-stained fingers.

I've never been to a funeral. Mack didn't have one for Memaw. They are a waste of money, he said. I didn't have any say, not at thirteen. She was buried with no service out in the cemetery next to my papa and mama. I visited it on my own after the burial, bringing her a bundle of wildflowers from the farm. I never learned the proper way you do a funeral or how to say goodbye. I didn't know how to grieve, how to send someone off. All I did was kneel beside her grave, spreading flowers in a way I thought she'd find pretty, and talk to her. In the midst of everything wrong, I learned to say goodbye in the only way that felt right.

"This is deep enough," Foster huffs, tossing the shovel to the side.

As I stand, I'm made aware of how tired my legs are. It feels like the earth is vibrating my body, starting at the soles of my feet. In my moment of pure exhaustion, the barrier I've held around myself with Foster and Levi begins to waver.

I'm so tired of resisting.

I watch in silence as Foster examines the hole he dug for this innocent animal, who isn't my dog. The moonlight illuminates the empty highway and the pine trees that act as barriers, and the only sound is Foster's faint grunting as he picks up the tarp and sets it gently into the earth. An owl in the distance whoos. It can see me, I'm sure, but I can't see it.

Foster begins to cover the tarp with dirt.

"How could someone do this?" I ask, anger and sadness bubbling inside me.

Foster stops for a moment, turning his head to me. A bead of sweat sits on his brow despite the chill in the air. "The world can be a cruel place, Callie."

But I already know that, know the cruelty of people, know neglect. I know what it feels like to be hit, left on the side, and forgotten about.

"This could've been Opie," I whisper. "Someone could've hit my dog and left him here like this." I shake my head, but it does nothing to clear the tears or the hurt gripping my chest. It hurts; it all fucking hurts.

My quivering hand holds my mouth. He pushes the unearthed dirt back over the hole until it's closed up. Until there's nothing but a mound of soil.

Kneeling down in front of the mound, I set the wildflowers on the top. Foster watches me without a word. I've spent more time with Foster this last week than I have with my own father over the last decade, and that hurts too. I feel exposed as I sit on the newly upturned earth, but I do it anyway. Tipping my head forward, my hands reach for each other until they awkwardly find their place over my heart.

I don't know how this works.

"I don't know if you knew love. I don't know if there was someone out there looking for you or if you were looking for someone. But, sweet girl, wherever you are now, I hope you are at peace. I hope the sun shines for you, and you no longer know the cruelty of this word. Rest easy."

Foster clears his throat, but I can't look up as I push myself from the cool ground. My legs are black with dirt, my arms aching from digging.

"I didn't know you were religious."

"I'm not," I admit, feeling foolish.

"That was kind of you. Not many people would do this, Callie." His palm gestures toward the fresh grave at our feet.

"I did what I'd hope someone would do for Opie, if this was him."

"Can I ask who you were talking to?" he asks, his voice low as he places the cap back on his head.

Letting out a low breath, I turn my face away from his. "To whoever is out there listening."

The lights in the cab flicker as I sit in the idling truck outside the trailer. There is so much to be said, but it feels like no words I can formulate are enough.

"You'll let Officer Williams know, yeah?" I ask, one hand already on the door handle.

"Of course." He hesitates, his hand sliding over the top of the leather steering wheel. "Hey, kid . . . I'm sorry about all of this."

I furrow my brow, taking my hand off the handle to turn toward Foster, just two feet away from me in the driver's seat. "I don't want you to feel sorry for me, Foster."

"I don't feel sorry for you. You're a strong young woman. I'm *sorry* for the cards you've been dealt. You say life is unfair, and hell, don't I know that." He rubs his jaw. "But you don't deserve any of this."

It takes a moment for his words to soak in. "Thank you. For everything. And Foster, I'm sorry too."

He nods, his steel eyes layered. We exchange glances. One glance that speaks volumes. I forgive him for what he said to Levi.

Once I'm inside, I quickly rinse myself of the smell of death and earth. I smell clean, my hair damp against my neck as I curl into bed in the same spot I was just two hours ago when Foster called me. As if nothing has changed tonight.

But my God, everything has.

Chapter Twenty-Eight

August

The packet from Charleston Photography Co. glares up at me from the passenger's side of my car. I don't know why I grabbed it on my way out of the trailer today, but I did. At the grocery store, I run into Carla from work, who smiles when she sees me and comments on how tired I look and that Peg is concerned about me. What am I supposed to say? I'm not about to tell her I'm exhausted from spending half the night on an old interstate, burying a dog that wasn't mine. Or that my eyes have been in a state of tiredness, sunken and swollen for the last nine days.

"Your boyfriend came in by himself last night. He is *so* cute," she taunts, twirling her thick, red hair around a finger.

My tired eyes snap up from staring at the sleeve of bagels. She isn't even looking at me anymore but scrolling on her phone now. "Who? Levi?" I ask, squinting against the fluorescent lights in the bread aisle.

Carla laughs as if I'm being cheeky. "Duh, the only guy who comes in to eat alone just to see you." She snaps her bubble gum.

"Oh, he's not my boyfriend. Levi's just a friend." I flash a quick, but unconvincing, smile and swipe the bagels from the shelf, plopping them into my arms like a football.

"Okay, whatever you say. He asked about you, though." Carla winks at me.

"Well, he has my number. He could've texted me," I deduce, but now I'm saying too much. I don't need the gossip mills churning in this town, if they aren't already.

I go to turn and grab peanut butter, not even sure if I need it, but Carla has turned the gears in my head, and now I'm not even sure what I was supposed to be buying here. She follows me down the aisle, and I grow agitated.

"Oh, girl. I was going to ask you, have you found your dog? Half of your posters with your pup's face on them have shriveled up or been damaged from the rain." She pouts, jutting her lip out, like her sad face is supposed to make me feel better.

"No, Carla. He is still missing," I reply with a bite and turn on my heel. "I have to go though. I'll see you later at work."

I hear her bubble gum pop, and without looking back, I know she is waving obnoxiously as she yells, "Goodbye!"

I leave the store with four bagels and a tub of peanut butter. That will have to be lunch.

Levi texted me after I left the grocery store, asking me how I was holding up. Said Foster filled him in on the dog we buried last night. I wanted to call him, to talk to him about anything but last night, but I couldn't get myself to do it without incessant chatter in my head telling me I was being a burden to him.

All I wanted was to text Levi with good news—or Foster for that matter. Instead, I race to the diner for my dinner shift, already late.

As soon as I walk into the kitchen full of clanging pots and sizzling grills, Peg hastily sets her tray down and waltzes up to me, pulling me into a hug. The smell of hairspray fills my nose as her white, permed hair tickles my face.

"Honey, I've been so worried about you. How are you doing?" She looks at me with worried eyes.

I exhale a deep breath, looking away. "It's been a draining past few days, Peg. But I'm happy to be here right now." That brings a small smile to her face. I *am* happy to be here. It keeps me occupied, and I need to make every dollar I can right now—my savings is nearly tapped.

The dining room is full, though, so we don't waste any more time chatting. I quickly tie my apron, lace my shoes, grab a pad, and make my way out. It's not until I only have twenty minutes left of my shift that I have a moment to breathe. I find Peg cleaning a table near the front window.

"Hey, Peg. I owe you an apology."

She pauses, leaving the white towel in a heap on the table, and looks at me.

I bite my lip and wring my hands. "For missing those shifts without reaching out. I feel really horrible about leaving you in a bind like that."

Peg grabs the rag and puts a hand on her hip. "Callie, in all the years you've worked here, you've never been late, never missed a shift, and you never complained. You've picked up every shift I've ever asked. You're allowed to make mistakes, dear. It's okay. We managed. We all know you're going through things right now." She rests the plates and rag on her hip and cups my chin with her free hand. "Chin up, sweet pea. It's going to get better. I've been praying for your doggy."

Tears well in my eyes, but our conversation is interrupted by flashing lights whizzing by the diner windows. A cop car is followed by a fire truck, their ear-piercing sirens halting the conversations around me. Everyone watches as the vehicles head in the direction of the hills, and then silence returns and everyone goes back to chatting. Peg and I get pulled in separate directions, but her kind words feel like a hug, one I desperately needed.

The bright white photography packet with a blue embossed logo still glares at me when I slide tiredly into my car after my shift. My body sinks into the seats, and my legs burn from nonstop movement, but I decide I have to do something with the packet because every time I glance at it, the start date flashes in front of my eyes like it's branded on my mind. I need to just throw it out, but I can't bring myself to do it yet. So, instead, I toss it in the back seat with all my clean laundry I never got around to bringing inside.

Waiting for a miracle is a dangerous game, Callie.

As I add the tips from tonight out loud, I stop mid-count, halfway up the hill to the farmhouse. Plumes of hazy smoke rise in the distance, dulling my view of the sunset behind it. That's where the fire trucks must've gone, straight out of town toward the hills. My heart sinks in my chest as I get closer, worried for whoever or whatever is caught in the fire. I wonder if it could be a car wreck. A lot of people wreck on this climb uphill with its windy, narrow roads.

I brace myself, not wanting to see any carnage, as the plumes of smoke get closer, though they are less thick now.

The second I turn into the driveway, past the crooked blue mailbox, it becomes clear where the smoke is coming from. Slamming my foot on the gas pedal, my tires spin on the gravel, but I don't let up until I'm whirling past the farmhouse and speeding down the narrow road that's freshly trodden by the giant fire truck that is cutting me off from my trailer.

I've smelled smoke in one form or another all my life, like Mack's cigarettes that he smoked outside on the front porch, the butts lining an ashtray that overflowed on the handrail. Or campfires that burned every weekend outside the farmhouse when he would throw parties and I would stay in my room, reading a book or nursing whatever animal I found back to health. But this smell was not the same.

I don't bother closing the door as I jump out of my car, my feet hitting the sodden ground heavily. Rounding the corner of the fire truck, I see him first: my father, sitting in the back of the open ambulance, an oxygen mask over his face. Then my eyes dart to the trailer—or what is left of it. My home. And all at once, everything goes out the proverbial window.

Everything, everything, everything.

My home. My safety. My sanctuary. My backup plan. My escape from Mack for a whole year. The last piece of my grandparents I had access to.

Opie's home.

Hazy, gray smoke feathers above the trailer as it sizzles into nothing but a black crisp. At first glance, it looks like a few things survived, but it doesn't really matter. Where I once peered through the front door, I can now see to the other side. The door is a melted mass, hanging from one hinge. The door that never latched, the door that betrayed me, hangs on its hinges like a cockroach. I rush over and push on it.

"Callie!" I spin around, and the lights blind me. Beyond the fire truck and police car, the sunset mocks me. It's more beautiful than any I've seen all summer.

"Hey, hey. Please step away from there. It's not secure yet!"

Officer Williams's voice pulls me back to consciousness, and I know my eyes match the scowl on my lips. There's no life in my eyes anymore, and I don't need a mirror to know that.

"How . . ." is all I can manage to mutter. My eyes rake over Mack. His head hangs low, his shoulders slumped and his clothes torn like he got attacked by a wild animal. The firefighters are rolling their hose back in, a few of them looking at me, but I keep my eyes on Mack.

"Your trailer caught on fire around eight-thirty this evening. It appears there was faulty wiring where you're plugged in. Looks like it was messed with, resulting in an electrical fire. It happened pretty quick, Callie. They got here as soon as they could, but it was nearly gone when we arrived on the scene."

Faulty wiring. In my 1970s camper. And a door that doesn't latch. My first thought is, *What if Opie had been in there?* and my second thought is, *He wasn't Callie. He's gone. Gone somewhere you don't know.*

"Why is he here?" I ask, pointing at my father, disdain coating my voice. *How is he involved?*

Officer Williams lowers his brows. He has to be tired of coming here. Has to be sick of the *Hayes* creating issues in this peaceful town. I want to tell him not to worry about it, that I'll be gone soon. I'll be in Charleston, and he will never hear from me again. But that's not true. It can no longer be true. Everything was in my little home. My camera, my laptop, my photography prints—all my worldly possessions. All I still had.

"Mack was in your camper when it caught fire." His voice is low, and the reverence sets me on edge. The hair on my neck stands up. There's no breeze, and the smoke feels heavy around me, but I refuse to cough.

"What do you mean . . . he was inside?" With each syllable, I straighten my spine, my voice growing louder and louder.

Officer Williams's eyes grow wide with concern, and he puts his hands up. If what I'm suspecting is true, then Mack has truly taken everything from me.

Mack barely lifts his head when I run toward the ambulance, which is parked directly in front of the trail to the creek. My entire body shakes with shock and anger.

"Ma'am, do you need assistance?" the stocky EMS worker, who's checking Mack's vitals, asks me.

I ignore him. "Mack, what did you do?" I stare at him as my finger points straight at the shell of my home.

He says nothing as his eyes drop to the ground. One hand is over the oxygen mask, and the other arm is still in a sling.

"Mack, I asked you a question! Damn it! For once, just tell me the truth!" I cry out.

The EMS worker stiffens, his eyes alert, ready to intervene if I start to get physical. He doesn't know half the truth.

My father remains silent, but his blue eyes lift slowly to meet mine. If I wasn't staring so intensely, if I didn't know Mack's telltale signs of when he was lying and when he was too afraid to tell me the truth, I'd miss it. *But I didn't miss it.*

A slight narrowing of his eyes and a nod like the wind simply blew his head. His chest slowly goes up and down.

I stand there, eyes locked on my father, who is supposed to protect me. But instead, he's done nothing but make it so I can't live here. So

I'm not welcome in this town, in my home, on the land that's been in my family for generations.

"How could you?" I burst out, shoving him back.

He does nothing to resist. As he falls into the equipment, he grunts, and I hope he is in pain. Officer Williams runs toward me, grabbing me from behind and pulling me out of arm's reach. All I see is red, but I let Officer Williams restrain me.

"It's your fault! It's all your fucking fault!" I scream at Mack, whose eyes are bloodshot and barely open. My voice cracks open like the sky, and tears spill unapologetically from my eyes. My body collapses backward into Officer Williams as I watch the paramedic gently nudge Mack to lay back on the stretcher so they can readjust his oxygen.

"We are taking your dad to the hospital to monitor his lungs. He inhaled a lot of smoke," the EMS worker says sternly, glaring at me like I'm the one who caused this.

I don't reply. They could take him away anywhere.

They shut the ambulance doors, and Officer Williams lets go of my arms, coming around to face me. The firefighter chief walks up to join us. They start a spiel, the chief looking serious and Williams looking concerned. I am barely able to hold onto their words.

Call the insurance company. Don't enter the trailer's structure.

The fire chief pats Officer Williams on the shoulder and walks away while caution tape is wrapped around the fire scene. When I look up, Officer Williams's cheeks are puffed out, and his arms are across his chest. He looks distressed, and I want to remind him that I'm the one who just lost their home. He runs a hand through his cropped blonde hair and looks over at me.

"Chief Kensey let me know they are going to be ruling this as an accidental fire, started by an electrical malfunction."

"So they don't care about the truth?" I scoff, kicking the ashy dirt with my black work shoes. I glance over my shoulder at the skeleton of my home. All the trucks start to leave the property, except the squad car. Williams takes a step toward me, and I notice how tired he looks.

"Callie, you have every right to be upset right now, but the truth is, there is no proof Mack started the fire."

Throwing up my hands, I swing around, facing away from Williams and gathering myself. He lets me.

"He shouldn't have been in my trailer to begin with!" I cry out, my hands covering my eyes, shutting out the world around me.

"You're right. He shouldn't have been. But legally, this is his property, Callie. If you want to fight this you can, but—"

"No. I don't," I say bluntly, slowly turning back to face him. I'm so sick of Mack being on the wrong side of the law when I'm the one who suffers most.

But more than that, I'm tired. I just want to get out of this mess.

"Do you have someone you can call, maybe somewhere to stay tonight while you get this sorted out? I'm happy to give you a ride wherever you need to go."

My mind quickly races through all the people I could call right now. Peg, Levi, Foster—all of them would put me up immediately. But I'm not ready to be around anyone. All I want is to be alone right now.

"I'll sleep at the farmhouse tonight. I still have a few things there." I attempt to muster a convincing look to show him I'll be all right. He doesn't believe it; I know.

I'll feel better when he is gone. When everyone is gone. When it's just me. When I can stand here and cry. Or not cry. When I can feel anything but this panic that's risen in me the moment I saw smoke. *How long ago was that? I don't know. I don't know.*

His hand presses into my shoulder, a gesture that's meant to be comforting. "I'm so sorry this happened. I'll leave you be, but please call me if you need anything, you hear?"

I nod and mumble my thanks, knowing I'll never call him.

Chapter Twenty-Nine

I lied to Officer Williams. I left some of my stuff at the farmhouse, like clothing and such, but those items were left because all they did was bring back old memories. Old sweatshirts of Darren's I never gave back to him. My outfit from the night of the wreck, shoved into the back of my closet.

I wait until Officer Williams's squad car is long gone before I drive to the farmhouse. It's dark, but the porch light flickers, and the key to the front door still dangles from my keychain. I don't want to go inside any more than I want to stay in this car. But the truth is, I decided to stay here, so I either have to sleep in my car or enter the house.

"Fuck . . . just do it," I huff, grabbing my purse as I walk to the porch. I unlock the front door and step inside, flipping on the lights as I go. It's stale and silent, like I expected. Beer bottles litter the kitchen counter, and only half of the light bulbs still work.

Walking through the hallway, my heart hurts in my chest, and I pause outside my bedroom door as my throat tightens. It's been over a year since I entered this room, and I've never had any intention of reentering. But what choice do I have left?

Gripping the brass knob, I push the door, and it opens, clanging against the wall. I stand, unmoving, my eyes assessing the space. The pink walls are empty, and my white furniture is still in place. The bed is bare—I took my bedding when I moved. It's clean, like I left it, and I think it's safe to say no one has entered this room for a year. There is nothing of value for Mack, and the dust and staleness in here remind me that I made the right choice by moving out. This room is nothing but a time capsule of past traumas.

Stripping off my clothes that smell like diner food and smoke, I take the hottest shower I can in the clawfoot tub in the hall bathroom. I stay in the shower until it runs cold, and I'm forced out by sheer discomfort. But I don't feel any cleaner after. I still feel the thick blanket of shame draped around my shoulders.

Your father burned down your home and walked away.

Normally, by this time, I'd be getting ready for bed, planning the next day of searching. But as I pull on sweatpants and a T-shirt, I don't know how to settle in this house that feels so foreign.

I shut my old bedroom door and make my way downstairs. There's tea in the cabinet, so I use the kettle to boil water and make a hot cup. Sitting on the worn plaid couch in the dimly lit living room, I pull my legs under me and let out a heavy breath. I remove several beer cans from the coffee table, not wanting to look at them anymore. They are the reason my home went up in flames. Why *everything* did.

Trying to will away the thought of the fire, I squeeze my eyes shut and place a shirt over my face as I lay back on the sofa. The moon peeks through the yellow, frayed curtains, mocking me, keeping me awake in a numb state. It's not until the sun starts to rise that my eyes succumb to sleep, and I fall into a nightmarish slumber. One where I remember what I've lost.

Everything, everything, everything.

Only mere hours after falling asleep, I'm roused awake. It takes me a few seconds to realize where I am and what has happened. The sofa feels scratchy under my skin, and a half-drank mug of tea sits on the coffee table in front of me.

It's quiet in the farmhouse, except for the song from a Carolina wren in the oak tree out front, but I can't take comfort in that. It's loud with the ghosts of people who've left me behind, both without meaning to and all too intentionally. At any moment, I know Mack could walk back through the front door of the house that was never really mine. It almost feels like Memaw could round the corner too, pulling her knitted shawl over her shoulders even in the midst of summer in a house without air-conditioning.

Or I could look out the kitchen window, like I am now, and see Opie running over the hill, energy and joy taking over his whole body, muscles moving back and forth so that he wiggles as he runs, unable to control the love bursting at his seams. I've pictured it so many times, trying to embody the whole "if you believe it, it will be" mentality, but when I blink, it's gone. And all I see out the dirty kitchen window are trees and grass that no longer feel like a safe spot.

I start making coffee, happy that at least Mack always has a tin of it, but the moment my mug is full of black caffeine, I lose my appetite for it. Instead, I set it down and walk to the front door, pulling on my ash-covered shoes. For once, I'm grateful for my laziness this past week because outside in my car, there's a large load of clean laundry I never brought in from the laundromat. Leaning into the back seat, I mindlessly sift through it and settle on something clean to wear, though it hardly matters. I'm not planning on seeing anyone today.

What I plan on doing is walking up to what remains of my trailer. I know I need to brace myself, and I tell myself I have time, that the walk is at least five minutes. But today, I swear it was ten seconds.

I've read enough about psychology to know that after most house fires, people go into shock. Shock, depression, anger. But what those books don't divulge is what to do if you are already in that state. The grief just stacks. What if you are already a shell of yourself?

I'm forced to pause that thought when my phone vibrates. I pull it from my pocket, and Opie's face, with his wide smile, pink gums, and black nose, shines up at me under a number I know. I've ignored Levi's texts. I missed a call from Officer Williams too. If I ignore them long enough, they will stop. People stop caring when it gets exhausting.

Seeing Levi's name stirs up tears in my eyes. I shove the phone back in my pocket, silencing it. It buzzes again, and I don't pull it out until the call stops. *Foster.*

"Fuck!" I scream.

What would they think of me now if they knew the truth about the fire? I was only now beginning to feel like I maybe belonged. Somewhere, with someone. That feeling was taken away in one night, one *more* night, of loss. I have nothing to offer them.

Foster is a hired *friend*. He would've never sought out a relationship with me. He would've never had the inkling to care about the nineteen-year-old daughter of a drunk. *No, he only cared because I was lining his wallet with all I had to my name.*

And Levi. His name hurts on my tongue as I whisper it to myself. It catches in my throat.

Maybe in another life, yeah?

In another life, he could've been something to me. He's the sun, and I'm the cloud.

It's not wallowing if it's true.

Levi would argue with me if he were here, if I ever had the courage to voice what was on my mind aloud to him. He would say, "*Callie, that's not true. You are the most talented photographer I know,*" and I'd scoff because in this nothing-town, I doubt Levi even knows any other photographers. I'd roll my eyes and smirk at him, and he'd smile back even brighter, lean in, and stare intensely with his honey-brown eyes. "*There's a whole packet of proof on your passenger seat,*" he'd remind me.

I never told Levi I got in. I never told him. He's probably the only person who truly cares about my future and my passion. And I never told him the truth.

The truth that I got in, and that there is no way I can go. If I don't tell him, there's no chance he will be disappointed in me.

Chapter Thirty

The trailer is a burned crisp wrapped in caution tape. The fire chief looked me dead in the eye and told me that under no circumstance should I attempt to go inside due to the instability of the floor. I nodded along, agreeing to obey. I had no desire to go inside, but I needed to look at it in the daylight, maybe just to see that it wasn't all just a nightmare. Chief Kensey also apologized. Sincerely, I think, because they believed there was nothing salvageable from the fire.

But that's not true. They don't know what still holds meaning to me. They don't know what I'd give to cling to anything.

Resting my hand on the blackened frame of the trailer, I close my eyes. Everything inside is melted, charred, or ash. I should be calling my insurance company, sending them the official report, and taking photos. That's what Officer Williams said to do, and I nodded along because I didn't have the integrity to admit the truth. *There was never any insurance.* Every extra dollar I had went into my escape fund. My new-life fund.

And now that is gone.

I exhale my shaky breath and open my eyes. That's when I notice it, out of the corner of my eye. A purple stuffed dinosaur. I don't turn my head to look at it right away, in case it's not real. In case it's a figment of my imagination. But I bite my lips together, my fists clenched in anticipation, and I turn fully.

Sure enough, there it is. Opie's favorite toy, sitting outside the camper, just under the cinder blocks holding up the frame.

I scramble, nearly tripping over my own feet as I slide down to my knees and reach for the stuffed animal. It's not totally unscathed, but by some miracle, this stuffed animal is not gone. I hold it to my chest, not caring about the charred bits rubbing ash on my shirt. My fingers graze the matted fur, and I think about Opie carrying it gently everywhere with him. Holding it to my chest, I feel Opie here with me, reaching through the layers of my skin that have hardened to metal and straight into my heart. Right where he belongs.

I spend another hour carefully walking around the rubble. The daylight shows me the truth of what's left and what isn't. Then I leave because there's nothing more I can do here, and it just makes me sad.

Back at the farmhouse, I find myself wandering the house until I come to the pull cord for the attic. It's been a while since I stashed anything up there, and for once, I'm grateful for Mack's negligence. The attic is exactly how I left it.

There are boxes of crocheted blankets Memaw made, some half-finished, dusty boxes of photographs, and a few items I left in my childhood bedroom. I take a few trips down the rickety ladder, carrying the boxes under my arms. Mack won't miss them, and wherever I'm going, I'm taking them.

I bring all the boxes down to the living room and wipe them off. Shaking out a crocheted blanket, I swear I can still smell Memaw and her ninety-nine-cent perfume. I place the blanket on my lap and am startled by my phone ringing. It's Levi again.

I know I need to talk to him, give him an explanation, but I don't know what to say. Not yet. I don't even know who knows about the fire. In this town, word spreads quicker than fire, but it won't be news that something on Mack Hayes's property went up in flames. Only Levi and Foster even knew I was living in the old camping trailer anyway. And I don't peg Officer Williams as a gossiper.

My fingers worry at a loose thread of the blanket, and I let out a soft groan. I should call Peg and let her know I'm okay. If she finds out, she will be worried sick.

But I can't bring myself to do anything. Except put on my shoes and walk to the creek. As I walk, it feels like I could be walking anywhere. I wait for a glimmer of sunshine to warm my face and remind me I'm alive, or the pine needles to rustle under foot and give me a feeling of grounding. I even tell myself Mack isn't here, that this land is all mine for the day, because that used to bring me peace.

Nothing comes, though, and it's as if I'm not even moving my own feet. The wind picks up, and it's as if it's carrying me along, whispering through the green leaves, and I stand here next to the bubbling creek, watching the wind carry leaves through the air. I wait for it to carry my heavy heart away with it too.

I don't have an answer for why I do what I do next, but I pull out my phone and make a call. It takes a few connections to get to the right person, but when I do, I get an answer that gives me no peace.

The nurse tells me Mack was discharged from the hospital this morning around nine. It's been hours, and he hasn't come home yet. For a second, part of me wonders if he will ever come back, but I know the answer. He will. This property is all he has.

There's no saying when he'll walk through those doors, but I know I want to be gone when he does. Though I can't seem to get myself to formulate any plan.

But right now, as I sit here under the blanket Memaw made, on the floor of the house I once called home, I reach for the box of photos and grab a stack. Leaning my back on the plaid couch, I don't expect the first photo to be *us*. Mack, me, and Mama. It looks like it was taken the day I was born, or maybe just a few later. My mother looks tired, but Mack has a smile as wide as the Mississippi on his face.

I drop the photos to my lap and take a deep breath, feeling the gnawing twist deep in my stomach. One look at that photo and I'm faced with the truth I've run from since the day Mack returned from prison: somewhere deep inside me, there's a dim light, one that still holds onto the hope that Mack will remember who he was before he let everything go, that he'll remember me.

I skirted around the house all day, anxious and avoiding calls. I check the forums for lost dogs and call the shelters to no avail. Around dinnertime, there is still no sign of my father, so I make myself food. I haven't eaten since yesterday evening. My hands find the pots in the same spot they always have been.

I eat noodles and make a sandwich, surprised there is anything still edible in this house. If he walks in right now, he might be mad I ate his food, but I'll remind him he burned down my home.

The food has no taste as I sit there in the dining room with floral wallpaper. I know I can't stay here forever, and in the silence, I work up the courage to call Peg. She picks up on the first ring.

"Oh, thank heavens, Callie. I have been so worried about you! Officer Williams stopped by this afternoon. He told me about the fire. I tried calling honey, but you didn't answer." Peg sounds like she is on the brink of tears, which makes me want to cry too. I never wanted to cause her this much worry.

I'm quiet for a moment before I clear my throat to speak. "I'm sorry. Peg. I'm okay. I just . . ."

"Callie Hayes, shush now. Don't say anything. Don't apologize for what you've been through. You come in here, and I will get you fed, okay? We will rework your schedule. I don't want you worrying about a single thing."

Her kindness is too much, and it floods me with warmth. I drop my fork on the table and pull my legs to my chest in the chair.

"You need a place to stay, honey? Where you staying?" Peg rattles off her questions as the telltale sounds of the diner play in the background. My heart jumps a bit with each sentence she speaks.

"Thank you. I promise I'm okay. I'm a little shaken up, but I'll survive. Things can be replaced. I'm just thankful I wasn't in the trailer when it happened." I take myself by surprise at my shift in perspective. I don't know if I totally believe it or if I'm just saying it because hearing Peg upset is unbearable. "And I'm staying at my father's house. I'll be in tomorrow to look at the schedule. I'll be back at work soon, I promise."

Silence meets me on the other end of the line. *She doesn't believe me, and it's okay because I don't believe myself.*

"Okay, sweet pea. You know where to find me when you need me."

"Of course. Thanks, Peg."

We hang up, and I exhale a shaky breath. After dinner, I pull back the curtains in the front window, and my heart picks up in pace. I don't know what I'll do if Mack returns today. But I guess I should prepare and gather up my stuff. I'd rather sleep in my car than near him.

That means going back to my bedroom, but this time I think of it like a task, putting all repressed memories aside as best I can. Storming into the room like I belong there, I walk to the closet and pull down some boxes from the shelf. There's quite a bit up there I hadn't realized I left. There are some old photographs I took with Memaw's Polaroid camera, including an album of photos of my pet bunnies that were actually wild rabbits. There are photos of flowers, and blurry selfies of me and Memaw on the front porch, drinking something sugary she blended together one summer afternoon. I bring the picture to my lips, kissing her cheek.

Next, I pull out a box of high school stuff. All the yearbooks remain blank because I never asked anyone to sign them. Under that are the art projects. I actually smile when I see them, and I sit on the floor, leaning on my bedroom door, taking my time to sift through a few.

At the bottom of my art box is a leather-bound journal. *The journal.* I flip through it, not intending to read any of my dramatic high school rants. It's full of sporadic details I decided to write with no rhyme or reason. Of course, a few pages are all about Darren, but I skip over those. One page catches my attention, though, because it's thick. I open it only to find a Polaroid taped onto the page. It's a picture of the creek from three years ago, and next to it, I wrote about the Charleston Photography Co. I'd just learned about it from my art teacher, and I was so excited apparently. Funny enough, that was the last thing I ever added to my journal.

Tossing it in the box, I stretch my legs out. I'm feeling a sliver better, a minuscule amount, but I'll take it. I lost a lot in the fire, but there are a few hidden gems I've discovered today. I'm trying to find something to be grateful for. If I don't, I'll stay on this floor forever, I'm afraid.

And of all the things I lost in the fire, the damn acceptance packet wasn't one of them. I have a couple more days to give them an answer.

If I don't reply, it will be over. I also know that saying no to this year means no forever. They don't allow repeat entries, and I've always known that.

I was okay with that fact, feeling pretty confident I would get it. As delusional or not it is, it was the only choice I was giving myself. I had a plan, just a few months ago, and everything was actually going according to plan. For once in my life.

I think now I can look back and say I was happy or, at the very least, on my way to being happy. But now that the rug has been pulled out from under me, I'm more lost than ever.

I promised Opie I wouldn't leave without him. But I'm so afraid that staying here in Miscruz Hills doesn't just mean I'd physically be here but mentally stuck in this moment. Like a carousel you can never get off.

Lost and heartbroken.

I must've fallen asleep because I wake up on my twin-sized bed to the sound of a car pulling up to the house. My heart jumps out of my chest, and I sit up frantically.

Shit, shit, shit.

Panic rises like bile in my throat as I rush to the stairwell, peering out the window to the front yard. Car doors open, but I don't see anyone. Darting down the steps, I nearly fall at the bottom but catch myself on the wall and place a hand over my heart.

Callie, get a grip. You can face him.

I still don't have a plan, and I have no inkling about what kind of mood Mack is in. All I can hope is the hospital sends him home with some type of sedative and he will just go sleep it off, giving me time to figure out what I'm going to do.

A knock sounds at the door, and I freeze. My bare feet pad along, crossing the wooden floors of the living room. Tucking my loose hair behind my ears, I walk slowly to the front door and pull it open, ready for whoever may be waiting for me on the other side of the door.

Ready for anyone but him.

"Levi?" I ask, my voice groggy as my knees grow weak. I clear my throat. Levi's hazel eyes grow wide with concern, then gentle as he steps inside and throws his arms around my shoulders.

"Callie, I've been calling you all day. I've been so worried."

His voice breaks my heart. *I wasn't prepared for this.*

"I'm okay, Levi. I fell asleep and must've missed your calls," I object, mimicking his low tone.

Levi pulls away and snorts, tipping his head back. His cheekbones are a stark contrast to his soft eyes, but they grow deep with concern as he settles his gaze back on me. I squirm under that look, unable to hide.

"Callie . . . please don't lie. Not to me. We are beyond that."

My heart hitches in my chest. I step back, but Levi steps forward. He reaches out, placing his hand on my chin, tilting my face up to his.

"I'll be okay. I always am." I muster up a crooked smile that I know looks like bullshit.

Levi peers into my eyes and shakes his head, dropping his hand from my face. His shirt stretches over his arms, and for a moment, I want to be inside those arms.

"Your home burned down, and you are holed up in this hell of a place." He looks around, scoffing, as tears well in my eyes. "And Opie is still missing. Stop pretending you are fine. Stop lying to me. To *me*."

The way he says it *crushes* me and reaches into my soul, where only Opie has ever reached. And for once, I'm defenseless. Because Levi is right. *About everything*.

I close the gap between us, crashing into Levi's chest. His arms envelop me, holding me. If he lets go, I truly believe all the contents of my heart will spill onto the floor. His other hand, large and strong, cradles the back of my head, and I let him hold my face there, my eyes soaking his shirt with silent tears. He holds me through sobs that rip through me, ones from deep inside. Tears that stem from before this moment, from before Opie. I barely recognize the feeling of being safe in someone's arms, and the thought makes me cry harder.

Levi presses his lips to my temple, and I squeeze my eyes shut.

"Callie, it's going to be okay. I'm here," he soothes, his hoarse voice.

I hold onto him harder, wondering how I stood alone for so long, because collapsing into him only took one second. I don't know how long he holds me like this as I cry and feel everything I haven't allowed myself to feel. I only know that when I finally pull away, Levi leans down and wipes my cheeks with his thumb, reassuring me again and again I'm not alone.

"I'm here, Callie."

Chapter Thirty-One

We sit on the steps leading up to the front porch while the sun sets over the tall pine trees. Levi keeps an arm wrapped around me as I lean into him, my head barely reaching his shoulder.

"You'll never believe what I found under the trailer this morning," I tease.

Levi inches back to look at me. "Under! Cal, it can't be safe to do that!" he protests, but I ignore him.

"Opie's toy didn't burn." I smile, even though it hurts a little.

Levi laughs quietly and gazes over the tops of the trees. "That's something." He exhales and looks at me. "But promise me you'll be careful. I don't want you to get hurt up there."

I nod and stare off in the direction of the ruins. "I don't think you need to worry about that . . . I don't plan on going back up there. Not for the trailer anyway. I got what was left." My voice fades.

"What did they say the cause was?"

As soon as he asks, my body goes rigid, and Levi pulls his arm away so he can turn to face me. But I avoid eye contact.

"It was Mack," I reply with an ironic bite. Levi extends a hand, brushing it across my leg, and I lean forward on my elbows.

"I'm so sorry. That's shitty. Damn, Callie." Levi runs his hands through his hair, visibly upset. It helps take the sting away.

The sting of shame that I'm related to Mack, and he's still ruining my life in ways I never believed possible.

When I nod and don't respond, Levi scoots back over, pulling me into his side. We sit a few minutes longer in comfortable silence. But then the silence grows heavy because there's one more thing I need to tell him. He deserves to know.

"I got into the photography program," I whisper.

Levi's eyes grow wide, his lips revealing a pearly smile that falls the moment I don't mimic the joy he feels.

"Wait, why aren't you happy?" He playfully shakes me side to side.

What a loaded question.

"It's not good timing, you know?" I cock my head, peering at him under my heavy eyelashes, glued together by earlier tears.

What a loaded answer.

Levi leans back while stretching out his legs in front of him. "Callie . . ." My name leaves his lips in an exhale. "You're right. *This* is horrible timing."

Levi sounds sad, which hurts me. I didn't want this, to drag Levi under with me into my mess and chaos and the stain of my father that follows me like a dark cloud. Because if I'm being honest, Levi is sunshine. And I selfishly want to soak up his rays, but you can't take without giving, and I'm not sure what I have to give him right now.

"Listen," he continues, rubbing his palms on his jeans, "you have worked *so* hard for this. I know what this means to you." He pauses to look pointedly at me. "Promise me you'll at least think about going to Charleston, okay?"

"Levi," I huff, mimicking his tone when he speaks my name, which makes him crack a lopsided smirk. "I promise you I will *think* about it. Right now, I just want to be anywhere but here in my father's house. I can't think clearly here," I admit. As soon as Levi showed up, something in me snapped. I can't stay here a moment longer.

Levi nods, and I know he wants to say more, but he accepts my answer, which is all I could've hoped for. What I don't say is losing the trailer wasn't just losing a temporary home for me. It was the only home Opie ever knew. Even though Foster said it wasn't likely Opie would physically return to it on his own, there was still a place for me to go back to where he once *was*. I could still picture him on the bed or sitting near my feet at the kitchen sink. It still smelled like him. His food bowl was still the first thing I tripped on every time I went to shower.

Now that it's all gone, it's like a piece of him is gone. A piece of Callie and Opie, our history, is erased. It would've been different when I willingly sold it and left, but this fire . . . It just took it from me. Without permission, without warning.

"Do you remember the field trip in fifth grade when we went to that farm and picked strawberries?" Levi asks.

I crack a tiny smile, confused but grateful for his mind that jumps from thing to thing. "Of course I do."

It was the end of the school year, we were eleven, and Levi was still my only confidant. I remember picking strawberries in the field for what felt like hours with my classmates, and afterward I had a whole basket full of them, so excited to come home and show Memaw. I was sure she'd know exactly what delicious things we could make with them. That's when I got shoved from behind. Stumbling, my woven basket, full of painstakingly picked fruit, was thrown in every direction, and I hit the ground hard.

The berries were smashed and ruined, and before I could even turn around to look at the boy who shoved me, Levi was next to me, pulling me up to my feet. Then he threw a punch only a scrawny eleven-year-old boy could.

"You know that's the first and last time I ever punched someone in the face." Levi chuckles, shaking his head, embarrassed. His gaze meets mine. The sun sets behind us, but the fiery color casts shadows across the front yard, making this moment feel like it could last forever.

"I never properly thanked you for that—or for giving me your entire basket of strawberries that day," I reply, only half joking. I never did tell Memaw what happened, but the next evening, we baked a strawberry pie fit for first place at the county fair, and I brought a slice to Levi at lunch. That was my thank-you. We never talked about it again. Until now, of course, nearly a decade later.

Levi shrugs, the corner of his lips tugging up. "I'd do it all over again, Callie." He pauses, his palm cupping his jaw. "I should've never stopped defending you. If I could do it again, I wouldn't have let you slip away."

When our eyes meet, every bit of shame woven through me, every year of isolation, every moment of pain these last few weeks, they stop buzzing inside me, calmed by the words Levi has poured before me.

"Thinking about the past only causes pain; trust me," I advise. "I pushed you away, too."

Levi leans closer, pushing hair out of my eyes. "Then no more of it, yeah? Let's leave it in the past and talk about *now*. Like how I'm starving. Let me get you food." He smiles softly, and I have to blink hard to pull myself back to now.

"I won't say no . . . but I'm a freaking mess." I half-laugh, half-cry, covering my face with my hands.

Levi moves from the step and squats in front of me, pulling my hands away from my face. "There will be none of that. You were the prettiest girl back then, and you're still the prettiest now. Maybe you inhaled smoke, too, Callie. I mean, if you can't see it." He smirks.

I swat his shoulder playfully. He extends his hand, palm up to me, and I place my hand in it. Levi pulls me to my feet as I dust off imaginary dirt from my clothes, unable to make eye contact with him.

"You're just being nice to me." I blush and turn away.

"I'm not always that nice."

I spin around. Levi has his phone in his hands now. My eyes dart from it to his apologetic face. "Levi, what did you do?"

"Don't be mad at me." He starts backing up, and I inch closer to him. "I texted Foster about thirty minutes ago when you were in the kitchen. He wants us to have dinner over there tonight with him."

"Okay," I start hesitantly. "That's fine with me." I try to read Levi's expression, unsure why I'd be mad over *that*.

"And..."

Of course, there is an and.

"He wants you to stay with him."

"What? Why was my lodging up for discussion? No, absolutely not." I scoff and turn away from Levi.

His fingers softly caress the back of my arm, and he nudges me to face him. "Hey, you said it yourself. You can't stay here. And you shouldn't. Foster cares about you. This was his idea. I know he's rough, but he cares. You don't have to stay there long. Just until you figure things out."

I consider this carefully, even though I know he is right. My eyes trail the driveway of the farmhouse. I can't see the blue mailbox from the front porch, but I know it's there.

If I leave this porch, if I get in the car and go to Foster's, I might not ever return. There's no reason to. This place doesn't belong to me. Not in the way I longed for it to.

I promised Opie we'd get out of here. I promised Opie I'd do better for him. And now he isn't here. But I still have to keep my promise. I have to do better for myself.

"Give me five minutes to pack my stuff."

Levi smiles softly at me, the kind of smile that makes me forget why I am so sad. I guess this is what it's like to let someone in.

It only takes me a few minutes to round up the very few items I have lying around the house. As Levi loads the boxes into my car, I stay inside, bracing for the goodbye. As I walk from room to room, my feet quietly padding on the wood floors, I know, in my heart, I'm ready. I said goodbye a long time ago, but somehow this feels different. This place is full of memories, both some of my favorite and some of the worst I've ever had. They hide in every wall, around every corner, in the chair by the front door, and in the kitchen sink in the back.

I'm glad there are no memories of Opie in this house, though.

"All done out here!" Levi hollers from the driveway, and I glance over my shoulder at him through the open front door.

This is it, Cal.

I slip on my sandals and pull the front door shut behind me. Levi's leaning on my car door, his hair messy and eyes soft. He waits patiently, like always.

"I'm ready," I say, and he reaches out his hand.

I don't lock the door behind me. I'm not sure Mack has a key.

Chapter Thirty-Two

Waiting on the front porch, leaning against the wood column with a soda can hanging from his fingertips, is Foster. A feeling of safety envelops me as he stands there watching over his front yard, with Daisy and May in their respective, but lazy, spots next to him.

His demeanor shifts when I slowly get out of the car, and he sets his drink down and starts down the steps. The air is starting to chill, so I pull a sweatshirt over my head and look at Foster as he stops in front of me.

"How you doing, kid?" he asks and places a hand gingerly on my shoulder.

My first instinct is to shrug it away, but I stand there, grounded, and gaze back at him, unsure what to say exactly. All I know is the moment I pulled into this driveway, I felt safe.

That scares the shit out of me, but I have to trust it. I have to trust him . . . and myself.

"I've had better days," I muster up, joking, "but . . . I'm happy to be here."

Foster nods. His blue eyes are warm, and he pulls his hand back, resting it in his pocket. "Glad you're okay. Lucky you weren't in that camper when it caught fire." He shakes his head, his eyes going somewhere else before settling back on me.

We just look at each other, but Levi interrupts as he pops open my trunk and pulls out the old duffel bag I packed for tonight. Foster looks quickly between the two of us, but I say nothing. I just thank Levi.

Foster leads us inside and points down the hall to the very last door. "You can take the guest room. There's a bathroom connected. There are towels and whatever you need. Levi can show you." He stops, and I follow Levi to the guest room. He drops the duffel on the bed.

"I'll give you a few to settle in." He smiles and closes the door behind him, giving me some space. It's an odd feeling to be in this area of Foster's home. It feels intimate and private, and my heart starts to quicken as I unpack my toiletries.

But moments later, there's scratching and loud sniffing at the big, pine door. I chuckle to myself and pull the door open. Daisy and May come bounding in, both immediately vying for my attention. Maybe it won't be so bad since they are here with me.

As I pet them, I take a look around the guest room. It looks pristine, way more put together and well-decorated than I thought Foster was capable of. There's no way Foster picked out the green bedspread and matching drapes. No, of course he didn't. He once had a wife only a few years ago. Beth Calloway lived here, too, before their separation. I heard through gossip at the diner that Beth and Foster separated the year Everett was in physical rehabilitation. The news back then was too hard to swallow. Now, in this room, clearly decorated by Beth, the reality settles in. I push away the pain of that realization and kiss May on the head.

I'm sure if it was up to Foster, this entire cabin would look like the inside of a camping store.

I don't bother unpacking. I just set up my phone charger on the nightstand. I don't plan on staying here long. It's nice. It's beyond nice, actually, for Foster to open up his home to me, but I can't overstay my welcome.

Two soft knocks sound on the open doorframe, and I look up to see Levi. My stomach flutters when I see him.

Levi gazes around the room, laughing when his eyes land on Daisy and May, who've taken up residency on the wood floors near my feet. I'm completely boxed in.

"Foster told me once that he thought these two would make better therapy dogs than search dogs."

"Oh, yeah. Why's that?" I question, squatting down to scratch their wrinkly heads.

Levi sniffs, his voice getting quiet. "He said they always know when someone needs them. They cling to certain people."

I stop petting May and look at Levi, who's biting his bottom lip, staring at me like he might've said too much.

He isn't wrong. I need them. I need everyone. And that's a hard pill to swallow.

"Hmm." I kind of laugh, and Levi narrows his eyes, confused by my reaction, I think. "You know, I spent all my life thinking if I just distanced myself from everyone, no one would associate me with my father. Like maybe I could disappear into the background and be a loner. But look at me now. Center of attention." I laugh ironically.

"Callie, you could never fade into the background."

My breathing shallows, and our eyes meet. I'm still kneeling between the dogs, and he's leaning against the doorframe. His eyes glisten, like he's looking at the stars and they are reflecting back at him. But he's just looking at me.

I know I told Levi I'd think about going to Charleston. And I meant that. I'm going to think about it. But I wonder if he realizes, when he says things like that, when he looks at me like he is . . . that he makes leaving even more complicated for my heart.

Oversized brown paper bags sit on the kitchen island, stamped with a logo that I could draw in my sleep. I look expectantly at Foster, but he throws his hands up.

"I went by the diner earlier today, looking for you, and Peg sent this home with me. I think she sent the whole menu to be honest," he remarks, eyeing all the food on the counter. "She told me to drop them off for you, but once Levi told me where you were staying . . . Well, either way, I hope you know you're welcome here. As long as you need." He doesn't make eye contact as his fingers drum on the other countertop.

"Thanks, Foster," I reply, and we exchange polite grins.

He nudges the food toward me. "Well, help yourself."

Grabbing plates, we each fill them up. My appetite is slowly coming back. I guess I feel safe here . . . with them.

"Shit, she sent the sweet potato casserole? That's my favorite," Levi says, scooping some.

I chuckle, rolling my eyes at him.

"Oh, my god, the brisket. I would kill for this."

"Let me guess. It's your favorite?" I tease, and Foster laughs. "Did I tell you that the first time I served Levi at the diner, he ordered eight different dishes?"

"What the hell's wrong with you, son?" Foster jokes, his eyes narrowing at Levi, who pretends to shoot me a dirty look.

"All this muscle requires a lot of calories. And I ordered it because I knew doing so would make Callie smile."

I feel myself grow red and change the subject. "This was really nice of her." I shovel French fries and green beans onto my plate, and then we all take a seat around the table.

"You've got people on your side. News spreads quickly in this town, and people want to help you," Foster adds.

"Hmm . . ." I still find it hard to believe.

"You're stuck with us now, whether you like it or not." Levi winks at me as he picks up another drumstick. My cheeks flush.

We eat quietly. The only noise is the country station playing on the radio. I think they both know by now I don't want to talk about the fire, or Mack, or the gaping hole in my heart that is Opie.

But it becomes crystal clear to me in that moment that these two men sitting before me, they are who I have to lean on. They'd do anything for me, which is still not easy for me to accept. But I feel myself wanting to open up to them.

I need to say something as we all sit here, like a weird, but incredible, dysfunctional family brought together by neglect and fear and hope and courage and loss. I have to tell them something, something I hope won't hurt them.

"Thank you for all of this. Really . . . I . . . I'm overwhelmed by it."

Even in all the loss, I gained them. I look across the table at Foster, who I know now would give the shirt off his back for me, who is rough and quiet at times but is really just a protective father.

Even of those who aren't his own blood.

And Levi. The quiet boy who used to play with me on the playground and invited me for ice cream after school, who still smiled at me after the accident. The selfless guy who hiked mountains to search for Opie and spent a whole weekend putting up lost dog signs. The only person who I've let hold me in years and who's seen me at my lowest.

If Opie had never run away, I wouldn't have found a way back to Levi. I wouldn't have found a friend who texts me when they know I'm not okay, who cares about my photography and if I've eaten that day. I wouldn't know I could still feel *something* for someone the way I do Levi.

Whatever that feeling is, it's growing inside me.

Levi and Foster begin talking to each other about something I don't know, and I let myself shut my eyes. When I do, I see Opie's amber eyes, swirling with life and curiosity. I feel his breath on my leg as he walks next to me and hear his paws softly pad along the dirt trail to the creek. But he keeps walking ahead of me and doesn't turn around. I open my eyes, my vision blurred, my heart pounding in my chest.

I wish I knew what this all meant.

Levi and Foster are still talking. Levi smiles, amused and animated over a story he's telling Foster. I clear my throat because if I don't, I might choke on the tears threatening to spill over.

They both look at me anyway, forks floating above their plates.

"You all right, Cal?" Levi asks, eyebrows knitted together.

I lay my paper napkin in my lap. It dampens and crinkles in my clamped fist. "I think I need to go." I swallow hard as I stare at the food on my plate.

"What are you talking about?" Foster begins, scooting forward in his chair, eyes crinkling with concern.

"I mean, I need to leave Miscruz Hills. I promised Opie I would get us out of here. I owe him that. I owe myself that. I just don't know how to leave." I pause and glance at Foster, who looks frozen in his chair. "It's been a month, Foster. A month of no Opie . . . and . . ."

He puts his hand up to silence me. "Do you trust me, Callie?" he asks, his voice clear and his eyes pointedly on me as he straightens in the dining chair. It's the kind of question that silences my mind and causes me to pause and sit up straight too.

"Yes, I do."

It's both frightening and comforting how easily that admittance comes forth from me.

He nods earnestly. "Then you need to go. Tomorrow you can call the school and accept the spot you've earned. You're going to Charleston, and I'll be here. Right *here*. Looking for Opie," Foster convicts.

A small whimper leaves my chest, and I pull my lips in. Because what he says breaks me.

I know he is right, but that doesn't make it hurt less. It doesn't make it less scary to leave Opie behind.

"I'm not giving up on him. And I can't let you give up on you. Do you understand?" Foster narrows his eyes a bit, his voice and face all business. But his words are all love.

I nod, unable to speak.

"And that makes two of us. I'm not giving up either, Callie," Levi adds.

I offer him a tiny grin because it hurts. All of it hurts. In a way I didn't know could hurt. Stitching my broken heart back together aches in a way I never knew possible. I have nothing to offer these two, and yet they keep pouring into me.

I've never had anyone fight for me so that I can breathe, too.

"What if he's gone?" I ask, my voice small. It's a question I can barely comprehend, barely be okay with, something I can't accept. But it's something I have to ask.

Foster takes a deep breath. "If he is gone, then I want you to know you did everything you could to find him. That you left no stone unturned. That you left, like you promised him you would."

"Don't give up hope yet, Callie. Charleston needs your brilliant work," Levi chimes in.

I laugh, rolling my tear-filled eyes at him.

He nudges me with his foot under the table. "Come on. It's time to stop being so humble."

I allow a tiny sliver of excitement to ripple through me, thinking about Charleston and all that it means. I'll have to find a job right away. Maybe I can rent a room or stay in a motel until I find something more stable.

But then reality sets in. I lost *everything* in the fire, and for a moment, these two lifted me up and filled me with so much love that I forgot about all that was lost. My face falls, and they can read it on me instantly.

"I can't go."

"What?" they both speak at once.

"Everything got destroyed in the fire. I don't have what I need for school. I don't even have a place to stay or a way to pay for tuition." Silence befalls the table, and I take a sharp inhale.

I hate how pathetic this makes me feel.

Foster pushes back his chair and walks to the kitchen cabinets silently. Levi and I watch him as he bends down to open something that sounds like a safe. I turn to Levi, confused, but he just shrugs. He returns a minute later, tossing an envelope down in front of me. The same one I handed him with all the money I paid for his services.

I don't touch it. *I'm not taking it.*

"Foster, what is this?" I ask, even though I know.

"It's your money. I've been holding onto it."

"I don't understand. You *earned* this money. You've been working for me."

"I was going to charge you like a normal client. But that day you sat right there, eating pancakes, telling me that you would not let *me* give up . . . that's the day I decided I'm not letting you give up either. I'm not taking your money, Callie. This was never about the money. This is about bringing home your best friend."

My fingertips gingerly run across the top of the paper envelope. It looks untouched. I know exactly how much is in there without counting it. I counted it multiple times on the hood of my car before I placed it in there.

I'd do it again. I'd do all of it again for Opie.

I don't know what I did to deserve this kindness from either of them.

I feel Levi and Foster looking at me, patiently waiting for me to say something. *How do you thank someone for saving you when you didn't even know you needed saving?*

"I don't know what to say." I smirk as my eyes meet Levi's.

"You don't need to say nothing to us, but you do have a call to make." Foster nods at me, looking over his eyebrows.

I bite my cheek to keep my grin at bay. This is not how it was supposed to be, but I'm accepting this is how it is.

Chapter
Thirty-Three

After dinner, Levi and I sit on the front porch with the dogs. He seems so at home here, sitting on the porch swing next to me. My legs barely touch the wood deck, but his do, and he keeps us rocking slowly. He's brought out a red woven blanket and has draped it over our legs as the sun starts to disappear in the sky. There's real peace here, and for a moment, I picture Levi and I with a home of our own like this. The thought startles me, so I push it aside.

"I'm completely unprepared for this. I don't even have pajamas... or a camera!" I laugh, but dread fills me inside.

Dreams are beautiful things, but reality is a bitch.

Levi clicks his tongue, turning to me and smiling. "Looks like we have to make a trip, then." He looks way too happy about that.

"We? You don't strike me as the shopping kind," I poke fun at him. He shakes his head back and forth. I sometimes wonder if this boy was born into this world with a grin on his face.

"Well shoot, Callie. You're not going to leave me out of the fun, are you? How about we take a trip up to Asheville tomorrow? I need to grab a few things anyway."

I only have to think about it for a split second before deciding yes. A month ago, I would've cringed at the idea of anyone coming with me to do anything. I hated that our grocery store didn't even have a self-checkout, forcing me to interact with people. But I find myself happy to be with Levi.

I guess the right kind of person can make you feel that way.

"Yeah, I'd like that."

He smiles, his honey-colored eyes sparkling as he does.

"Levi, can I ask you something?" My thumb rubs against the metal chain of the swing as I catch the worry in my voice.

"Anything," he replies.

"Do you think I'm making the right choice? Leaving like this."

Levi stops rocking us and leans his elbows on his legs as he thinks for a moment. I don't interrupt, just watch him intently.

"I think you're finally choosing *you*," he says after a moment.

I know that should make me feel better, but I can't shake the guilt festering inside my heart. "My dog is missing, and I'm leaving," I rebut.

I'm being selfish. I'm abandoning Opie.

Levi sits up, twisting in his seat to look at me. His hand settles over mine on the blanket, and my heart catches in my chest.

"Whatever negative thoughts you're feeling toward yourself, they aren't true. Your dog *is* missing, and you are leaving . . . but you're by no means giving up. You're the most selfless person I know."

My chest feels heavy with his words. I stay silent.

"You know, Opie's really lucky."

As always, my heart squeezes when I hear his name. *Opie.* I'm forever grateful that Levi doesn't talk about him like he is something of the past. He is still out there—in the trees or the mountains. He is somewhere, staring up at the same moon as me every night. We just have to find our way home to each other.

"Why's that?" I swallow my tears away and ask as *some* foreign emotion replaces my sadness and shame.

Levi's hand envelops mine, and he squeezes it once. "He's got someone who would do anything for him. Someone who really loves him. What more could anyone want?"

We stay silent, listening to the summer song of the cicadas. Everything in my vision goes narrow as Levi leans in toward me, pausing briefly to cradle my neck in his hands.

That feeling . . . Maybe it's love.

My heart stops beating as I feel the heat of his lips come close to mine. Our lips barely brush against each other, but the moment is interrupted by the front door creaking open.

Foster steps out, engrossed in his phone, and I quickly stand up, the blanket dropping as Levi runs a hand through his hair. My cheeks are still flushed, and blood courses through my veins.

Foster says something, but I don't hear him. Because the feeling of Levi's mouth on mine has consumed me, and I can't bring myself down.

How long has Levi wanted to kiss me like that?

I sensed it, but it was easy to dismiss because I was too busy trying to find Opie, too busy worrying about what everyone else was thinking of me, what Mack was doing.

"I'm heading to bed. Just lock up when you come in. 'Night, y'all," Foster says.

I nod diligently, humiliated by something that *almost* happened. I turn to Levi once Foster's inside, but he is already standing, folding the blanket and setting it on the swing. Standing there, stunned, I pull my arms across my chest and look away.

"I should get going actually. We have an early start tomorrow," Levi reminds me, and I get nervous butterflies thinking about spending tomorrow in Asheville with him.

One moment at a time, Callie.

I walk beside Levi to his car, where he opens the driver's door. He pauses, leaning against the frame. Reaching out, Levi pulls me by the hand, bringing me closer to him, and I move like I have no self-control.

"Maybe I can try that again," he whispers.

I don't say anything, just smirk, looking up at his hazel eyes as the stars dot the sky above us.

Levi cradles my face in his hands, his lips landing softly on mine. I settle my hands on his hips, steadying myself against his strong, tall body.

I don't think anyone is prepared to go through the range of emotions I have in the last twenty-four hours.

I come up from the kiss feeling breathless, missing the heat of his body against mine the moment he pulls back. It was just one kiss, but it felt like years of emotions settled in the mere moments our lips touched.

"Goodnight, Levi." I smile gently as he nods at me, and we slowly part ways, but when I look back at him, he's still looking up at me.

That night, as I settle into a bed that's not mine, I have a hard time falling asleep. Daisy and May find their place on the bed with me, and I leave the curtains open so I have a view of the trees and stars.

It's been mere hours since deciding I'd go to Charleston. My mind is still reeling with all I need to do and mentally prepare for. And my heart, that's another story.

That kiss.

I'm slowly coming to terms with the fact I'm not just leaving Opie here either. I'm leaving Foster and Levi.

Through the windows, the landscape I've memorized lays before me, and a sense of truth settles in my gut. This is what I know to be true: Opie's in these waters. He's in the mountain air and the buzz of this sleepy town. There are endings and new beginnings. The fire ended something. A lot of things really, but it ended the home I thought I had. Though it was really never home. It was just a crutch, a place for Opie and me to find our footing in the world. Or maybe just my footing, because I think Opie knew right away what his mission in life was: to love endlessly, forgive without question, and to make me smile when the world was cruel.

Tomorrow is a new beginning, but it doesn't mean I'll ever give up my search for Opie. He saved me in a way no one else ever could, and I have to believe our story together isn't over yet.

No, I'm not giving up. But I am moving on.

And as I drift asleep, I'm still trying to trust that those two things can coexist.

Chapter Thirty-Four

The next morning, Levi picks me up, and I run down the front steps of Foster's house to greet him like it's something I do every day.

It feels natural.

We drive out of town. The small back roads merge onto bigger highways, leading right to the city. I mentioned yesterday to Levi that there is a store in Asheville that sells used camera equipment. He takes me straight there and patiently peruses the shelves with me. I settle on one that isn't as great as my first camera, though nothing could compare to it. Buying this camera is the first step toward my future. The first time I choose me.

But Levi reminds me, as we head out of the store, that I am choosing me again today.

The sun shines on us as we walk the city streets, heading to lunch. I tell Levi we can just grab a sandwich and explore a park, but he insists on taking me to a restaurant, one where we sit down and get waited on. During lunch, Levi asks me a million and one questions about Charleston Photography Co.

At first, I give him simple answers, but he won't accept it. He keeps asking. He keeps pulling words from me until I feel myself open up and accept it. I'm excited about this. Nervous as hell, but excited. On the back of the receipt, Levi writes a list of places and eateries to try in Charleston. He put stars next to a few of them, and when I ask him what it's for, he says very seriously that I can't try those places—not until he comes to visit and can take me himself.

Levi pays for lunch and for the afternoon in Asheville. Everything feels light.

Maybe this is how it can feel, being somewhere new.

On the car ride back, we crank the windows down, letting the summer sun soak us in its rays.

"You know, Charleston doesn't have these mountains. I spent a summer with my grandparents in Wilmington, and man, I missed these hills. Kinda took it all for granted," Levi remarks as we wind through the Blue Ridge Mountains we call home.

I hum a song while looking out the window, letting the breeze wash over my face. *I think I want a chance to miss this.*

"You might miss it . . . *though* on second thought, the city fits you, Callie." He looks at me contemplatively, and I feel myself blush under his watch.

"Yeah? Let's hope so. I don't know the first thing about city living."

"You'll be fine. I promise. And I'm just a phone call away."

"Thanks, Levi." I smile back at him and then down at the camera equipment between my feet. I hope he is right. I always believed that new places would fill me with hope, with the promise of a new beginning.

A blank slate, like when you first uncap the lens of a camera.

"I'll miss some things. But I'm excited, I think," I let myself say. I deserve to feel excited about this.

Levi reaches over and gives my leg a squeeze. It's his affectionate thing; it's what he does. Over the past weeks, I've picked up on a lot of little things Levi does.

I already miss Opie more than I can articulate, but now, my heart is going to have to make some more space because I think I'll miss Levi too.

That evening, when we arrive in Miscruz Hills, Levi helps me unload what I bought today. I didn't get much. Only the essentials.

It's crazy to think it's only been a couple of days since the fire. Grief comes to me in waves, and mostly when it's silent and I'm alone. At times, it feels like maybe I should be more upset, but after losing Opie, nothing really compares. With a plan to move forward, it's easier for me to see the truth of what I lost. It was just shirts and photos. Shampoo bottles and twinkle lights. *All of it is replaceable*, and I proved that today when I filled my bags at the shops with new stuff.

As for things that aren't replaceable in life, I feel well-versed. However, there is one very expensive thing I couldn't replace today—after calling the school and paying tuition—and I don't yet have a plan. I'm working on one when Foster knocks on the door of the guest room.

"So much for loyalty, huh?" he asks, scratching his newly grown beard and smirking at the two dogs curled up on the bed next to me. They are tired from today. Foster took a private job for an elderly couple who lost their dog. He left this morning, driving an hour away with Daisy and May. They were there for nearly six hours and found the dog shaken up but alive.

I gave the girls treats when he told me, bent down to scratch their ears, and told them they were good girls. Levi was right; Foster is really good at his job.

"To be fair, I am eating cookies in here," I admit, looking at the empty cookie box on the dresser.

"Well, anyway . . . I found this in my office. It's Everett's from his first year in school. He upgraded to some new, expensive thing, who knows, but it's just collecting dust." Foster extends his arm, holding a laptop out toward me.

My mouth falls open a bit. "Foster, I can't take that."

He places it on the dresser next to him, his eyebrows shooting up, which I've come to learn means he is serious. I imagine Everett didn't get away with anything in high school.

"You need a computer for school, right?" he asks bluntly.

I swallow and nod. "I do, yeah."

"Then don't question it. Take it."

"Thank you," I say, feeling like that's all I will ever say to him. There is simply too much to thank him for.

Chapter Thirty-Five

It's a chilly morning, unusually so for August. I pull my thick, red flannel tightly around my shoulders and get in the car, hoping I catch Peg before the Sunday breakfast rush. She graciously took me off the schedule after the fire, but I still haven't been in to talk to her about my availability. I've been dreading the chat, dreading telling her I'm leaving. Turns out, saying goodbye to Peg is harder than I imagined it would be.

The diner door chimes as I walk in. It's quiet with only the chatter of a few older women in the corner enjoying coffee and sizzling griddles. As I walk to the counter, Carla lifts her face from the coffee machine and smiles at me. I smile back as a bolt of guilt sears through me. Now that I'm leaving, it's become clear to me that I could've been friendlier to her.

Before I can say anything to Carla, the swinging door whooshes, and Peg walks out with a plate of biscuits, her eyes widening upon seeing me. She hurriedly drops the plates on a couple's table and beelines for me, wrapping her fingers softly around my wrist and guiding me to the back. Her perfume is sweet, and her white hair is piled extra high on her head this morning.

"Oh, sweetie. It's so good to see you," she says the moment we are in her office. Peg pulls me into a hug, and this time I let her, feeling her soft arms wrap around my shoulders as I hug her back.

"It's good to see you too, Peg."

She grips my shoulder but pushes me back, a worried look creasing her brow.

"Thanks for all the food the other night; that was really kind of you."

Peg waves it off. "It's the least I can do for you, Callie."

We exchange sad smiles, and she searches my face with her warm, brown eyes.

"I need to talk to you about my availability." I break the silence, nervously tracing circles on her green desk with my finger.

"Yes, yes. Take your time. I've got help covering all your shifts." She smooths her apron out.

I pause, wringing my hands together, and take a shallow breath. "The thing is, Peg . . . I'm actually not coming back." My mouth twists anxiously, feeling horrible for giving short notice.

Peg places her hand over mine. "Oh? Is everything okay?"

I nod. "Yes. It's good actually. I'm . . . I'm leaving Miscruz Hills. I got accepted into a photography program, and I'm moving to Charleston," I say and hold my breath as the weight of my words settle around me like dust.

Peg shrugs back, her hand now clutching the dainty gold cross necklace hanging from her neck. Suddenly, a smile spreads across her face. "You got in," she states in awe with a shine in her eyes.

"How did you know?" I ask, but then I remember who I'm talking to. She knows things about people in this town before they even know them.

"I hear everything, honey. You don't own a diner for fifty years and not become the queen of town gossip." She winks at me, then turns around to riffle through the papers on her desk. She pulls out an envelope and hands it to me. It's my paycheck that I forgot to pick up a few days ago.

"Go show Charleston who you are." She looks me up and down, and I laugh, feeling tears prick the corners of my eyes. "Chin up, sweet pea."

I nod, and this time, I pull her into a hug. "I'll visit. I promise."

Leaving without a trace is out of the question now. But somehow, this is better.

I wipe my eyes as Peg pulls her pad and paper from her apron and starts scratching a name and number. "Now I don't know where you're staying down there, but my neighbor's daughter, Megan, lives down there right outside town. She used to rent a room to college folks. It's worth reaching out, okay?" Peg rips the paper off and hands it to me.

I look down and smile. "Thank you, Peg. I appreciate the help."

Baby steps.

There is only one way to get to Foster's house from the diner. You have to pass the farm, which was easy enough to ignore on my way into town, with my mind obsessing over telling Peg goodbye. The farm and Mack have been easy enough to push out of my head since I've been getting everything together for school, making phone calls, getting my car checked.

I did work up the courage to ask Levi for one more favor. Of course, he didn't hesitate to say yes the moment I asked him to replace the ruined lost dog signs. I refuse to let anyone in this town forget about Opie's face. Every morning and every night, I still check all the lost dog forums, shelters, and vets. I'll keep going until there's a reason I shouldn't.

But today, as I pass the little blue mailbox on my way back from the diner, I feel a pulling, like a magnet, so I slow down and turn into the gravel driveway. I roll down my window slowly, feeling the breeze on my face as I hear the crunch of the pine needles under my tires. There's no rusted truck parked in front of the farmhouse, but a few crushed cans of beer line the porch railing. I sigh because somewhere deep inside me, I feel relief knowing Mack returned home. I don't want this land to be abandoned, even if he is barely living.

I pass the farmhouse, winding up the little dirt path that feels foreign, but I don't stop until I'm at the base of the trail to the creek. Getting out of the car, I quickly scan the shell of the trailer, half expecting an overwhelming sadness to wash over me. But there's nothing. I only see what once was and what is no longer.

But that's not what I came here for.

I start down the path to the creek. Rabbits dart under bushes as I approach, and the holes from Opie remain unscathed. If I close my eyes, I can almost feel him next to me, trotting along like he never left my side.

Water flows slowly today over the rocky creek bed, and the wind rustles the leaves with a gentleness that contrasts the rapid beating of my heart. As I scale the path to the water's edge, where Opie always slid into the water without a care in the world, silence falls around me.

This is the kind of day where I would've spent all afternoon with a camera around my neck and Opie trotting happily beside me. We would've stayed here until I couldn't take the hunger any longer, and we would've gone back to sit outside the camper under the strand of lights that paled in comparison to the stars. Opie would've fallen into a peaceful slumber, right next to my feet.

Rolling up my flannel sleeves, I bend down to dip my fingers into the water. The creek is cool, no matter the time of year, but today the iciness numbs my hand as my eyes well up. I stopped questioning weeks ago how many tears a human body can produce because, at times, I feel like this creek—endless with no source in sight.

The rock behind me is grounded in the earth, so I sit, gingerly pulling my knees to my chest, holding myself tight like I've done for so many years. Flipping my hair over my shoulder, I reach around my neck to unclasp the dainty chain that hangs from it. I got this necklace a few days after Opie wandered up to me. I had gone into the pawn shop to search for a trailer part when a single opal on a chain caught my eye. It was serendipitous, so I left the store with it around my neck, and I haven't taken it off since that day.

Until now.

Wiping a salty tear from my cheek, I watch the opal necklace pool in the palm of my open hand and stare at it.

"It's all for you, Opie," I whisper, feeling my voice vibrate in the confines of my rib cage.

I squeeze my fist around the opal and bring it to my lips, then place it on a crater in the boulder beside me. A shaky breath releases from inside me, bringing more tears to my face. But I don't try to stop them. I just feel. *Everything.* I let it flow from my heart through my veins and into this water.

Tipping my chin toward the clouds, I shut my eyes as a few sunrays peek through the clouds.

"We got into the photography program, Opie. We did it," I announce, a laugh escaping between the sobs. "I promised you, didn't I?" I wipe my running eyes on my sleeve. "I have to leave town tomorrow. But I'm not giving up on you. Levi and Foster are still looking for you, boy."

I pause, taking a deep breath.

"You'd love Foster. He seems mean at first, but he's not. He's kind. He'd love you too. When he finds you, you'll see. You can trust him, Opie."

My fingertips mindlessly draw swirls on the rock beneath me.

"You might be jealous of Levi now, though. He is always with me. Just like you were. You'll remember him. He's like you, Ope . . . a ray of sunshine."

I talk to the wind for a little while longer. For so long, Opie was all I had. And then all I had was the traces of him.

And now I'm not alone. *Because of him.* His disappearance brought people into my life that I never knew I needed. Even in his absence, Opie is finding ways to save me.

"I love you, Opie. Wherever you are, boy." I kiss my palm and place it in the water, hoping it will carry my love to him.

Chapter Thirty-Six

I can't help but wonder, as my tires crunch the gravel and the farmhouse comes back into view, if this will *actually* be the last time I drive away from here. My childhood home is occupied by a man who never felt like *home*, and my other home is in a crisp pile of rubble and ash.

I can't fathom a reason to come back.

Mack's truck sits haphazardly parked under the oak tree in the front yard. I take one long stare at it and then slow the car until I'm merely inching toward the road so I can turn around and look at the house. Somehow when you're saying goodbye, everything looks different, more clear—like goodbyes awaken the senses, like I can see all the details I once missed.

I want to remember this place the way it was when Memaw was alive. With the scents of her baking filling the kitchen, her contagious laughter on the front porch. That's how I'll choose to always keep this place in my heart.

As I'm getting ready to gun it out of here, having soaked up enough visuals of a place that's nothing but bittersweet, I notice Mack waving his only good arm back and forth, signaling me. My brows stitch together, and I think about ignoring him, but the better half of me pumps the brake, keeping my hands firmly on the wheel as he saunters closer.

If only to keep them from shaking.

"Carolina, wait!" Mack yells.

My heart stings as it always does when Mack says my name. *My mother's name.*

He's out of breath. His beard is unruly, his hair needs combing, and his shirt is stained with grease. When he stops beside my car, I put it in park, and for reasons I can't explain, I get out. Mack shifts uncomfortably on his feet as I shut the door and lean against the side of my car, arms tightly over my chest.

"What is it, Mack?"

"I just need to tell you something," he sputters.

My heart pounds as I stare at him. I say nothing, waiting for him to speak first.

Mack scratches his beard, his eyes nervously tracing lines on the ground between us. "You got to believe me. The fire was an accident. I was just looking for some change and dropped my damn cigarette. Shit luck I've got." His lips curl like it's funny.

Heat rushes up my throat, and I swallow, digging my boots into the ground, attempting to stay standing. *Don't let him see you bend, Callie.*

As my mind whirls with how to possibly respond, wondering what Mack is possibly *expecting* from me, he opens his mouth.

"Letting the dog out was an accident too."

The words rush over me like floodwaters, drowning my senses. A dull buzzing sounds in my ears, and all I see is red as my father sways in front of me.

"M-my dog?" I stammer, taking an unsteady step toward Mack.

His red-rimmed eyes widen.

"You have two seconds to explain yourself, so help me . . ."

Mack's arm goes up like a white flag, and his chest puffs up. "I didn't know he'd run out like that! Honest to God, it was an accident!" Mack fires back, with no right to be angry.

My fists start to shake by my sides as hurt courses through my limbs. "All this time and you knew! Why didn't you tell me? How, Mack? How?" Disbelief turns into confusion and anger as Mack stutters and takes another step away from me.

"We ran out of beer, and Wendy thought to check your trailer. I didn't break in, if that's what you're thinking. I knocked, but you were gone, and the damn door wasn't even latched—it flew right open! The dog bolted out. I hollered for him, but he never even looked back!"

Of course, he didn't. Opie knew better. I trained him not to trust Mack. Opie was only doing what I always showed him was right.

The ringing in my ears grows louder, and I can't functionally think of a reply. He's the reason Opie is gone. Every night, I beat myself up over not fixing the door latch. The confusion I felt over why Opie would just leave me like that. The hope I held for him, and the hope I still wrongfully harnessed for Mack.

I now see my mistake wasn't that I had hope in him. My mistake was not remembering Mack's ability to destroy everything in his path.

I can't let him destroy me. Not when I'm this close to getting out.

I wish I could say I had the right words to hurl at him. That there were words in the English language that would convey the hurt raging in me like a wildfire. But my mouth comes up empty, my tongue is dry, and my eyes sting as I peel them away from the man standing in front of me.

At one point, I thought my father would see the light of day. That me moving out, leaving him all alone, would be a wake-up call. But I was wrong. I was wrong all this time.

It's time I leave this mess. I won't let Mack haunt me anymore, showing up in shadows where the light should be shining. He may be the reason that everything crumbled around me the last six years, the reason I lost Opie, and at times myself. But I'm going to be the reason this cycle ends *now*.

I leave the conversation without another breath, pulling the car door closed behind me. I don't say goodbye to the house, to the last spot I saw Opie, or to the front porch Memaw rocked me on. The things I love, the people and animals I cherish—they aren't *here*. They live inside my heart now.

And I'm carrying them all out of here with me.

Chapter Thirty-Seven

Ten minutes pass before I can get out of my car. I've been parked in Foster's driveway, staring out the window with my seat belt still on. What's done is done; Mack's made his choices. He's destroyed all he can, but I still have my choice—my choice to keep moving. So I center myself as best as I can and get out.

When I walk into the house, Foster is perched in a worn leather chair by the stone fireplace with a book propped in his lap. It's quiet, except for the low hum of music on the radio and the jangle of collars when Daisy and May lift their heads at my arrival.

He smiles briefly at me over his book, and I drop my head down in response, biting my lip, and walk into the kitchen to get water. A few minutes later, after I've drank nearly two glasses, Foster comes in, his novel tucked into the nook of his arm.

I was fine when I left the farm. Well, not *fine*, but I was feeling confident and strong in my decisions. But now, in the quiet of this house, the urgency of everything strikes me. Time isn't on my side, and there's something I need to say to Foster. Something I can't leave town without addressing.

I can't leave things unsaid. Not to the people who deserve to hear them most.

The tears beat me to it, though, and start streaming down my face as I turn away from Foster and set the glass cup down, gripping the back of the wooden kitchen chair. My eyes rake over photographs of Everett on the wall. There's one that looks recent with him in a wheelchair and Foster next to him, both smiling at the camera with fish in their hands as they stand next to a lake. These pictures in here aren't new. I just haven't been able to look at them for more than a second. Until now.

"I'm sorry about what happened to Everett," I say simply, my eyes never leaving the face of the handsome young man in the photos.

Foster clears his throat, coming closer, standing at the other end of the round table. The table feels like a sea between us, a barrier I'm not sure how to cross. For a while, I don't think he'll reply, his eyes also lingering on the photos. A small smile tugs at his lips finally.

"We never blamed you, Callie. I need you to understand that," he insists, but instantly I fight back.

"I was in that car. I knew Mack had been drinking, and I got in the car. I naively thought he'd be smart enough to let me drive. I never imagined..." I can't finish my sentence, though, and cover my mouth with my palm.

Foster leans across the table toward me. "Callie, you were just a kid. None of it was your fault. And I'm sorry people have led you to believe it was. He was your father. He should've protected you! What he did is unimaginable, and yet it happened to you." Foster shakes his head.

Tears blur my vision. "But it destroyed Everett's life. And you...you and your wife...you two divorced...all because of the accident." I can't hold it back anymore. The wall collapses, and with it comes the surge of shallow breaths that threaten to knock me to the ground.

Foster rushes over, pulling out the seat next to me, his hand guiding me to sit at the table—the same table his family all used to eat together at before everything.

"Callie, listen to me." Foster's voice is stern as he sits next to me. We face knee to knee, and my eyes snap to his. "Mack would've wrecked that night with or without you in the car. If he hadn't hit the shop and Everett, it would've been someone else in town. Another innocent person. And if not that night, then another time. Do you understand?" he asks, his voice strained but stern as he searches my face, and I nod. "Your father . . . he is reckless and put you in harm's way. But not once did I or Everett or Beth blame *you*."

Silence befalls us as our eyes lock in on each other. I know this hurts. And I hate that I've brought this back into his life, that I'm a reminder of everything.

"I don't understand how you can take me in like this." I bite my lip hard.

Foster leans back in his seat and shakes his head for a moment, and I know he remembers that terrible night as well as I do. His voice goes soft as he leans forward.

"When Everett was in the hospital, just one floor below your father, he received a lot of visitors. His room was overflowing with flowers, cards, cookies—everyone showed up for him."

I don't understand why he is telling me this, but I keep listening.

"One day, after he was there for a few nights, I got word that your father was being discharged and taken away in handcuffs."

I nod ever so slightly because I remember that day in a haze. *I was at the hospital too that day, but not to bid Mack farewell.*

"I watched from my son's window as Mack got taken away into custody. It didn't help me feel any better, though, as Everett lay there being told he would never walk again with a year of rehab ahead of him. It couldn't take away that pain." Foster balls his fist and clears his throat, his glossy eyes searching my face. "But as I was leaving the room, needing a moment alone, I saw you."

I look at him as he stares back at me, and my heart skips a beat, my lungs restricting in my chest.

"You were standing at the nurses' station with a bouquet of flowers in your hands. A bouquet of yellow sunflowers. There was no card attached, no way to know who they were from. I only know they were from you because I saw you leave them with the nurse." A single tear rolls down Foster's face, and he quickly wipes it. He looks away from me. "You had a black eye from the wreck. And I remember worrying about who was looking after you. My heart broke for you, Callie."

It all comes rushing back to me. The smell of the gift shop, picking sunflowers for Everett. Writing *I'm sorry* in a card but throwing it out before handing it to the nurse. And leaving the hospital that day alone.

Foster continues. "Has anyone ever told you that you look like your mother?" he asks.

I freeze. It never occurred to me that Foster knew my mama. She moved here as a teenager after being in the foster care system, and after Memaw passed, there was no one to talk with about her. Especially not my father.

"I haven't heard that in a long time." I sniff, my lips tugging up gently.

"Your mom was one of the kindest people I ever met. She lit up a room with her laugh. She had every boy in town falling for her, and I'm not embarrassed to say I was one of them. She just had a way of making everyone feel special. But as you know, she only had eyes for Mack." He shakes his head with half a smile on his face.

"I didn't know . . . any of this," I mutter, trying to piece it together.

"Callie, all I'm saying is you're nothing like *him*. You've got all the goodness of you, of your mother, and your memaw in you. And you're going places. If anyone can take a crappy hand and make it into something, it's you. You're going to be okay. Understand?"

I wonder if he knows how badly I want to understand, to fully believe, it will all be okay.

"How are you so sure?" I question, wishing I could steal some of his confidence in me and bottle it up.

"Because I'm not going to let you fall. Like it or not, you're part of the family now."

I pinch my lips together. *Family.*

Foster lightens the mood. Despite the tears and the heaviness of all that's surrounding us, after all that has brought us together, we're both still trying to figure out how to convey how we feel. I think we are learning from each other.

"And don't get me started on my nephew. My god, that boy thinks you hung the moon."

He rolls his eyes, and a warmness bubbles up in me, and I feel myself hiding a blush.

"I know. I'm lucky to have him. Both of you." That's all I have to say, and Foster and I exchange a nod with a knowing look.

He squeezes my shoulder, and when I close my eyes, it's nothing but yellow sunflowers.

Around six that evening, after much of my packing is done and Foster has checked my car twice to make sure I'll make it the six-hour drive to Charleston, he asks if I want to get dinner at the diner. One last hurrah, as he puts it.

I don't really want to go to the diner again. I've already said my goodbye to Peg and eaten enough food off that menu for a lifetime. But Foster has on a shirt that actually appears ironed, so I say yes and pull out a new outfit I bought on my trip to Asheville.

I'll be leaving tomorrow, giving me a few days to settle in before classes begin. Foster sat me down this afternoon, making sure I had everything I needed, something my own father has never done. He told me the places I shouldn't go and the places I must see. He wrote down the number of a mechanic he knows down there and reminded me again that he's only a phone call away.

It's no secret Foster is a great dad to Everett. I'd heard many stories about how he retired to dedicate all his time to being with his son through his rehab, retrofitting the cabin so Everett could navigate in his wheelchair. He is the kind of father a person dreams of having.

And somehow, along the way, I went from fearing him and being skeptical of his motives to knowing what it feels like to be cared for by Foster. I have a glimpse of what it feels like to have a father. I'm not used to it, and I still fight the instinct to push him away, to tell him I'm fine, to remind him I've survived all these years on my own. But the truth is, losing Opie showed me one thing. *To no longer want to be alone isn't weak.*

And though I'm going to Charleston by myself, I'm not alone. So when he asked me to have dinner with him, I said yes. Because he's done more for me than I could ever repay him for.

"My, my, my, if it isn't our little photographer!" Peg exclaims, slapping her hands to her hips when I walk through the door ahead of Foster.

Carla beams at me, and I smile back, waving quietly.

"I had to have just one more meal. I'll miss this place," I say for the sake of Peg, but as I do, it rings true. It hits me in the gut. I *will* miss this place.

Even on the most painful days, when all I saw here were reminders of my past, Peg invited me with open arms and provided a safe place for me to work. Because of her diner, I was able to save for my great escape and pay Foster to search for Opie.

I let Peg hug me again.

"Put them in the good booth," she instructs Carla, winking and smiling at me before she greets the next customer.

I have to laugh. To Peg, the "good" booth is the one in the front window, where you can see all of Main Street. I used to feel bad for people who sat there, thinking they must feel like fish in a tank. But tonight, when I scoot in across from Foster and peer down the tree-lined street, I feel something different—I'm proud to sit across from him.

"Anything you want, it's on me. We have to send you off right." Foster smiles briefly before pulling the menu in front of his face, blocking my view of him.

I don't need to see the menu. I could recite it in my sleep. So I glance outside. My eyes catch the several white pieces of paper with my boy's face on it.

Lost Dog. Responds to Opie. Do not chase. The number has been changed from my number to Foster's. I don't know when Levi found the time in the last few days since he's been busy in the print shop, but he did. He replaced almost all the signs down Main Street with new ones.

We aren't giving up, Opie.

"How's the Oreo creme pie here?" Foster asks, putting down the menu.

I tilt my head at him. "You've never had Peg's famous pies?" I tease.

Foster shakes his head, taking a sip of water. "When Everett was in high school, he came here all the time. It was *his* place. You know, I was the uncool dad. I couldn't hang out in the same place as the football team," he says, shrugging.

I laugh, even though I don't fully understand. I think I would've loved to have anyone to eat dinner with in high school. The closest Mack and I ever got to sharing dinner was when he'd order pizza and pass out on the couch before it was finished. I'd sit in the chair watching TV, finishing the pizza, while he drunkenly snoozed a few feet from me.

I think dinner with Foster would've been nice.

"Are you going to see Everett soon?" I ask, letting myself feel uncomfortable for a moment, as this is all still so fresh.

Foster's face lights up as he rolls the straw paper in his fingers. "Yeah, actually. Next weekend, he's coming up. He's bringing home his girlfriend for the first time," Foster responds, and I think I detect nervousness in his voice for the first time.

"That's good, right?"

"Yeah. It will be nice to have him home for a bit." He smiles, nodding as our server comes over.

"You two ready to order?" she asks.

I am about to tell her what I want when Foster gestures toward the window.

"Actually, we are waiting for one more person," he reveals.

I follow his eyes out the window where, sure enough, a tall guy with a grin on his face is crossing the street. To my mortification, he's holding a bouquet of balloons and a present. I want to duck my head under the table and army-crawl out the back door, but it's too late because he sees us looking and he nods his head at me. Even from inside, I can see his dimple and hazel eyes staring right back at me.

I cross my arms and put my head down on the table momentarily before Foster lets out a full-bellied laugh, something I've never heard before.

"You know it wouldn't be a proper send-off without him, Callie," he elaborates.

I lift my gaze to his. His eyes twinkle with mischief, and I know this is giving them both so much joy, so I give in. I was imagining a more intimate goodbye for Levi and me, but this is fitting too.

Levi pops inside the diner, his eyes lighting up when he rounds the corner and sees us. I cover my face with my hands for show and uncover them, smiling at him. He sets the balloons to the side and I cringe, but I manage to grin at Levi.

"I know you hate balloons. You said they were pointless. But I had a feeling you hate a bouquet of flowers even more, so I went with balloons. Plus, I wanted everyone to know you had something to celebrate." He smirks at me, and my stomach somersaults at his gaze.

I do hate balloons, but maybe it's only because no one's ever gotten me any.

"It's really thoughtful. Thank you."

Levi seems genuinely surprised and pleased as he sits next to me. I don't look at the gift bag Levi brought, hoping it's not for me, but I also feel bubbly with the thought that it is.

Like he's reading my mind, he turns to face me. "I got you a going-away gift."

My cheeks redden. "You know it's only for a few months."

"Yeah, but after you complete this program, you're going to be a hotshot. You'll get a fancy job in New York City or LA, and you'll forget about Miscruz Hills. Plus, it's nothing big. It's just something. Actually, it's two parts—"

"Just give the girl the gift," Foster juts in, and I smile graciously at him. He rolls his eyes at me as Levi nudges the gift bag toward me.

Under the billows of tissue paper, haphazardly thrown in there, I pull out a gift card. It's for a coffee shop I never heard of. I hold it gingerly in my hands and turn, confused.

"It's a coffee shop near the school. I won't be there to hand deliver you coffee anymore, but I thought if I could at least buy you it, that counts for something, yeah?" Levi explains.

My eyes mist, but I quickly blink away the oncoming tears as I sip my water before setting the gift card down. "Levi, this is truly the nicest thing anyone's ever gotten me."

And I mean it. My memaw used to bake me my favorite cake every birthday, but most Christmases and birthdays, there wasn't money for gifts.

Levi nods. "Had to make sure you had your caffeine fix. Here, there's something else." Levi pushes the bag closer to me, and my heart speeds up.

I hope I'm reacting the right way for receiving gifts.

Reaching in, my fingers land on something soft, and when I pull it out, my voice unexpectedly catches in my throat. I set the stuffed animal down on the table in front of me. It's a replica, down to the black spot over the right eye, of Opie. There's a tag around the dog's neck that says his name too.

"I know it's weird. It's what you would get a kid, so I totally get it if you don't want—"

This time *I* cut Levi off, wrapping my arms around him and pulling him tightly into me. He pauses in surprise and wraps his arms around me. The lean muscles in his arm stretch across my shoulder as I breathe in. I pull back, wiping my eyes, and lay my hand on the stuffed animal. It looks just like him.

"I thought you needed to take a piece of Opie with you. Until we can deliver you the real thing." He smiles, and I appreciate his optimism. He's always been the one to hold the hope when I couldn't see it.

Every day that passes, it gets a little more painful to wonder where Opie is. All I can hope for is that until we are reunited, he is safe. Even if that's not with me.

"It's perfect. It's really . . ." I can't finish my thought, but I smile at both of them. "Thank you."

Levi leans over, squeezing my shoulder and kissing my temple. I put the gifts back in the bag, my heart bursting with gratitude.

After we order our food, conversation flows like this is what we three do every Saturday night.

"So Charleston is next for Callie. How about you?" Foster looks to Levi, who pauses midbite, pondering the question. I wait intently, too. In the chaos of the search, the fire, and now the move, Levi and I haven't spent much time talking about the future—well, his at least.

"For me? I'm thinking about enrolling in some online business classes. Haven't talked to my parents about it yet, but I doubt they will be *against* it."

Foster nods, a smile on his face.

"And I'm sure you've heard," Levi starts, his eyes darting to Foster, then over to me, "my brother, Robbie, is engaged. Mom and Dad are *enamored* by the whole thing." He rolls his eyes as he smiles at me.

Foster doesn't seem to care about that news, unlike the business school idea. I see now why Levi favors his uncle over his immediate family. I would too, I think.

Just when I think dinner is over, Peg comes out with three different desserts, and the guys let me choose mine.

"I feel like it's my birthday or something," I say bashfully with a dessert spoon dangling lazily from my fingers.

"May as well be, kid. It's the start of something new for you," Foster retorts, pulling the apple pie toward him.

He's right. And I'm still no good at goodbyes, so when dinner is over, I slip out of the diner and escape to my car. Tomorrow, I leave, and I don't know how to properly do this. After loading my stuff into Foster's truck, his eyes roam over Levi and I standing awkwardly to the side.

"I have an errand to run. You okay to catch a ride with Levi?" he asks, his hand already on the door handle of the truck.

"Yeah, of course," I reply. I'm glad to have a few more minutes alone with him so I can figure out how to do this, how to process everything. If anyone will get it, I think it's Levi. And if he doesn't understand, he will still sit and listen.

We slide into the car, and he turns it on but doesn't move from the dim parking lot.

"I'm gonna miss you, Callie. What am I supposed to do every day?" Levi jokes.

I shove his arm, laughing. I guess he is no better at goodbyes than I am. "Looks like you'll have to actually run the print shop," I tease.

He smirks at me. But then his smile fades into a serious look, his jaw tense but his eyes soft as they gaze into mine. "I'm not going to stop looking for him either. I want you to know he will be on my mind as much as you will be . . . and that's a lot."

A silence sits between us, and I reach out to place my hand in his. "A lot?"

"All the time," he proclaims without hesitation, and my heart constricts with his admission.

You're always on our minds. Not just mine. There are a lot of people who care, Opie.

"Thank you, Levi," I say softly, my eyes settling on our locked hands.

"Thank *you*—" Levi chuckles. "—for coming into the print shop right before we closed."

We both laugh as Levi runs a hand through his hair.

"It would've been a real shame to never get to know you *again*, Callie."

I could say a million things to tell Levi what he means to me or to thank him for never giving up on me, but none of it seems like enough. So I lean over, lace my fingers behind his neck, and kiss him deeply.

Thank you for showing me I'm worthy of love again.

Chapter
Thirty-Eight

When I arrived in Charleston the next afternoon, I was greeted by a smiling face. It turns out, luck was on my side, because Peg's connection did have a room to rent in her townhouse for the fall and was happy to have me. The townhouse wasn't far from my classrooms, and I could walk most places.

"Thank you again for letting me rent on such short notice," I say for the second time as I finish hauling my boxes from the car to my room. The house smells like vanilla and is decorated so nicely. I keep pausing to look around in disbelief that I get to live here too.

"Of course. I'm gone most of the time. I'm working on my PhD and in labs a lot, but please, make yourself at home," Megan replies, showing me around the kitchen.

Once I'm alone in my bedroom, I shut the door behind me and look around my new temporary home. Megan rents it fully furnished, and the room is easily bigger than half the trailer was. The view isn't as good, of course, but I laugh to myself, looking out at the single tree in the front yard, thinking about what Levi said only a few days ago.

You'll miss these mountains. I promise you, Callie.

It doesn't take me long to unpack my clothes and put my photography equipment on the desk. The last thing I do is pull the gift from Levi out of the bag and set it on my bed. The Opie stuffed animal rests right next to the remnants of his purple dinosaur toy.

My last step is to spread Memaw's quilt, the same quilt I snagged from the farmhouse on the bed. Sitting on the bed, I trace the stitched outline of flowers with my finger, and my throat unexpectedly gets tight.

This is all better than I had imagined. This room, this safe haven, I get to call home. A friendly person to live with. A beautiful new city, begging me to explore. And the photography program of my dreams starting soon. But still, my eyes tear up, and I fall back on my bed, letting them.

It's okay to miss him. It's okay to be sad.

Inhaling a steadying breath, I know I have to take this day by day. This is what I always wanted.

It's okay to be scared.

"Callie Hayes?" the instructor calls out, and on instinct, I keep my eyes averted and lift my hand to signal that I'm present. But then it dawns on me that the shadow of Miscruz Hills doesn't loom over me here.

It took me a few days after moving to Charleston to truly accept that through the gossip and hurtful words, the souring of my reputation was very real. But so was all the good. Like Peg taking me under her wing through it all and the Calloways never holding a grudge against me. And Levi, my oldest friend, who helped me when I needed him most. Who is still helping me.

Mack's shadow isn't here in this new city, and I'm no longer burdened with being *just* his daughter. I am so much more. And I'm ready to prove that here.

In class, I meet the students I'll be working alongside for the next five-odd months. A lot of them are older than me. One girl, Ellie, who sat next to me, invites me for coffee afterward.

I tell her I know a place, and we walk together to the coffee shop Levi found for me. Of course, Levi was right. The coffee shop is really good, and I managed to get a part-time job there.

"So tell me about yourself!" Ellie claps, her grin large as she plops down in the worn green chair across from me.

My thumb messes with the paper coffee cup sleeve as I try to think of what to say. I silently hope it isn't so painfully obvious how little experience I have with making friends.

"I'm from a tiny town in the mountains. Miscruz Hills."

"Oh my gosh, I've been there! There's a summer wine festival!" she exclaims.

I chuckle. More for myself than for her response because all I can think of is Peg cursing all the young people who "clutter up the streets" during the festival week.

"Yeah, there is. It's a small town . . . and I didn't think I'd miss the mountains, but I do," I admit, feeling strange about reminiscing this complicated topic with someone I just met. But Ellie is sweet and smiles back at me.

"I don't miss home yet. I'm from Texas. But I do miss my mom! I've only been here for five days. How embarrassing is that?" She blushes, scrunching her face as I brush it off, reassuring her it's not.

My phone lights up with a text from Levi asking me how my first day of classes went, and behind it, as always, is Opie's face. Quickly, I silence the vibrating alert, but Ellie's eyes wander to the screen before it goes dark.

"Is that your dog? Did you bring him with you?" she prods.

Ellie's inquisitive smile remains steady as she swirls her iced coffee, and in that moment, I know I don't want to hide this. I hesitate, shuffling the coffee cup between my hands. "Yeah. That's my dog, Opie." I pause. "He actually went missing a few weeks ago. There's still a full search going on for him back home."

Ellie's face crumbles, her mouth falling open, and I wish for a moment I would've said nothing. It feels like I scared her away, ruining my first chance at having a friend in this foreign place. She probably thinks so low of me for coming *here* while my dog is *lost*.

But she doesn't say any of that, she reaches out, lightly touching me on the arm.

"Oh my gosh, Callie. I'm so sorry." She shakes her head, her eyes cast down. "That is so brave of you to come here. This must mean so much to you."

My breath stalls before I can swallow and blink away the negative self-talk bubbling in my mind. "Thanks. It means everything to me . . . and so does Opie."

Ellie takes a sip of coffee. "I can't even imagine the stress you must feel. I'll be praying for your dog's safe return."

"Thanks, Ellie." I offer her a small smile of gratitude. "He's got the best people looking for him. I know that for certain."

Ellie and I talk more about the program and what we are excited for. I've never had anyone to share my love of photography with. I'm tired by the time we're done at the coffee shop, but when we split ways and I walk home, the dusky sky makes me stop in my path.

The hazy sky peaks between the majestic oak tree leaves, lining the historic city streets. There's no trail to run barefoot down or creek that's all my own, but even in the bustling of the city on the uneven path of brick, I pause and find solace in all that's alive around me.

Pulling my camera from my bag, I quickly snap a photo of the street that's lined with weeping trees and roots that poke out of the sidewalks like strokes of paint on a canvas. Peering down at the screen, I admire the photo I captured and think one thing.

Opie would love it here.

Chapter Thirty-Nine

September: Four Weeks Later

It was finally overcast, a rarity in Charleston in mid-September, but we took the opportunity to drive out to the National Wildlife Refuge to get photos. *We, as in Ellie and me.* She became my friend these last few weeks, and while we spoke a lot about the program and our assignments and explored the city together, she didn't pry about my past.

My phone started to ring as we drove the bumpy backroads.

"Do you mind?" I ask, holding up my cell, and she waves and mouths no. Ellie knows I will answer my phone at any time of day if it's Levi or Foster. Any phone call could be *the* phone call.

"Hey, Levi." I'm not able to stop the smile from spreading across my face when I hear his voice on the other end of the phone.

Charleston's sunshine was beautiful, but nothing compared to the rays that were Levi.

"Hey! I know you're on your way to the park, but I wanted to ask if you'd like to come to Robbie's engagement party next Saturday with me—in Charlotte?"

The line goes silent because I don't know what to say.

I don't get invited to parties or family gatherings or social events.

"Cal?" Levi's concerned voice breaks through my spiraling worry.

"Yeah. Yeah, I'm here. I, um, I would have to be back for my shift Sunday afternoon, but I think I could go."

"You don't sound so sure. And in all fairness, I'm being selfish. I know you hate parties. But I miss you."

I'll never tire of hearing him say that.

"I just . . . Will it be weird? I don't think your mom likes me and—"

"How about I promise you this: when it starts to get boring or weird, or you want to leave, we will. I'll take you anywhere you want. You deserve a night to just have fun."

I breathe out, feeling less tense, and nod even though Levi can't see me in the passenger's seat of Ellie's car.

"Okay, deal. I can do that," I reply and can feel Levi's smile in his response. When I get off the phone, I peer out the window as the park comes into view, and eagerness blooms inside of me.

"Sounds like you have a hot date next weekend." Ellie wiggles her eyebrows at me, and we both laugh.

Ellie and I go separate ways in the park, splitting up to photograph different things. We have different styles. She moves around a lot, searching for animals and angles. I find one spot on the side of the marsh and wait. I wait for the elusive animals of the refuge to show themselves to me, and they always do once they realize I'm not a threat.

With my camera balanced on a tripod, I look down at the grass near my feet, half expecting to see Opie's paws padding next to them.

I'll never not think he is with me. Just a step behind.

I remember the first time I took him on a long hike with me, all for the purpose of photographing an owl I'd spotted days before. Opie was still a pup but had learned commands quickly and picked up on nonverbal cues even quicker. When I stopped walking, so did he. When I crouched down, he paused, steeling his limbs. I knew that day that there would never be another dog like him.

Both Foster and I remind each other the search isn't over until it's over. Even if most days feel like searching for a needle in a haystack. Kind of like waiting here to see an animal in its natural habitat.

There's peace out here, behind the camera, the one I thought I'd never pick up again. There's peace being somewhere new, where I can breathe, and form who I am without the cloud of Mack. But inside, in my soul, I know there won't ever be complete peace until I know what happened to Opie. I can't heal, not fully, without knowing.

A small splash takes me out of my thoughts and back into the moment. In the water, not far away is an otter, floating with her baby. I inhale a sharp breath, quieting myself in the sweetness of the moment and quickly get behind the lens to capture it.

Thank you, my sweet boy.

Ellie and I walk away from the day with a lot of good shots. She's nervous to present hers tomorrow in class because wildlife photography is new to her. But for once, I feel good about this. My wildlife photography is what got me into the program.

However, at the end of the five months, all of our work goes into a portfolio, and we have to present it in a formal gallery setting. It's a big deal, but I'm trying to take it day by day, or else I'll start to second-guess myself. Every time I say this to Levi, he reminds me I'm the *best he ever knew*, and it makes me laugh, every time.

I hope one day I feel that way about myself, too.

And Opie . . . Well, I think of Opie often and thank all my lucky stars for Levi and Foster, who continually search for him. But I don't think of the past, not in the way I used to. It used to feel like a dark storm lingering just behind me. And there was no turning point I could put my finger on. It just *happened*. I decided it was time to be the Callie Hayes I wanted to be, to form myself in my own likeness. Something else that's been happening—or not happening since I left Miscruz Hills—is I've barely thought of Mack at all. And I know he doesn't think of me.

Though, every night, when I curl up in bed under the color quilt, I think of Memaw.

She would've been so proud, Cal.

Chapter Forty

One Week Later

It's still dark outside my bedroom window when my phone rings loudly. Fumbling in the darkness, I reach out until my hand collides with my phone, and I silence it. I set an alarm to wake up early and drive down to take sunrise photos by the bay, but I'm exhausted and contemplating going there tomorrow instead. But moments later, my phone goes off again, and I grimace, grabbing it to silence it, but the time glares back at me in the dark room.

It's four-thirty in the morning, and it's not my alarm. It's Foster.

My heart thuds audibly in my chest, vibrating my body awake as I tap my phone screen with shaky fingers.

"Foster?" I barely stammer his name, and low static sounds on the other end of the phone like the sound when a call is about to get disconnected.

Immediately, my gut sinks, and I throw back my covers, scooting to the edge of the bed, repeating myself. "Foster, are you there?" My voice echoes through the sleeping house.

"Callie, can you hear me? I don't have good coverage." Foster's voice comes through tired and strained, and my heart starts to thud against my rib cage.

Is it Opie? Is it Levi?

"I can hear you. Wh-what's going on?" I ask, breathing heavily even though I'm only sitting still. I pull the cord on my bedside lamp, casting a yellow glow throughout my room. The stuffed animal Opie is on the floor near my feet, tossed during my sleep, so I reach down to grab it, needing something to hold onto just to keep myself breathing.

"I think we found him," he blurts out.

I stand abruptly, tears filling my eyes faster than I thought humanly possible. My lips part, but I can't think. I can't formulate what to say, what to ask.

Is this all a dream?

"Where, how . . . Foster . . . I . . ." I can't finish my sentence. My limbs burn, every nerve on fire as I start to pace my small room, pausing to grip the bedpost when he cuts me off.

"He's alive, Callie," he says, and I want to ask more. I want every detail. But my body collapses to the floor. Every muscle in me goes weak as I fold in half, tears streaming down my face. Every tear is a purge of fear, relief, worry, confusion. Foster stays quiet on the other end of the line, and I know he hears me crying into the phone. He lets me weep for a moment before I grab a tissue, wipe my face, and pull myself together long enough to speak.

"Is my boy okay?"

I hear Foster fidgeting. "A hiker found him nearly twenty miles east of Miscruz. He brought him to the vet in town, and they called me immediately."

The news absorbs slowly as I try to wrap my mind around it. I haven't eaten in hours, but my stomach floods with nausea. Foster inhales another sharp breath, and I hear chatter in the background.

"I need you to know . . . Opie is in bad shape. I can't sugarcoat it, kid. He's been on his own for a while. He's pretty weak."

"Are you there now with him?" I ask.

"I just walked to the parking lot to get fresh air. I'm here. They just took him back."

I nod, though he can't see me, and stand on shaky legs. I put the phone on speaker, tossing it on my bed so I can pull on my pants. "Don't go anywhere. I'm on my way.

My movements are on autopilot. Putting all my emotions aside, I gather a few things, toss them in a duffel quickly, and head out the door into the early morning hours. My phone says it will take six hours, but I don't think about the time.

Every mile, every minute I'm in this car, heading toward the mountains, I'm one mile, one minute closer to holding Opie in my arms again. Whatever condition he is in, whatever the vet tells me, I know we can weather the storm. I told Levi I'd risk everything; I'd do anything to find my dog. And now, I will do whatever it takes to save his life.

Life has thrown me a second chance to get out of Miscruz Hills and start all over. Now it's giving Opie a second chance, and as I drive the long stretch of dark freeway, I promise him we won't let this *chance* go.

He's going to be okay. He has to be.

At eight a.m., I stop to fill up my car and go through a drive-thru to grab food because I know the moment I am with Opie, it will take an army to pull me from his side. My phone rings as I get back on the road. It's Foster.

"Hey," I start, having so much to say, so much to ask, but all I can manage is a greeting.

"Hey," Foster replies. He sounds just as tired, and I take a mental note to tell him to rest the minute I get there and take over.

"What's the update? I'm two hours out."

"They have him in the emergency division. He needed a few wounds cleaned and stitched, and now he is resting, hooked up to fluids, and being monitored."

"What are they monitoring?" I ask, my hands growing clammy on the steering wheel.

"His organs. But please, don't worry. He is in good hands here, and they know you're on the way. I'll call you with any updates. Drive safe, okay?"

Tears choke my throat. I wipe my eyes with the back of my hand while keeping my eyes on the road. Quickly, before I come loose, I blurt one last request.

"Can you call Levi for me, let him know?" I ask, and my voice breaks, my palm snapping to my mouth.

Two more hours. You can do this. Just hold on, Callie.

"Sure thing. I'll tell him. Drive safe, okay?"

"Mm-hmm," I murmur and hang up the phone. The moment I do, a sob rips through me, shaking my shoulders.

I watch the sun rise over the highway as I blink away tears for the next two hours. For months, I thought I'd lost him, and now that he is found, losing him suddenly feels so much more real.

Chapter Forty-One

Driving through town, on the edge of my seat, I pass all the places I didn't think I'd see for a while. Peg's Diner is bustling with all the regulars. Main Street is sleepy, but as I turn up the street and into the vet parking lot, it hits me like a ton of bricks.

I'd daydreamed about finding Opie many times, but I never let myself imagine finding him like *this*. This is too painful, and I successfully fooled myself into thinking he'd be okay. Opie is a fighter, a survivor, but it didn't make it hurt less that he's inside this building right now in pain.

I shut my eyes as I sit, parked in the lot, with both hands on the wheel. Two small knocks on my window jolt me, and I see Foster peering at me through the glass.

"Callie," he calls softly, my name muffled through the door.

I open the car door and silently get out. We don't exchange words. Because what could we say? But I lean into him, and he pulls me into a hug.

"You ready?" he asks.

I nod. I've never been more ready, yet less prepared, for anything in my life, but with Foster walking by my side, I feel a silent strength I've never had before.

You aren't in this alone.

Inside, we walk past the receptionist, who flashes me a sympathetic smile. Foster glances her way, his hand on my upper back as he guides me through the brightly lit animal hospital. We keep walking past the exam rooms and into the back, where the small surgery and emergency center are located. I swallow my fears, but they stick in my throat. Suddenly, I feel so small.

"You want me to come back there with you?" Foster asks, pausing next to me outside of the gray metal door.

"No, I can do this."

He places a rough, but warm, hand on my shoulder. "I know you can. I'm going to run and get coffee. I'll be back soon, okay? You need anything?"

"Thank you, no. I'm okay," I reply. The door opens and a vet tech slips into the hallway with us.

Foster nods and walks back to the lobby, leaving me with the vet tech.

"You must be Opie's owner," the young girl says.

I nod, desperate to push open the door. Opie's on the other side.

"We have him resting. He has a few flesh wounds that need to be cleaned out and stitched. He's hooked up to an IV and a heart monitor," she informs me, putting her hands in the front pockets of her blue scrubs.

I nod slowly, feeling my cheeks grow damp with more tears.

The vet tech, whose nameplate reads *Lisa*, tilts her head and smiles softly at me. "He's doing better. He's a little fighter."

"Can I see him?" I ask, terrified they will tell me no. I don't think I can physically handle not seeing him with my own eyes.

"Of course. We need to keep him calm though. He is on a mild sedative and pain management meds, so I just ask you stay calm and quiet around him." She runs a hand through her black ponytail, and I nod. "I know this has to be extremely emotional for you," Lisa adds.

I almost laugh, despite crying. Because *extremely emotional* is a gross understatement.

Lisa leads the way, pushing open the door, and the room instantly shrinks. My eyes focus on one pinpoint in the room.

My whole heart.

A small gasp escapes my lips, and I quickly cover my trembling mouth, not wanting to startle him. *Opie.* With one hand on my heart, one on my mouth, I glance at Lisa, who nods toward Opie, and I rush to his side, where he lies on an elevated table, resting in a nest of colorful blankets. She adjusts the IV drip, and I blink rapidly, ricocheting between bouts of laughter and tears.

I am both overjoyed to see my sweet boy and scared of all the tubes and bandages surrounding him.

Lisa backs away from the table. "I'll be right out here. I'll give you a minute," she says softly, and I thank her.

Gently, I place my hand on Opie, watching his ribs expand up and down. He is in a drug-induced slumber. His front leg is wrapped in blue bandages, and I lightly run my finger over his dirty white fur. It takes everything in me not to wrap my arms around him. His face looks peaceful like it always did when he was napping in the sunbeams outside the trailer, dust coating his white fur. But right now, his eyes are slightly sunken, and his ribs poke out from under his skin. He's held on for so long.

I have to bite my trembling lip to keep from crying, knowing that if I do, I might not be able to stop, and I don't want to disturb him. Moving my hand gingerly up his back, I pause on his heart, feeling the beat drum against my palm.

He's alive. Opie is alive.

Opie's eyes open a tiny sliver, and he looks up at me. He can't lift his head, so I bend down and lay a kiss on his black nose.

"Opie, you're home."

The tip of his tail lifts, tapping ever so lightly in response to my voice.

I don't leave Opie's side all morning until it's time to change his bandages and the vet asks me to step out to talk with her. She squeezes my upper arm, giving me a reassuring, but loaded, smile.

"How are you holding up, Callie?" Dr. Hollack asks, and I let the tension from my shoulders drop.

"I'm so happy. I can't explain it. I just . . . I can't believe he's here. I think I'm in shock."

"We are all so happy he was found. It's a miracle, really," she says wistfully and then pulls out a clipboard with notes in front of her. "I want to talk to you about what's next. Opie has a long road ahead of him, but he is a young, strong dog. I really believe he is going to make a full recovery with proper care."

"He's a fighter, isn't he?" I marvel with a closed-lip smile on my face as I look through the tiny window in the door at him. The vet tech is petting him, smiling down at him.

"He's a special dog. I see why you couldn't give up on him," she expresses, and I nod. "The best thing for him is to keep him here for four to five more days while we get his fluid levels back up and can monitor his cuts for any signs of infection. After that, it will be mainly helping him get his strength back, gain weight, and get into a routine again. Being lost that long puts a lot of stress on dogs, but they are resilient little creatures. How's that sound?" Dr. Hollack asks.

I nod vigorously. "Anything. Anything he needs."

She excuses herself, and I head to the parking lot for fresh air. I told Foster to go home and sleep, though I highly doubt he listened to me. He went home to feed the hounds and get food but assured me he'd return before lunch.

I have several texts from Levi, too. He's in Charlotte, where I was supposed to go today, too, for his brother's engagement party. As I'm about to go back in, my phone lights up with a call from him.

"Hey, Cal. How are you holding up? How's our boy?" he asks, and I smile, wishing so badly I could hug Levi right now.

"He's getting all the love and all the treatments. He's going to be okay. I mean, he is in rough shape, but I'm going to make sure he has everything he needs to make a full recovery."

Levi chuckles. "I wouldn't expect anything less. I can't wait to see him. And you," he adds.

I bite my lip, hesitating before telling Levi the bad news. "I'm so sorry, but with all this, I don't think I can go to the party tonight, Levi. I was really looking forward to seeing you."

"I can't go either."

"Oh?" I ask, confused.

"I'm on my way back to Miscruz right now. Did you really think I would pick a dumb party over you and Opie? This is the most important day of the year. I'm coming home," he says, and my throat grows tight.

How did I get so lucky?

"You sure, Levi?"

"Of course. I'm already on my way. I'll see you in forty minutes."

I bite my lip from smiling too hard.

"One more thing, Callie."

"Yeah?"

"What size coffee do you want?" he asks, and I hear him smiling like a fool on the other end of the call.

The vet doesn't usually let owners stay with their pets for more than an hour, but it becomes clear this isn't a normal situation, and I'm not leaving Opie's side. They bring me a chair and let me sit beside him while I wait for Levi to arrive.

They leave me alone in the room with Opie, and it's quiet here except for the fan blowing through the vents and the beeping of the monitor. I know the drugs are making him even more tired than he already is, but he wiggles his tail when I come to sit. Slipping my hand under his heavy head, he gives my hand a tiny lick.

"It's been a long road, boy." His eyes peer up at me as I talk gently to him. Just him. "Did you hear me talking to you, Opie? I went to our favorite spot when I missed you most and prayed that the wind would carry my love to you." I laugh to myself, knowing it sounds crazy and knowing only a love like this could make you crazy. "Guess what? I live in Charleston now. And I'm going to take you there with me. You're going to feel better soon, I promise you."

Opie's amber eyes flutter shut, and I stay quiet, letting him rest. But not before placing a kiss softly on his nose. Time moves quickly as I sit there and watch Opie sleep when the sound of a door opening startles me.

"You made it," I whisper, smiling up at Levi, whose face is both happy and sad. He marches over, pulling me out of the chair and into a bear hug. I'm surrounded by his woodsy scent and reminded why I've missed him so much.

"I'm so happy, Callie. I don't even have words." He pulls back, my head still cradled in his large hand. "And that's a first."

We both laugh, and I swipe away a single tear. The emotion of today has flooded my body like a wave . . . ebb and flow.

"Thank you," I whisper.

"For what?"

"For being here, for everything. From the beginning."

"I will always be here," Levi says, and my eyebrows shoot up at him. "As long as you'll have me," he clarifies.

His words sink into my skin, wrapping themselves around the part of my heart that permanently has his name inked on it. I grab his hand, slowly turning us around to my sleeping dog. Levi gently strokes Opie's head with a look that can only be described as *awe* in his eyes.

The door swooshes open again, and Lisa comes in smiling at us both, then glances at Opie. "I know you'd prefer to stay here all day, but I really need you to trust us. He will be okay. He's already showing signs of improvement."

She readjusts the blankets around Opie. His skinny body gets cold quickly, they let me know.

"Opie needs to rest, but we will call you with any update. You're welcome to come by tomorrow first thing," Lisa says.

I look at Opie, then Levi, whose lips pull up in warning. *Listen to them, Callie. Don't be stubborn.*

"Thank you, Lisa, for everything y'all are doing for my boy. I'll be back in the morning. And you'll call me with any update, right?"

She nods, and I'm sure she does this a lot. I sympathize, but it doesn't make it easier for me to tear myself from his side. It feels like he could so easily get lost again, even though I know where he is.

"Absolutely. Go get some rest," she replies.

Slowly, I gather my stuff, then I kiss his sweet face one more time. "Rest up. I'll be back in the morning, Ope," I whisper. My eyes linger on him until Levi grabs my other hand, gently guiding me out of the room and down the hallway into the parking lot. I have to look back through the door on my way out to remind myself it's not a dream.

"What's the plan, Cal?" Levi asks, and once I stop moving, I feel the exhaustion take over my bones. Suddenly, I just want a bed to curl up in until tomorrow. His phone buzzes, and he pauses, mouthing *one moment* to me.

"Hey, Foster . . . yeah, we just left." There was another moment of silence as he looks at me. "I'll ask her."

I rub my eyes to bring more energy into me. "Foster's for a late lunch . . . and maybe a nap?" He winks, and I nod.

They get off the phone, and we agree to meet at Foster's. Levi kisses me goodbye, and I watch him drive out of the parking lot. In my car, facing the front entrance of the clinic, I pause with both hands on the steering wheel.

What's the plan, Callie?

Chapter Forty-Two

As I pull up to Foster's house and park right beside his truck, the front door opens. I look up in time to see the hounds dash out and halt outside my door.

"Hey, girls. I've missed you!" I say, stepping out and crouching down to pet them. They sniff me all over. I smell of Opie.

"They never get *that* excited for me to come home," Foster hollers from the porch steps.

I chuckle tiredly, leading the dogs to the house. "They know it's a big day."

Foster grins, agreeing.

Inside, I'm greeted by a big stack of pancakes and everything you could want for a breakfast feast. He doesn't even have to explain himself, and I'm beginning to wonder if this is the *only* thing Foster knows how to cook. Either way, I'm so grateful and begin to fill up my plate immediately.

Levi joins us, and before I know it, we're all around the table. It's like old times, but it's all different now. The mission that brought us together is complete.

"So now that Opie's found, are you two done with me?" I joke, looking over my plate at Foster.

Foster feigns insult. "You wouldn't be so lucky."

"I'm sorry you both are missing the engagement party," I say between sips of the orange juice in front of me.

"Are you kidding? I wasn't going anyway. I work for you. Finding Opie was my job. Though the hikers are the ones who can take all the credit."

I scoff because that's not true entirely. They might've found him, but without Foster and Levi, I'm not sure I would've made it this far. Actually, I know I wouldn't have.

"Did you happen to get any of their names or info? I need to thank them."

Foster nods and says he can get that for me. As we eat breakfast for lunch, I fill in both of them on everything Dr. Hollack told me. The plan is to keep Opie at the vet until Wednesday or so, then take him home to transition him. They listen intently, exchanging glances.

"That sounds good, Cal. They'll take good care of him there. He's on the road to recovery now, yeah?" Levi reassures me, squeezing my hand under the dining table.

I nod and ask Foster if I can rest a little in the guest room. Daisy and May follow me in, more than happy to curl up on the bed with me, their heavy bodies like heating pads on my legs. Before long, I fall into a deep slumber.

When I wake, the sky outside the window is dark, and a slight panic rises in my chest. The dogs aren't in the room with me anymore, and I roll to look at my phone. It's nearly seven, and I've been asleep for five hours. Frantically, I check my phone, but there are no missed calls from the vet. I do have a text from Ellie from two hours ago asking if I want to grab dinner.

Shit, I didn't even think about classes. Or work.

Two voices from the front porch make their way to the bedroom, and I get up to wander out there, padding barefoot down the hallway.

Levi and Foster's backs are to me, both sitting on the front porch steps. They stop talking when I open the screen door. Levi smiles at me, crinkling his honey eyes, and Foster is unreadable. He must be exhausted.

"I'm so sorry you guys had to have a long day with me."

"Don't apologize. This is a day worth celebrating." He tugs me down so I'm sitting on the steps with them. Levi wraps his arm around my side, and I settle into the softness of his gray sweatshirt.

"I wanted to ask you, Foster, would it be okay if I stay here, just for a few more days, until they release Opie?" I don't look up, not *wanting* to ask for anything more from this man. A long beat of silence sits between us before he replies.

"I can't allow that, I'm sorry."

"Oh . . . okay. I understand, I—" I stutter, not expecting that answer.

"You can't stay here at all in this town," he elaborates, and I lean back, peering across the steps at him. His blue eyes are soft, not matching his words.

Levi chimes in. "I'm with him on this, Callie. I'm sorry."

"What the hell is this? I don't understand," I counter, my eyes darting between them.

"You've got to get back to Charleston," Foster says, and I stiffen, my eyes widening at his obscene request.

I can't control my tone and whip my head toward Levi. "You really expect me to leave Opie right after getting him back? I'm *not* leaving him." My words come out hurt and sharp.

Foster doesn't budge. He just kicks his boot on the wooden steps and hangs his head. "We *can't* tell you what to do, but you've come so far . . . you can't miss a class. You told me yourself." His words ring true, though harsh.

I hate this. I really hate this.

"I'll stay for a week until Opie's good enough to drive back with me," I say, but as the words tumble from my lips, I know it's not possible. The program has a two-class strike. I can only miss two sessions, and if I call off a whole week of work, I won't be able to afford *to go* back. I start to crumble, but Levi's strong hand tugs at my clenched fist, and I turn to look at him.

"It's going to be okay. You have to go back and finish what you started there."

"Are you two insane? I'll answer that. *Yes*, you are. I can't leave him. I can't." My voice breaks, my body begging me to stand and run, but I know that will do me no good. I glance at my car, wishing I could jump in and go to the clinic right now. If I could just hold Opie, everything would make sense.

But nothing makes sense.

Levi wraps his arms around my shoulders. "You trust me, Callie?" His voice is warm against my ear.

"Where are you going with this?" I reply skeptically.

"Go back. You can leave tomorrow morning after checking on Opie and get back for your Monday morning class."

I turn to ask, but he already has an answer.

"*I* will take care of him. I'll stop by daily until they release him, and we can video chat. The day he is released from care, I will bring him to you. Opie and I will come to *you*."

Levi's small smile is full of warmth, and I don't doubt anything he's saying. He is full of love and kindness and fierce protectiveness, and I know he'll take care of Opie like he is the most important thing on this earth. *Because he knows Opie is the most important thing on this earth to me.*

"It's going to be okay. I promise." Levi pulls my head tight to his chest, resting a peck on my forehead.

"And I'm here. Anything he needs, anything you need," Foster chimes in, raising his eyebrows at me.

I break away from Levi's hold and flash a tiny grin to Foster.

Nothing about this is easy. But maybe I can do this. Maybe with them, I can.

The following day, I head to the clinic. Levi offered to go with me, but I told him I'd like to do it myself. I'll see him in a few days, and the fewer hearts I have to say goodbye to, the better. I'm still not good at *goodbyes*.

On the drive to the vet clinic, I call the coffee shop in Charleston and let them know I had to come home due to a personal emergency but would be back in town tomorrow for my shift. As I hang up the phone, I pass the farm.

The crooked blue mailbox doesn't make my heart hitch like it once did. It's weird driving past a home I have no reason to return to. I find myself hoping Mack's arm is healed and that nature is taking over where the trailer once stood, reclaiming the land. Part of me still grieves for the sanctuary I had created for Opie and me, and I think it always will.

I still dream of the trail and creek and the meadow that greeted me like an old friend every morning. In my heart, I know it's not a *forever* goodbye. Nothing is forever. But it's my *for now* goodbye, and that I can accept. There are greater things ahead for me. For us.

When I make it to the vet and walk through the clinic doors, Lisa instantly recognizes and greets me, leading me to where Opie is. She opens the door ahead of me, and I let out a small, joy-filled gasp. Opie is sitting up on his own, eating wet food from a bowl. When he sees me, he starts to cry and shake. Tears fill my eyes.

"I think this is the first time he's realized it's me," I say, choking through my tears. *Happy tears.*

"He is alert enough now to recognize people, but he is still so tired. We're introducing food slowly so his stomach doesn't get upset," she responds, and though he looks rough and like he was alone in the wilderness for a few months, I see the light trying to shine through his eyes.

Lisa lets me sit beside Opie on the floor, petting him as he eats breakfast. He takes one bite, then looks at me and starts crying again, shoving his nose into my collarbone. He can't get close enough to me, so I wrap my arms around him.

"It's okay, buddy. I'm here. You're safe," I whisper.

I tell him what I've always needed to hear. What I know settles a scared heart.

It breaks me when an hour passes, and I know I have to get on the road. I care about the photography program, and I know Foster and Levi were right to push me. Without them, I'm afraid I wouldn't be leaving. I would stay here, sacrificing everything. And that wouldn't be the correct answer.

Opie grows tired quickly, and Lisa puts him back in a penned-off area where he is safe.

"I brought this for him. Can I leave it here?" I ask her, pulling the purple dinosaur toy from my bag. She looks at me with confusion for bringing a ratty old toy for him. "It's his favorite toy. It's all I have left of him. I think I'd feel better knowing he had it," I add.

She flashes a look of understanding, reaching for it. "I'll give it to him after his next dose."

"Thanks," I reply as I ball my fists, trying to relieve the fear flooding me.

"I'll see you soon, buddy," I call out and quickly peel my feet from the floor, walking down the hallway and out of the clinic.

On my way back to Charleston, I stop at the last gas station in town before getting on the freeway. The smell of gasoline fills the air as the gas pumps slowly, and there's a chill to the fall air around me. A police car pulls up to the pump next to me, and I don't think much of it until Officer Williams steps out.

"Callie, hey."

"Oh, hi. How are you?" I respond, making eye contact with him over the hood of my car.

He pauses and looks down at his feet momentarily. "I heard you were going to school in Charleston. Peg told me," he adds, and his face breaks out in a genuine grin.

I nod, returning the slight grin. "Yeah, I am."

"That's great. I'm really happy for you."

"Thank you. And we found Opie. He's at the clinic in town right now actually."

Officer Williams's whole face lights up, and he pinches his lips together, chuckling. "I'm so happy to hear that. That's amazing. I'm really sorry . . . about not being able to help more."

"It's okay. It's in the past," I say, hearing the gas click behind me, then reaching to stop it. I don't know when I forgave him, but I think somewhere along the way, I realized he wasn't the bad guy. He was just caught in the middle.

Officer Williams returns the look but hesitates like he wants to say something. I open my car door, and he takes a step closer to me. "I know you didn't ask. But I want you to know I'm looking out for Mack."

The sentiment catches me off guard, and we hold each other's gaze. I don't say anything as I pinch my lips together and nod. By the look on his face, he understands.

Thank you.

"I should get on the road." I point toward the highway.

He chuckles and backs away toward the patrol car. "Of course. Drive safe, Callie. And good luck."

I say thanks and duck inside, then drive away from Miscruz Hills.

Chapter Forty-Three

"I have a new strap if you want it?" Ellie asks, eying my frayed camera strap hanging around my neck. Today's class was inside, where we learned how to set up lighting in a studio, and it's the last class of the week. Tomorrow is a work day, and typically Ellie and I will meet at her place to work on assignments together. But tomorrow will be different for me.

"I love my broken strap. It adds character." I stick out my tongue at her and she laughs, rolling her eyes at me.

We part ways, and I drive to the townhouse, preparing the space. The space that's already been prepared for four days now. New bowls sit in the corner of the kitchen, and a basket of toys sits near the sofa. A soft blanket lays on the bed. My roommate, Megan, didn't even bat an eye when I told her about Opie. She told me it was my home too and that she couldn't wait to meet him.

As the day stretches on, though, I can hardly concentrate on anything. I cleared my schedule, got my shifts covered tomorrow and Saturday, and already made a huge portion of lunch for myself and Levi. Though I haven't been able to touch food. I'm too nervous, waiting by the doorstep, checking my phone every few minutes. Any moment, he will be here, and Opie with him.

This is what I've been waiting for. Pins and needles scale my legs as I stand, bouncing on my heels. I slide my phone into the pockets of my jeans and rebraid my hair as I pace the sidewalk in front of the townhome.

Then the truck comes into view. And next to Levi's smiling face and messy hair is Opie. White face, black patch over one eye, and tongue hanging out the side of his mouth. A brand new red collar sits loosely on his skinny neck, but he looks as happy as can be. The leaves rustle on the oak tree as I run to the parking spot, waiting for Levi to pull up. The moment the tires stop on the pavement, my fingers release the door handle, and I'm greeted by my best friend.

Every ounce of worry that's riddled my mind, every sleepless night, every roadblock in the way of our plan disappears as Opie licks my face, and I'm reminded not of all that was lost but everything I've gained.

Epilogue

January

The murmur of voices in the gallery fills the air, and I shake out my arms to release the nerves for the hundredth time. Ellie makes a silly face at me from across the room, and I laugh. Her whole family came from Texas to see her.

As I rock back and forth in my shoes—heels for once—I look around at the other students I've grown to call friends, exchanging little moments of knowing smiles and nerves. I puff my cheeks in an exhale and check my phone. He should be here any minute.

I smooth the front of my black dress down, realizing Levi's never seen me dressed up. I haven't either. Moments later, my eyes lock on the gallery doors, and butterflies flood me as Levi walks toward me. When he catches my eye, I can't help but beam.

"You made it!" I exclaim and quickly pull Levi into a hug. He kisses me softly.

"I couldn't miss the *best photographer in the world*'s first exhibit." He winks and snakes an arm around my waist, turning me toward the wall with my work. "Foster is only a few minutes behind me. He should be here soon." He glances down at his watch, then back at me with an amused smirk.

"And holy shit, Cal. You look incredible."

"Thank you." I blush. Levi's wearing a sweater and dress pants, and it hits me how crazy this all is.

"Levi, this is wild . . . I can't believe I'm *here*." After five months in Charleston, I'm not bogged down by self-doubt or fear anymore. But some days, when I pause to look back on this year, I have difficulty understanding the full transformation of my life.

"You made this happen, Callie. This is all *you*."

I kiss him on the lips again and spin him to look at my work. He goes still, his attention slips away from me, and he zones in on the photos on the wall before us. Levi rests his hand on his chin, studying the two dozen photos I have pinned to the wall with small blurbs beneath them.

I wasn't nervous when I presented my portfolio to my nineteen classmates or my professors, who still intimidate me, but I am now. I feel like I'm stripped of all my layers of protection when Levi's eyes scan my art.

I stand off to the side while he observes silently. I wouldn't let him look at anything beforehand. My exhibition portfolio consists of wildlife and nature photos. Those come naturally to me. Then, of course, I have photos of famous Charleston architecture and the weeping oak trees lining its historic streets. They are classic *postcard* photos.

Then, there is one that's unlike the rest. It sits in the middle, oversized in black-and-white. It's my *highlight* photo, the one with an achievement ribbon on it. It's the one that's not technically the best or the most interesting subject matter. But it's the one that tells a story. The story of the dog who never strayed from my heart.

Levi pauses on it, his lips tugging at the corner as he looks lovingly at me. "This is the best one." He pulls me to him, and I nod, agreeing because it's my favorite, too. "I'm so proud of you."

The photo may look like any other dog in a beautiful park. But when I pause to really look, I see what it truly is. Opie's eyes look back at me with an ocean of depth. In Opie's black-and-white eyes is everything he is to me: hope in the dark, grit on the roughest days, and trust in the people who've come and never left.

Project Opie || Callie Hayes || Black & White Film

The city moved around us. It was just another Tuesday in Charleston. But for me, it was the day everything changed. For over two months, I didn't know where my dog was. My best friend in the world, the one who got me through my worst times and the one who made me love photography, had strayed. When I came here, I not only left behind Opie but I also left behind the only place I'd ever known. I was questioning everything and wasn't sure when, or if, I'd be okay again.

When Opie was miraculously found, my world flipped upside down again. Now, I wasn't only learning the ins and outs of a new city and honing my skill behind the lens. I was also taking Opie on his path to recovery. I was relearning life with him. But this place, full of new friends, gave me new strength, and Opie healed. His bandages were removed, his weight regained, and his trust restored. Mine too. He once again became my shadow, keeping me company on long nights and endless hikes.

It took some time for Opie to become the carefree and goofy dog I once knew again. But three weeks after he was found, I woke up to him beside my bed with the leash in his mouth. His tail wagged, and his honey-colored eyes were full again.

That day, we made it all the way to the park, where Opie explored the Spanish moss hanging from oak trees and the bridges over the ponds full of ducks. People stopped to pet him, and we spent hours in that park, letting the sun shine on us.

That day, I took this photo of him lying next to me in the grass. As I turned to look at him, I knew at that moment, we were going to be okay because this was just the beginning of our story.

The story we get to write together.

Acknowledgments

First, thank YOU, the reader. Thank you for picking up this book, for reading Strayed and giving an indie author a chance. When I say it means the world to me - I'm dead serious. I've been wanting to write Callie and Opie's story for years.

Thank you to my beta readers - Racheal, Haley and Danielle. You all took the time to discuss this book with me, cheer me on and give me feedback that gave me so much confidence. I am so grateful for all of you. Thank you to my amazing editors - Allie, Kimberly, and Amy. Without you all, this story would be a jumbled mess.

I may be a solo indie author, but it takes a team to bring a book to life. Thank you Brian, my husband, who reads everything I write and supports me through this crazy adventure. I love you endlessly. For my family, who keeps buying my books and insisting I sign them at family gatherings. Y'all make me feel like a superstar.

And of course, to Wilbur, my dog, who will never read this but inspired this whole story. His love and ability to save me over and over again, even in my darkest moments never ceases to amaze me.

If you enjoyed Strayed, I would love if you could leave a review! Goodreads, Amazon, or wherever you bought the book is wonderful. Reviews help small authors like me get seen, and matter beyond measure.

XO Katherine

Other books by Katherine Bitner:

Time To Bloom
The Way You See Me

About Author

Katherine Bitner comes from a long line of passionate storytellers and loves to write gritty, realistic stories – with a sprinkle of romance woven in! When she isn't writing, you can find her spending all her time with her rescue dog, Wilbur, and her husband. She resides in beautiful North Carolina.

You can connect with Katherine on Instagram at *thekatherinebitner* and at *www.katherinebitner.com*

Made in the USA
Middletown, DE
02 November 2024